# THE SWAN AND THE JACKAL

D1526369

# THE SWAN AND THE JACKAL

## #3 - IN THE COMPANY OF KILLERS

### J.A. REDMERSKI

Cover photo by Mayer George/Shutterstock
Cover Art by Michelle Monique Photography |
www.michellemoniquephoto.com

AISN: B00ISCB0OW
ISBN-13: 9781496123725
ISBN-10: 1496123727

J.A. Redmerski | THE SWAN & THE JACKAL | 2nd Edition
Fiction – Crime – Psychological Thriller - Suspense

# PRAISE FOR IN THE COMPANY OF KILLERS

# ABOUT THE SWAN & THE JACKAL

---

Fredrik Gustavsson never considered the possibility of love, or that anyone could ever understand or accept his dark and bloody lifestyle—until he met Seraphina, a woman as vicious and blood-thirsty as Fredrik himself. They spent two short but unforgettable years together, full of lust and killing and the darkest kind of love that two people can share.

And then Seraphina was gone.

It's been six years since Fredrik's lover and sadistic partner in crime turned his world upside-down. Seraphina went into hiding and has eluded him ever since. Now, he's getting closer to finding her, and an innocent woman named Cassia is the key to drawing Seraphina from the shadows. But Cassia—after sustaining injuries from a fire that Seraphina ignited—suffers from amnesia and can't give Fredrik the information he desperately seeks. Having no other choice, Fredrik has been keeping Cassia locked in his basement as he not only tries to get her to recall her past—because she and Seraphina share it—but also to protect her from Seraphina, who clearly wants her dead.

But Cassia is a light in the darkness that Fredrik never believed existed. After a year subjected to her kindness and com-passion, he finds himself struggling with his love for Seraphina, and his growing feelings for Cassia—because he knows that to love one, the other must die.

Will light win out over darkness, or will something more powerful than either further destroy an already tortured soul?

# TABLE OF CONTENTS

# PROLOGUE

———

*Six years ago...*

There is blood on the furniture and smeared across the wall, a beautiful crimson color that only blood can be, stark against the bright white sheetrock even in the darkness of the room. This wasn't done by a gun. The nearly-naked body of the woman lying on her back against the floor in a thick, dark pool of the crimson stickiness was dispatched by a knife. A very sharp one. Probably with a curved blade and an engraving down the length that reads: *Taste the sugary thorns upon my lips.* But this wound...I'm all too familiar with the handiwork. The gash in the lowest part of the neck, just above where the center of the collarbone meets. Seraphina, my wife, has been here. Just moments ago. I can still smell her perfume in the air.

I've been spying on her for months, since the day I allowed myself to believe she had been betraying me all the time she claimed to love me. But before that she had been betraying my employer, Vonnegut, and The Order by working for another employer and leaking information to our rival. I couldn't let her die for what she had done. I wanted to help her, to change her, to make her choose a side, *my* side. So I began working with her against Vonnegut. It was the ultimate disloyalty, an instant death sentence betraying The Order. But love came first.

Love *always* comes first.

Though I learned the hard way that love is cruel and dangerous and more fiendish than a man like me could ever be. Because Seraphina played me for a fool, after all. After everything we had been through together. She threw it all away.

Tonight I'll find her. And tonight I'll kill her.

I step over the body, remembering the little brown mole on the woman's lower stomach, close to her hipbone. I remember the shape of her slender thighs, the way they felt in my hands while I was fucking her as Seraphina watched. It had always been our thing, something we thrived on—dark, forbidden sex.

This dead woman is the second I've found in two days. Both of them women who Seraphina and I have shared. Both of them doomed to suffer this brutal fate the second Seraphina's jealousy switch finally flipped. That, along with her needing a way to get back at me for figuring out her secrets and no longer falling for her lies. These dead women are messages. *Come and find me,* they say. *I'm not hiding from you, my love, I'm just enjoying the game,* she's telling me.

She always did enjoy the game. So did I. Only now I know I have to end it. And I have to win.

I let the body fall against the saturated carpet. As I rise back into a stand, headlights blink on across the street and shine blindingly into the large living room window, illuminating the sheer white curtains that dress it. An engine revs. *Come and get me,* she's telling me. With my gun gripped in my hand, I walk, not run, briskly out the front door and into the frigid air. I raise the gun in front of me pointed at the car as I approach it brazenly from across the street. A dog barks vociferously in the backyard of the house on the corner, violently heaving itself against the chain-link fence that confines it. Teeth gnashing. Bloodthirsty. Like all animals, it knows evil when it sees it.

"What are you doing, Seraphina?" I ask in a low, threatening voice as I get closer to the car, my gun still pointed at her, my finger on the trigger. "This is beneath even you."

Seraphina grins from the driver's seat, her long slender fingers draped over the top of the steering wheel. Her shiny jet-black hair, cut short to the bottom of her cheekbones is always in perfect order, not a strand out of place, even in times like this.

The echo of blaring sirens approaching from afar sounds in my ears and I snap my head around toward it. Then I hear a thumping. *Thump, thump, thump, BANG!* It's coming from the trunk. My eyes dart to and from it and Seraphina and the south street from where I hear the sirens. I can't decide which is more imperative.

"What are you going to do?" Seraphina taunts, grinning in such a wicked way it can only translate as complete confidence. She knows she has me in this moment. Even with a gun pointed at her beautiful head, she *has* me.

I take a deep breath and look behind me again, expecting the police cars to drive up any second. The sirens are getting closer, but I still don't see the sporadic flashing of their lights reflecting in the darkness of the late hour, so I have a little time. But only seconds.

I look back at Seraphina in the car. My breath exhales visibly in the winter air.

"I'll give you what you want," she says, changing her tune to something more serious and less taunting. "But you have to hear me out. Do you fucking understand me, Fredrik?!"

I feel my teeth grinding behind my cheeks, my nostrils flaring, the bones in my hand aching as my grip tightens around the gun handle with crushing force.

We look into each other's cold dark eyes one last time and she presses her foot on the gas pedal and speeds away. Reluctantly

I drop the gun to my side and let my breath out in a long deep sigh of defeat and enragement. Seraphina knows that I can't kill her until I get information from her. Like an obsessive compulsive need, the information must come first or I'll never be able to sleep again. No one knows but Seraphina, not even my employer, Vonnegut, that I've been torturing and interrogating criminals associated with The Order since I *met* Seraphina. She was the one who opened me up to it, who…gave me a release for my greatest imperfection as a member of the human race. Seraphina helped me and for that, though not that alone, she knows I can't kill her. At least not yet.

With only seconds to spare, I tuck my gun into the back of my pants and walk briskly down the sidewalk, slipping into the shadows of the trees lining the street. Heading toward my car parked four blocks away, I leave the house with the dead woman behind me as well as the police who are coming from the opposite direction.

Seraphina wants to talk. After all this time she has eluded me, kept me in the dark about what she's been doing behind my back, she finally wants to tell me. More lies? Is this her way of getting me off her back so that I'll let her go and let her live? So she can be free of me? But it's not her style. Seraphina, for all that I love about her, is as sadistic as I am. Begging for her life even in the most sardonic of ways, is very out of character for her.

There's something more to it.

I'm back at our house in Boston in under thirty minutes and her car is parked in the driveway. How bold this woman is, how defiant and fearless. She knows what I'll do to her. She knows how much I'll enjoy it and that not even *she* is immune now that she has betrayed me so unforgivably.

I park next to her car, my eyes skirting the trunk before I pull in all the way, remembering the sounds I heard from it before. But I don't care about that right now.

Slamming the car door behind me, I rush up the stairs and burst into the house, the front door slamming into the wall.

"Seraphina!" I call out as I close the front door and begin my search.

But in the back of my mind I know exactly where to find her, in the basement where I keep my interrogation chair and tools.

The basement door is unlocked. And cracked.

I place my full palm against it and push. It opens without making a sound and I waste no time and descend the concrete steps. A single light glows in the distance, casting faint swaths of light against the steps as I take them one at a time. The familiar sound of a woman whimpering, slowly fills my ears. But this is another kind of whimper. Not one of pleasure inflicted by sexual pain, but of fear and pain of another kind.

I step off the last step to find Seraphina standing there in all of her dark and sinister glory. A woman in a long t-shirt and a pair of panties is strapped to my interrogation chair—an old dentist chair—with a gag in her mouth. Blood is still wet in her long disheveled hair, staining the blond color just above her hairline, indicative of being hit over the head with something. Tears stream from her wide and frightened eyes, running streaks of mascara down her reddened cheeks. I know now that it was her who had been banging inside the trunk.

Seraphina smiles at me across the space between us, so lovingly, yet so darkly. Her knife hangs from her hand down against her thigh covered by the fabric of a skin-tight black bodysuit. The black lace-up boots with six-inch heels appear to make her tower over the frightened woman. But I don't remember this woman. She's not one who Seraphina and I ever ravaged together.

"Why are you doing this, Seraphina?" I walk closer, slowly. "Why did you bring her here? Who is she?" We're not coldblooded murderers—of innocent girls, anyway. We've never done something like this to any woman who wasn't willing—unless she was a target. Seraphina has taken this to a whole new level and I don't like it.

She clicks her tongue and puts the blade to the woman's throat. "Not too close, love," she warns me, shaking the index finger of her free hand side to side. "She's the one with the information. She's the one you want to talk to."

This isn't about sex, I realize now. This is about something so much more.

Confused, but thoroughly invested, I crouch down and set my gun carefully on the floor beside my scuffed dress shoes. Then I rise back up slowly into a stand, both hands level with my shoulders to let her know that I'm not going to make a move. The blond-haired woman's eyes grow wider, darting between me and Seraphina though with her head fixed against the chair by a leather strap, she can't see much of my wife behind her.

Seraphina's eyes stray briefly to the wooden chair sitting against the wall to my left. Knowing it was an indication for me to sit down, I wrap a hand around the back of the chair and drag it on its back legs into the light before doing so. I cross one leg over the other and fold my hands on top of them after I sit.

"Why do I need to talk to her?" I ask calmly.

"Because she's the reason we're here," Seraphina answers and then slowly moves the blade away from the woman's throat. "She's the reason I am what I am. And just like I helped you kill that bastard pig who raped you when you were a boy, you're going to help me kill *her*." She points the knife at the woman. "Because you owe me, Fredrik, just like *she* owes me."

I remain quiet for a long moment, trying to take in her words, seeking some kind of understanding in them and how this woman has anything to do with why Seraphina betrayed me. Why she has betrayed The Order. I want to feel out the details she's already given me and have some kind of idea of where this is going before I speak. Because I like to have the upper-hand right at the get-go. Always. Only this time I'm beginning to think that's not going to be the case.

Not being the one in control makes me very anxious.

"Why does this woman owe you?" I ask. "What has she done to you?"

Seraphina's darkly painted eyes grin before her lips do. She reaches around and touches the woman's hair, spearing the ends of it in between her fingers with gentle, motherly strokes. "So blond. So pretty." Then her hand comes up in a swift motion and falls back down across the woman's cheek; a sharp slapping noise zips through the air. "I hate blonds. I've always hated them. But this one in particular, I've been looking for her for *years*, Fredrik. Because of what she did to me."

"What did she do?"

She slaps the woman again and this time blood springs from her nose. The woman's hands are shaking against the leather restraints securing them to the arms of the chair. The muscles in her legs harden and relax repeatedly as she struggles. Her eyes are pleading for me to help her. I can't tell her that I'm not here to rescue her, that I'm a heartless bastard who only needs answers. But it's the truth. I don't *want* the woman to die, and if I can stop Seraphina from killing her, then I will. But sadly she's not my priority. And if she dies, I'll still be able to sleep tonight.

Yes, I am a monster.

"Why don't you ask her?" Seraphina says as she steps around in front of the woman and snatches back the gag tied around her head, removing it from her mouth.

"PLEASE! PLEASE LET ME *GO!*" The woman's cries pierce my ears, filling my senses with pain and heartbreak.

*I only feel this pain when the victim is innocent,* I say to myself as I've done many times before. It's how I know when I'm being lied to. It's how I know that when I'm torturing a victim in my chair whether they deserve to be set free or not. It's an instinct, one that only my heart knows, but sometimes my mind refuses to listen.

*I only feel this pain when the victim is innocent...*

She thrashes violently within the chair, trying to break free, but to no avail.

"P-Please...I'm *begging* you...*please* just let me go!" Sobs roll through her chest, causing her whole body to shake.

I push myself out of the chair and grab Seraphina from behind just as she's slamming the hilt of her knife into the woman's face. She fights against me, swinging her fists in the air blindly at me behind her until I grab them, too, and pin them against her chest. I hear the knife clink against the concrete floor. And then black spots spring before my eyes accompanied by a white-hot pain as the back of Seraphina's skull smashes against my face. Instinctively I release her, trying to shake my eyesight back into focus. Finally when I do seconds later, Seraphina already has the knife in her hand again and she's heaving herself away from me and toward the woman.

"SERAPHINA! STOP!"

I don't get to her in time.

Time stops. *Everything* stops. My answers, if they were truly to come from this unknown woman, seep out of her throat with the gush of blood pouring down her chest.

I stumble back and fall against the chair again, sitting in a slouched and defeated position with my legs splayed out across the floor. I watch the woman from my seat, the way her eyes begin to glaze over, how her eyelids flutter in some soft yet sickening way. I watch helplessly as she chokes, and how her body fights to hold on to that last breath, her bloodied chest heaving desperately.

And then her fingers uncurl and lay heavily over the chair arms. Her dead eyes look upward at the ceiling, filled with nothing. Blood drips from the chair into a dark puddle beneath it. It won't stop. I wonder how much blood this woman's body holds.

I sigh with pain and remorse and softly shut my eyes.

*I only feel this pain when the victim is innocent.*

Seraphina, standing with her back facing me, finally turns around. Her soft, plump mouth is partially agape. There's something called confusion and maybe even regret swirling in her brown eyes. She looks down at her hands, the right one with the knife covered in blood, and then she drops the knife as if it's a dirty, evil thing. She brings her hands up and looks at them, it seems as though asking herself how she could've done this. How could she have *done* this? I don't understand it. Seraphina is a killer. An executioner. Many lives have been taken by her hands. But they were, for the most part, deserving deaths. These three women she killed since yesterday were the first—that I know of— who were killed in cold blood.

Was it because of me? Am I to blame for her madness somehow?

No. She was *already* mad. She was a sadistic bitch when we met and when I fell in love with her. But *this*. What I'm witnessing now…

*I am so goddamn confused…*

"It wasn't her," Seraphina says, her voice cracking.

She looks at her hands again, one covered in blood, and then she looks back at me.

"I'm so sorry, Fredrik"—tears begin to stream down her cheeks—"I'm so sorry."

She falls to her knees on the concrete floor and buries her face in the palms of her hands, sobbing into her fingers.

I rush the short distance to her and pull her against my chest, enveloping her in my arms. I rock her against me, pressing my lips to the top of her black hair as she weeps. I let her cry, but I don't let it go on for long. Because I need answers now more than ever. I need to know everything.

"Tell me, love," I whisper, holding her tightly in my arms. "Tell me who you thought she was. I can help you if you'll just tell me. Make me understand."

She shakes her head against my chest.

"I-I can't. I can't tell you because you'll hate me."

"I could never hate you," I say with truth. I *love* her. Parts of her I don't love, like who she was moments ago when she killed that woman. But right now, the person she is wrapped in my arms, I love with everything in me. "You said she owed you, Seraphina. What did she owe you?"

At first she doesn't want to answer. I wait patiently, hoping that if I don't push her she'll feel more confident about telling me. I squeeze her gently for good measure.

"I was ten when I met her," she says, but then becomes quiet again.

Anxious. Desperate. Perplexed. They are among a thousand different emotions I'm feeling right now. But still I try to remain calm.

"I never meant to betray you," she says.

I feel like she's jumping subjects, evading the one about the woman.

"But I knew you had to get away from me," she goes on. "I couldn't leave you on my own. I tried. But I couldn't bear it. So I lied to you about everything. I started sleeping at Safe House Sixteen."

This is the part I don't want to hear, but know that I need to.

I brace myself, gripping her tighter, both out of preparation for the pain I'm going to feel, and the pain I'm going to inflict on her before this night is over, because of it.

"I-I did sleep with him, with Marcus who ran the safe-house."

I grit my teeth and take a deep breath.

I stay calm.

I stay quiet.

*I want to skin her alive.*

"I did it because I wanted you to find out."

"Why did you want me to find out?" My voice is composed, careful.

"Because I wanted—."

She stops.

I'm growing more impatient. Subconsciously I feel the leather straps on the chair slipping through my fingers as I bind her against it in my mind.

"You wanted what?" I ask with my chin resting atop her head.

"I wanted to hurt you."

"Why did you want to hurt me?"

*I love you.*

*I despise you.*

"Because love is pain," she says and I swallow down the truth of her admission. "Because love is the greatest scam of all time. And because as much as I fucking love you, I *hate* you for inflicting it upon me!"

Suddenly I feel a pinprick.

Warmth moves from my thigh upward, spreading out through my veins.

The room begins to blur, faintly at first, but enough that I instantly know I'm in trouble. I try to shake my mind free of the drug, but it's too strong, wrapping around my consciousness like a spider's silk around its prey.

I didn't even realize when Seraphina left my arms, or when I fell against the concrete floor.

Gasoline. The cool air is rife with it, so much so that it's beginning to burn my nostrils.

"Love…where are you?" I call out, but can't tell if the words ever actually left my lips. "Sera…"

My lids are getting heavier. Flames. The air isn't cool anymore. It's hot…so fucking hot. I want to loosen my tie to let my neck breathe, to strip off my suit jacket, but I can't move my arms.

"I love you, Fredrik," I hear her voice whisper near my ear, soft like powder, fatal like poison. I want to kiss her, to feel her lush lips on mine. I want to grind my hips against hers until she cries. "I love you…and because I love you"—I feel my body moving across the floor—"you have to let me go."

Smoke. It's scratching my throat and my lungs, seeping into my pores and suffocating my blood vessels. I feel like I'm being cooked from the inside out. The heat is becoming unbearable, the flames engulfing the wooden beams holding the basement ceiling up. I can't see them through my heavy lids, but I can hear them, licking the walls like a thousand demons that sprang from Hell to torment me.

"Seraphina…" I call out, my voice hoarse with pain, every kind of pain, "…Sera…"

———

I wake up the next morning lying in a cold field with the sun on my face. The thin layer of white snow around my body is stained black by soot from my clothes. I look up at the sky, so clear and so blue, and I see a sliver of gray smoke rising into the air in my peripheral vision.

With difficulty, I try to get up, but can only go as far as rolling over onto my side. Dead grass pricks my cheek. Snow melts in a little indention near my face as my hot breath expels from my lips and nostrils against it. I'm freezing, yet I'm warm and it doesn't make sense.

The thin layer of smoke rising over the tops of the trees in the short distance is coming from what was left of my house.

She didn't leave me there to burn.

*Why did she drag me out?*

Upon realizing, finally I feel the pain in the back of my head and I reach up weakly to massage the area with my fingertips. She had to have dragged my body up the concrete steps.

I'm aching all over. But I'm alive. And I wouldn't be if Seraphina didn't want me to be.

I will find her.

I'll never stop looking for her.

It's a dangerous game that she and I play, that we've always played. Only this time she has upped the ante.

And I'm all in.

# ONE

*Fredrik*

———

*Present Day...*

Five men, two on each side of me and another seated at the head of the dinner table my opposite, watch me with guarded eyes— my gun was taken at the door.

"It is a peaceful dinner, monsieur," the door man had said. "No weapons allowed."

"Very well," I had said and removed my gun from the back of my pants, placing it on the table.

I knew not to wear more than one as I'd surely be patted down before they allowed me inside. And I was correct.

But I need no gun.

Unarmed, I walked past a dozen guards carrying a bottle of wine and stepped into the belly of the beast surrounded by four of François Moreau's most experienced men.

I knew in advance also that the wine I brought would be whisked away by one of the waiters and placed in the center of the table. François thanked me for the gift. It was an expensive French wine, after all, and it would have been quite rude of him not to thank me, even knowing that I came here to kill him.

"Is it true?" François asks casually, looking over the length of the table at me seated on the other end. "Vonnegut has a bounty on three of his former men? Including you?"

I nod. "I suppose the rumors are true for once."

A slim, confident smile pulls the edges of François' hard, weathered mouth. He has short graying hair, cut smoothly at the back of his neck and combed over to one side in the front, plastered to his small head by thick amounts of hair gel.

"And I suppose tis' good that I have no interest in filling bounties for a man like Vonnegut." His smile becomes more arrogant, as if I have him to thank for being alive in this moment.

I nod again and bring my lips to my wine glass, which isn't the wine from the bottle that I brought.

The dark-haired man sitting to my left with a scar above his left eyebrow removes his white cloth napkin from the table in front of him. He unrolls it from its neat little arrangement and places it within his lap. The other three men sitting on the outsides of the table follow suit when they notice the waiters entering from a side door balancing full plates on their hands. François remains in the same position, not looking away from my eyes even when the waiter places his plate in front of him.

François steeples his hands, his elbows propped on the table.

"So Monsieur Gustavsson," he begins, "it is my understanding that you were sent here to get information from me on my employer, correct?"

"Yes," I answer, but offer him nothing else. I prefer to make him work for the details I know he wants before he has me killed.

"And what makes you think that I am at liberty to give you such information?" He appears amused by the very prospect of it.

My expression remains standard. Cool. Calm. Unruffled. And he grows more nervous by the second by my absence of tension. I'm only one man. Weaponless. Sitting at a table amongst five other men who, most assuredly, are packing heat despite the doorman's claims. I'm but one man in a mansion on a private land just outside of Nice, France, where at least nine other men armed with guns patrol the outside.

He must know that I am not just *one man*, after all.

I steeple my hands the same as his.

"Before this"—I wave one hand at the wrist briefly—"*lovely* evening is over, I can assure you that I'll have the information I came for." I point my index finger upward gently. "But not only that, you'll give it to me freely."

He looks surprised. And amused.

François shakes his head and lifts his wine glass to his lips, afterward setting it gently back on the table. He takes his time, the same as I have, by making me wait for more of a response. The blond-haired man sitting to my right eyes me from over the rim of his wine glass. All four of the men are dressed like François and myself. Tailored black suits and ties. Though I definitely look better in mine. And as if they were a collective, they pick up their forks and begin eating at the same time. François finally joins them, though I'm confident it has nothing to do with being hungry. He's simply wanting to drag out his moment of pause longer than it needs to.

He chews and then swallows.

"Is that so?" François finally says with an air of authority and a smile. His shiny silver fork clinks against the glass plate as he sets it down.

"As a matter of fact, it is," I say with confidence, as if I were simply telling him that, yes, it *is* raining outside, and welcoming him to step over to the window and see for himself. "I know your

Order to be run by a man named Monsieur Sébastien Fournier. He took over last year after Monsieur Julien Gerard was killed in Marseille." François wipes his mouth with his cloth napkin and continues to listen. "I also know that your Order is strictly black market and that many of the men under Fournier are American, running American hits on innocent American women."

François tilts his graying head to one side thoughtfully.

"Oh come now, monsieur, you cannot make me believe that you, of all people, care what happens to a few innocent women," he taunts me.

I remain unruffled on the outside, but on the inside, his words sting. And he knows this, otherwise he wouldn't have brought it up.

Bringing my lips to my glass again, I meet François' eyes from across the table, challenging him to test me further, without having to move a muscle in my face.

He smiles faintly and takes another sip.

I set my glass on the table.

"Well, I must say," François cuts in, looking down at his food, "if you know all of this, what more would you possibly need from me?"

"I want the key to the safety deposit box in New York," I say.

The lines around François' mouth deepen with his smile. He looks up toward the waiter standing at the ready to his left and the waiter goes over to him.

"Please, do us all a kindness and open that bottle of wine that Monsieur Gustavsson was so generous to bring this evening." He gestures toward the bottle with two fingers.

The waiter does as he is told and sets the opened bottle in the center of the table.

The other four men at the table all place their silverware back onto their plates, knowing that something other than dining is going on now and that they need to remain sharp. All of them wipe their mouths with their cloth napkins after taking a sip from their wine glasses.

François snaps his fingers and a small-framed woman with honey-colored hair pinned to the back of her head steps through a side entrance and scurries over to him. She is exquisite. Vulnerable. Frail. She wears a short black skirt that clings tightly to her hourglass form. I study the gentle slope of her bare neck and the fullness of her plump breasts underneath the thin white fabric of her blouse. She's not wearing a bra and her nipples are like little beads of sex inviting me to devour them.

I would love to break her beneath me.

Briefly, she meets my dark gaze but looks away before François catches her. And in just that small moment, I could sense the tiny jolt between her legs.

"New glasses please, mademoiselle," he orders and she scurries off to do his bidding.

"You like what you see?" François asks, noticing my attention on her as she leaves the room. "Perhaps I could offer you her services before our meeting comes to a close? I *am* a generous man, after all. Just because I do not plan to let you walk out of here alive does not mean I cannot treat you to life's luxuries before you die. Think of it as a parting gift."

"That won't be necessary," I say. "But I appreciate the offer."

"Well, you should at least eat something," he says, gesturing at the food in front of me that I haven't touched.

I shake my head and sigh. "I did not come here to dine, monsieur, as you know. I came here for the key. That is all."

"Well, you won't be getting it," he says and offers another smile.

Then he points to the blond-haired man sitting next to me and says, "Bring me the black box on my desk."

The man glances at me coldly, drops his napkin on the table and stands up. And as he's leaving the room, the woman with the honey-colored hair and heat between her legs re-enters the room with six slim wine glasses wedged strategically between her fingers. She sets one in front of each of us, walking over to me last. She takes her time about pulling her slender hand from the glass. I don't offer her the luxury of my eyes.

François points at her. "Come here," he says and she walks over to him.

He looks across the table at me in a sidelong glance with a clever look in his eyes. He points at the opened bottle of wine I brought. "He will drink first," he says indicating me.

The woman takes the bottle and approaches me with it.

"You think I did not anticipate your intentions?" François says waving his hand in a dramatic fashion at the wrist. "I know more about you than just your…mishap…in San Francisco. Killing that woman. That *innocent* woman." I'm seething beneath my skin, but I can stay calm. Taunting me in this way only shows François' true level of worry. "I know *all* about you." He grins maliciously and instantly I get the feeling he hasn't brought out the big guns yet, that he knows something worse about me that I did not expect him to know.

For the first time since I walked through those mansion doors, I'm unsure of my next move. But I can keep my calm. It takes much more than the provoking words of a dying man to trigger me.

The woman pours the wine into my glass and steps over to the side.

Seeing that I'm not going to ask François exactly what else he knows, he proceeds to tell me anyway.

"I've heard of your past." He takes another sip of the wine he's been drinking since before dinner began. "About how you got that nickname of yours." He rubs the fingertips of one hand together and looks up in thought. "What was it? Ah, yes, I remember now. They called you the little jackal. A scavenger boy. Rabid and worthless."

*I'm going to enjoy watching him die.*

I pretend to be unaffected and simply raise my brows inquisitively. "Seems to me you're trying to buy time." I glance briefly at my Rolex. "You don't have much left, I'm afraid."

François chuckles and smiles at me with teeth. He leans forward against the table and relaxes both arms across it. The blond-haired man re-enters the dining room with a glossy black box that fits in the palm of his hand. He places it on the table in front of François.

Without taking his eyes off me, François opens the box and removes a gold key dangling from a thick gold chain.

He holds it up in the light so that I may see it.

"I do not fear you, monsieur," he says as he opens his suit jacket and carefully drops the key into his hidden breast pocket. "I did want to give you an opportunity to, perhaps, negotiate your terms. But you really do possess more confidence than any man should." His deep-set light-colored eyes drop from mine and fall on the new wine glass in front of me. "Why don't you do the honors and drink from the wine you brought." He smiles vindictively and brushes his hand in the air toward me, urging me to drink it. "That is what you expected, isn't it?"

The dark-haired man on my left suddenly appears uncomfortable, shifting on his chair with a look of agitation. He reaches up and slides his index finger behind the neck of his dress shirt and moves it back and forth, trying to pull the fabric from his sweating skin. His face is growing pale and sickly.

François looks at him with little concern. "Is something wrong?"

The dark-haired man stands from the table. "Forgive me, monsieur, but I am not feeling well. Perhaps I should sit the rest of the evening out."

François nods and waves him away.

The man pushes his chair out and steps away from the table, grasping his napkin in his hand. He wipes the sweat from his forehead with it as he leaves, stumbling just before he rounds the corner and disappears from sight.

"I'm certainly glad I didn't eat the food," I say with a raised brow. Touching the edge of my plate with my finger, I push it away from me.

The other men, including François, look down at their plates simultaneously and then toss their napkins on top of the leftovers. Two waiters act immediately to remove the food from the table.

François looks irritated, as if he's already addressing the issue in his mind of firing his head chef as soon as this is over.

"Why don't you have a drink?" he suggests, getting back to the matter at hand. "Or did you forget?" He points at my glass.

"What, you think I poisoned it?" I ask.

François smiles and steeples his hands again. He looks at me knowingly.

"I would like for you to drink the wine," he repeats, ready to get this over with.

All eyes are on me. The three men left at the table. François. One waiter standing against the wall behind him. The woman with honey-colored hair standing in wait on François' right.

Finally I nod and curl my index and middle fingers around the stem of the glass. Hesitantly I bring the glass to my lips and slowly take a drink. As I'm doing this, I notice another one of the men starting to show signs of distress.

François only notices me.

"Drink it all," François instructs.

"As you wish." A grin tugs the corners of my lips just before I touch them with the glass.

A hard *thump* sounds from the area on the other side of the wall where the dark-haired man went just moments ago. A woman's scream pierces the air, followed by shouts in French:

"Call an ambulance!"

"Monsieur Bertrand has collapsed!"

Clearly rethinking this whole situation, François' eyes dart back and forth between me and the other men. But then he can only look at them when he realizes they are also sick. One collapses from the table, the chair that had been holding up his weight knocked onto its side.

François looks right at me, his deeply lined eyes wide with worry and rage.

"What have—" he shoots up from his chair and points at me with a bony finger. "You did this! *How* did you do this? You will tell me!"

He clutches his chest and falls back into the chair.

Another man stumbles away from his chair and collapses on the floor, vomiting and convulsing.

Gun shots sound outside the mansion.

The waiter standing against the wall tucks his tail between his legs and takes off running. The sound of glass shattering and metal trays clanking against the marble floors echoes throughout the halls.

"*Bastard!*" François shouts, still pointing a finger at me while he tries desperately to cling onto the edge of the table with the other hand. His face is turning colors, a very nice shade of burgundy and ash. I'll have to remember that when I buy my next tie.

I stand from my chair and casually straighten my black Armani suit, tugging both sides of the lapel. Then I take up the glass of wine I brought as a gift and I drink the rest of it down in front of him, setting the empty glass back on the table. François watches with horror, barely holding onto his life. Then I take the other glass of wine into my hand, the one I never really drank from but only pretended to, and I approach him with it. His eyes dart back and forth. He tries to reach into his jacket to grab his gun but he begins to vomit instead. I stop and wait, not wanting to get any of it on my shoes. François chokes and throws his head back, pressing his back against the chair. He gasps for air to fill his lungs with, but it just won't come, and he falls over forward onto the table, his cheek pressed against the expensive wood grain.

He is already dead before I can tell him how I did it, how I managed to poison a bottle of wine that I never touched.

More gunshots sound outside. And they're getting closer.

I set the glass down beside the balding spot in the top of his head and then I grab him by the shoulders, pulling his dead weight away from the table. His eyes are wide open. Lifeless. His vomit-laced mouth remains open partway in a ghastly display. His tongue is swollen.

I reach inside his hidden breast pocket and retrieve the safety deposit box key, afterward slipping it down inside my own pocket. In a way, François did freely give me the key. I simply needed to know where it was and he played right into my hands with his arrogance by revealing it to me.

"You did well," I say to the woman with the honey-colored hair still standing in the same spot near François' chair.

She smiles…no, she blushes, and glances briefly at the floor. So demure. So fragile. So fake. So willing to do anything that a man asks her to do when promised enough cocaine and sex to send her into oblivion for the next week.

Suddenly she doesn't look so shy anymore, but rather needy and quite repulsive. Such a pity, really, I looked forward to fucking her later. She crosses her arms over her large breasts and swallows nervously.

Her little green eyes move back and forth at each of the dining room entrances. Staff are still running frantically through the mansion.

"Where is it?" she asks anxiously about the cocaine.

She rubs her hands up and down against her arms.

Just then, as the last of the gun shots abate, Dorian Flynn, known by Izabel Seyfried as the 'blond-haired, blue-eyed devil', walks into the room with his 9MM down at his side.

The woman jumps at the sight of him and springs over next to me.

"Did you get it?" Dorian asks.

I nod.

Dorian's short, blond, spiky hair, I notice has blood in it. I cock my head to the side inquisitively.

"Can you ever get through a mission without making such a mess?"

"Fuck no," he says. "I *like* a fucking mess." Then he smirks and adds agitatedly, "Can you ever get through a mission without lingering? I'd like to leave before the police get here."

"Hey, wait a minute!" the woman says, stepping from beside me. "What about *me*?" She crosses her arms and glares at Dorian, but then looks to me for the answer. "You're not leaving until I get what you promised me."

Growing more anxious every passing second, Dorian takes things quickly into his hands. He raises his gun and a shot zips through the room. The woman falls against the marble floor with a bullet in her temple.

"Fucking druggie bitch," he says and jerks his head back. "Let's go."

I dust off my suit and step over her body.

# TWO

*Fredrik*

———

I'm back in Baltimore the next day, waiting for my employer and friend, Victor Faust, to arrive. It's three o'clock in the afternoon and it has been difficult to refrain from going into the basement. I usually visit her long before the afternoon hours, but today is a different day and sometimes things must be done out of order.

She gets very distraught when she doesn't see me for a long time. It kills me to leave her like that, but she understands that my job requires much of my time and attention. But I make it up to her the best I can. And she always forgives me.

Besides, *she* is also a job—a private and very personal one—and no matter what my responsibilities are to Victor Faust, I *make* time to spend with her. There has been progress and I'd hate to lose any of it by being away from her for too long.

After a late lunch, I'm sitting in the kitchen with my laptop open on the bar when Victor arrives.

"It's good to see you." I offer him a smile at the front door and gesture him inside.

Victor takes a seat in the den in one of two black leather chairs with carved wooden legs—imported from Italy—beside a matching wooden table. I take the one opposite him.

Reaching into the pocket of my white dress shirt, I retrieve the key I acquired from France and set it on the round table between us.

Victor leaves it there for the moment, his eyes only skirting it.

"I take it Moreau wasn't very cooperative," he says.

He sits with his arms resting across the length of the chair arms, the sleeve of his black suit jacket barely covering the thick silver watch he wears on his right wrist.

I smirk and shake my head.

"Monsieur François Moreau was exactly as you said he'd be. A stubborn and overly confident bastard." I motion two fingers in front of me when I see my maid, Greta, enter the room. "Please, get my guest and I a…" I glance over at Victor.

"A beer would be fine," he says.

I hold up two fingers to Greta. "Two Guinness."

She nods her gray head and slips into the kitchen.

Victor finally takes the safety deposit box key from the table between us, sliding it carefully across the shiny wooden surface. He examines it closely, the gold chain draped across the backs of his fingers.

"So this box in New York," I begin, propping my right ankle atop my left knee, "it contains *all* the information you need? Or will I be making another trip to France soon?"

Victor drops the key into the secret pocket of his suit jacket and shakes his head. He props a foot on a knee just as mine is.

"It contains enough," he tells me. "Sébastien Fournier may be difficult to track down, but I don't need *him* to take over his black market operations. He entrusted the identities and personal information on his operatives to François Moreau. Called him the

Gatekeeper. Moreau did an excellent job keeping the information hidden by securing it on an independent device and clear across the ocean. But he was a fool to think it would stay hidden forever."

Greta enters the den with an opened bottle of beer in each hand. She offers the first to Victor.

"Would you like me to prepare extra for dinner this evening?" Greta asks after she hands me my beer.

She stands before us dressed in a calf-length navy skirt and a short-sleeved, button-up pink blouse. Her long gray hair is fixed into a bun at the back of her head. She is of average height and weight, but her legs truly show her age, with tiny, varicose veins running along her thick calves and ankles.

I look to Victor again, curious myself if he'll be staying for dinner.

"No, I will be leaving soon," he says to Greta. "But thank you."

She nods to both of us and then I dismiss her, but just before she turns and leaves, her eyes catch mine privately, giving me a look of concern I'm all too familiar with.

She leaves the room, knowing she has made her point clear—Cassia has been asking for me.

I turn to Victor.

"Well, I have to say that you were right," I speak up. "I didn't think it would be as easy as it has been to take control of these black market operations."

Victor takes a sip of his beer and sets the bottle on the table.

I grasp mine firmly in my fingers over the end of the chair arm.

"Easy is too light a word," Victor says with a small smile. "I believe I used the word *do-able*."

I return the smile, because it's not often I ever see the statue of a man actually smile. For a long time, when I first met him, I never knew he had teeth.

"All right, yes, easy is putting it lightly," I agree and take another sip. "But I'd say taking over three operations in under three months is pretty damn good."

Victor nods.

"It's been a group effort," he says, always giving credit where credit is due. "I couldn't have done it without the four of you."

Victor is being modest. I know that, yes, he *could* do it without us. Very easily, in fact. Without myself, or Dorian Flynn, or his brother, Niklas Fleischer, or even that redheaded spitfire of a woman of his, Izabel Seyfried, who I've grown rather fond of in the past year. And Victor may treat us all with respect, but I also know that he wouldn't hesitate to kill any of us if it came down to it. Victor Faust is the epitome of 'iron fist'. I don't fear him. I fear no one. But I *do* respect him and I owe him my life.

However, if he were ever to find out about Cassia, he would likely take back the life he saved by getting to me before Vonnegut did a few months ago. Vonnegut is our former employer, head of The Order, which myself, Victor and Niklas were all a part of before we went rogue.

Now there is a heavy bounty on our heads and we've been laying low ever since.

"Where are we at now?" I ask. "What are our numbers?"

"Six black market operations are now under our control. Four in the United States. One in Mexico. And one in Sweden. All totaling one hundred thirty-three active members. Aside from what we had before obtaining them."

"One hundred thirty-*three*?" I ask, looking at him inquiringly.

"One operative was eliminated by Niklas yesterday. He did not pass the final tests. Spilled all of the false information we gave him, to Izabel."

"Ah, I see," I say, tilting my head briefly. "And how is Izabel doing in the field?"

"She's doing well," Victor says, but offers me nothing more, which strikes me in a curious way.

"It's not my place to ask," I say, "but is there anything to worry about?"

Victor looks over at me. He shakes his head. "Nothing *you* need to worry about," he clarifies. "My brother, on the other hand, I wonder every day if I'll get word that she has finally slit his throat."

I try to force my smile at bay, but it pushes its way to the surface. I shake my head and bring the bottle to my lips again just to attempt to conceal as much of the smile as I can. "Well, that doesn't surprise me. Surely you didn't think it would."

Finally I set the bottle on the table near Victor's.

"No, I did not," he says with a faint hint of a smile in his voice. "I doubt they will ever get along. It doesn't help that Niklas doesn't know when to shut his mouth. But Izabel..." he shakes his head with his short brown hair, as if he's concluding in his mind that there's no hope in their situation, "...she is just as bad as he is."

"As long as their...differences, don't get in the way of our operations," I say, "then it's probably best to let them ride it out." I shrug. "Besides, you know as well as I do that Niklas deserves the shit beat out of him every once in a while. He's almost..." I point my index finger up in front of me in emphasis, "...*almost* as bad a Dorian."

Victor switches feet, propping his left on his right knee. He drops his arms between the chair arms, leaving his elbows propped on the intricately carved wood, and he interlaces his fingers.

"Speaking of Dorian," he says, "how did he do in France?"

I sigh, shake my head and glance upward at the ceiling for a moment, expelling a burst of air before dropping my head.

"Like Niklas, Dorian is a train wreck," I say. "I admit he gets the job done, and he never makes a mistake, but he shocks even me at times. And, as you know, that's not an easy thing to do."

Victor raises an inquisitive brow. "Shocks *you*?" he says. "Yes, I do find that hard to believe."

I nod quickly. "Well yes. He's trigger-happy."

"That is his job," Victor says. "To kill the enemy and anyone who steps in the way."

"Yes, but"—I chew on the inside of my mouth in thought—"he's quite brutal. Kills without thinking."

Victor actually laughs, throwing his head back once and *laughs*. It stuns me for a moment, but I recover quickly.

He picks his beer up from the table and points at me with it in his hand and says before placing his lips on the glass, "You of all people accuse Dorian of being brutal because he kills without thinking about it." His laughter begins to fade but it's still present in his voice. "Don't you think that perhaps it shocks you because, *unlike* you, Dorian doesn't play with his food before he eats it? He's your polar opposite. How do you think he felt the first time he witnessed you in the interrogation room?"

He takes one more drink and sets the beer back on the table.

"OK, yes, I do see your point," I say with a faint smile.

"So then he's doing well?" Victor adds, dropping the humor and getting back to business. "I trust that he hasn't set off any red flags since he became your partner?"

I shake my head. "No, he hasn't. And so far he has passed all of the tests." I shake my head again, though this time with a long deep sigh. "I hate to say it, but I think you were right about him, too."

I hated to say it because when I first met Dorian Flynn, I wanted to strap him to a chair and pump his veins full of poison. He talked too much. Was cocky, arrogant, and incredibly impetuous. He's still all of those things. But he is, unfortunately for the sake of my killing him being put on hold probably indefinitely, an excellent operative.

But this poses an important question.

"How long exactly is Dorian expected to be my...partner?" I ask, practically having to scrape that dirty word right off my tongue. "I prefer to work alone. Unless of course, you're involved. *You* I can work with if necessary. Dorian, well, he kind of makes me want to stick the needles into my own veins at times."

Victor smiles faintly again.

"A few weeks more at the most," he says. "Just until he helps with the mission in Washington. After that, I'll put him on his own."

Then he adds, "I put the two of you together for the same reasons I put Niklas and Izabel together. You all need to learn to work together without killing each other."

I smirk. "And you just get along with everyone?" I ask with sarcasm, though entirely innocent and Victor knows this.

He simply nods. "I suppose."

Silence passes between us for the first time since he arrived. I hear Greta moving around in the kitchen, the sound of pans clanking on the stove and then the water running in the faucet as she begins to clean the vegetables. She always leaves the water running when she's cleaning vegetables.

"Fredrik," Victor says, breaking the silence.

He looks over at me and I meet his eyes, his painted darkly with concern and questions.

"I hear that you've been looking for Seraphina again," he says. "Is this true?"

I keep a straight face, not letting him know that his question has stirred something dark inside of me.

"Yes, I have," I answer honestly. "But I'm not letting it interfere with our operations."

Victor nods, but I get the feeling he doesn't believe me entirely.

It was just a few months ago, after he helped save my life from an ambush orchestrated by Vonnegut, head of our former Order, to take me out. I came clean and admitted to Victor that I never did kill my ex-wife, Seraphina, like he believed long ago that I had. I *couldn't* kill her. She may have betrayed me and tried to kill me, but there was still a part of her that I didn't want to let go. That in the end even when Seraphina was within reach of me, I couldn't force myself to take her life. Seraphina was the first and only interrogation that I could not break. And she was also the first and only interrogation I could not finish.

She escaped—because I let her, and I let her three innocent women died at her hands. I never saw her again after she set my house ablaze until nearly a year ago in New York. I was watching the nightly news and I saw her walking through a small crowd behind the news reporter.

I've been searching for her since.

Victor drops his foot on the floor and leans forward, draping his folded hands between his knees.

"Fredrik," he says, looking right at me with his head tilted to one side, "you do know that all you need to do is ask and I'll give you all the resources you need to help find her."

"No," I reject the idea quickly. I shake my head and lean forward, too. "This is on me, Victor. I appreciate the offer, but I have to do this one on my own. Surely you understand."

He nods a few times more, now looking out in front of him. Then he rises to his feet, straightening his suit jacket.

I stand with him and follow him to the front door.

"Keep me posted on Dorian," he says. "I'll send you details about Washington as soon as I have them ready."

"Will do," I say.

Victor bids me farewell and heads back to his current residence in Philadelphia.

The second he leaves the driveway, I head into the kitchen to get an update on Cassia from Greta.

# THREE

*Fredrik*

———

She's looking right at me, impatiently waiting for permission to speak, the moment I enter the kitchen.

"What is it?" I ask, standing at the entrance.

Drying her hands on a dish towel, Greta says, "Cassia is restless, Mr. Gustavsson." She sets the dish towel on the black granite countertop. "It's been three days. Forgive me for saying so, but it would've been better if you saw her when you first came back, rather than waiting until this evening."

I nod gently. "Yes, I know, but I have my reasons." Those which I don't feel obligated to explain to Greta. She is my maid and Cassia's caretaker when I'm gone. Not my mother.

I step up to the counter, my bare feet moving slowly over the cool tile floor, black and shiny like the countertop, and I enclose my hands down in front of me, loosely interlocking my fingers. I notice her throat move as she swallows nervously, her aged blue eyes falling away from me to look downward at something, anything other than me.

Tilting my head gently to one side, I say, "You're still afraid of me. After months in my home. Why? I've never harmed you."

Greta hesitantly raises her eyes to me, but can't hold the contact.

"I am sorry, but you're the first assignment I've ever had who"—she wrings her hands below her pelvic bone—"...does the things that you do. It is not something I'm used to. And probably never will be."

Greta—and Dorian—became two of our new 'employees' when Victor took over one of the black market operations here in the United States almost a year ago. Just like the one that is still—though not for long—run by Sébastien Fournier in France, we killed off the leaders of Greta's former Order and obtained all of the information on the identities of its operatives. Having this delicate and damning information gives us control over everyone involved. In a way it's no different than one large company buying another one out and new ownership moving in, making drastic changes and submitting all of the employees on the payroll to extensive background checks and running them through new tests. Most of them really don't care much who their leader is so long as they continue to be paid, but this makes it difficult to separate the loyal from those who would sell us out to a higher payer at the drop of a hat. But Victor Faust knows what he's doing. And I've become one of his key weapons in weeding out the unstable and untrustworthy. Each operation we take control of has had at least ninety or so members. All men and women, assassins and spies and safe-house operators who each go through me and my interrogation chair. If it comes to that, of course. But then again, most never get past Victor and Niklas to be unlucky enough to have to face me. I'm the one they are sent to when even after all tests have been passed, there is still suspicion.

Some of my...*victims*, as Izabel Seyfried calls them, might say that the way Vonnegut in The Order deals with suspicious employees—killing them quickly at the first sign—is a more humane way. Perhaps she's right. But there is no such thing as humane interrogation in this business. And besides, if there were, I'd certainly be old school.

Greta has never been in my chair. I trust her. Sometimes you can tell just by being around a person a few times if they're trustworthy. Greta is solid. A little skittish around me, though I can't blame her, but she has had every opportunity to call the police about the woman I keep locked in the basement. She has had ample opportunity to tell Victor or even Dorian. But she's done nothing. Maybe it's her fear of me keeping her loyal, which is never a good combination, but only time will tell.

I unclasp my hands and let my arms drop at my sides.

"If you'd like to be reassigned," I say. "I can arrange that, but I would need you to keep quiet about Cassia. I will tell Victor on my own time about her. Keeping her here is not a betrayal, it's simply a choice. One that I will face the consequences of when that time comes."

Greta shakes her head gently and momentarily drops her gaze to the floor. "No," she says, looking back up at me, her hands still clasped together in front of her. "I prefer to stay. I've grown to care for Cassia. I would like to make sure she is well taken care of when you're not here to care for her yourself."

"Thank you," I say and I truly mean it.

Not only did I not look forward to replacing Greta, but I really didn't want to have to kill her. And I would've had to if she chose to take the offer. She is the only other person who knows about Cassia and I can't let the little birdy leave the roost.

Greta sighs and unclasps her hands, resting them atop the counter.

She's growing nervous again.

"I have to tell you," she says and I prepare myself for it, "I truly believe, deep in my heart that she doesn't know where this Seraphina person is. I'm a pretty decent judge of character, Mr. Gustavsson, and when I look at that girl, I see a girl who is telling you the truth."

I bring my hands around clasping them together behind my back and then pace the floor a couple times.

"Perhaps," I say in response, staring off toward the floor-to-ceiling kitchen window overlooking the backyard, "but I believe that in time she'll have more to tell me."

"But I don't understand," Greta says with a hint of motherly desperation in her voice. "How can she tell you now *or* later where a person is whom she claims she doesn't know? And not that I would ever want you to interrogate her and do the awful things you do to others, *to* Cassia, but if you believe she's holding the truth from you, what is sparing her from that?"

I look right at Greta, disciplining her with only my eyes.

She blinks nervously and looks downward at the counter, grazing the bottoms of her fingers over the tops of the knuckles on her other hand. She knows better than to question my tactics. Her concerns may hold merit, but my reasons for not torturing Cassia are very personal.

Silence fills the room.

"You're free to go tonight if you'd like," I say. "I'll be in town for a few more days."

"Thank you, sir, but what about dinner?" She glances over at the fresh vegetables sitting in the strainer inside the sink, and the pans on the stove; one has been boiling for the past few minutes.

"Leave it," I say. "You can clean up tomorrow."

She bows her head and walks over to turn the fire off the stove. Afterward she removes the strainer from the sink and places it in the stainless steel refrigerator.

After taking up her yellow purse from the chair near the kitchen window and shouldering it, she walks over and places a silver key into my hand.

"Would you like me here at the same time tomorrow, sir?" she asks.

"Yes, that'll be fine," I reply, dropping my hand to my side with the key confined in my palm behind my curling fingers.

Greta disappears around the corner and seconds later I hear the front door closing behind her.

I turn and look toward the hallway, where just at the end of it a door is set in the wall which leads down into the basement. I picture Cassia's face, so soft and doll-like, her big light brown doe eyes and perfect, plump lips. And that treacherous little black heart that sits behind my ribs, as always when I think of her, begins to beat to a slow and ominous rhythm, betraying me so cruelly that I wish I could rip it from my chest and be free of it forever.

Moments later I'm standing in front of that door and sliding the key that Greta gave me into the lock. And without another thought, I head down the dark staircase and toward her. Cassia. The woman who if I let live, will certainly be the death of me.

# FOUR

*Cassia*

———

I love this spot, the way my back almost fits into the corner of the wall. The length of my spine running along the space where one wall meets the other. Sometimes I try to press myself against it so that my spine will touch the cool sheetrock, but my arms and shoulders are always in the way.

Something is *always* in the way—the shackle binding my right ankle, secured to a chain that stretches across the length of the room so that I can walk about; the ivory-painted walls unaccompanied by even the smallest of windows; the bottom of the concrete staircase on the farthest side of the room, at least six feet out of my reach; the door at the top of them that I know is always locked from the outside, so even if I could make it out of these bonds, I'd never see the other side of it. But more than anything in the way are the unanswered questions that constantly elude me.

Answers are the keys to my freedom.

Freedom to be able to feel the sun on my face whenever I want. To be able to sit underneath the stars and stare into their infinite silence. Or when I hear the rain pounding against the roof, I'd love the freedom to go outside and dance in it, to splash about the puddles like I used to do when I was a little girl.

But I happen to like where I am, confined in a sunless, starless, rainless room with only my thoughts for company on some days.

I guess it's the price I pay for being in love with the Devil.

I'm not ready for freedom yet. Fredrik needs something from me that I can't give him. But I still try. Only when I can will he give my freedom back. And only when I can, will I accept it.

Fredrik frightens me. But he isn't cruel. He is an enigma, that man, and I've never known another man like him. But then again…I can't remember.

I hear the door at the top of the stairs clicking open and I wrap my bare arms around my thinly-covered legs, drawn up against my chest. I'm wearing the sheer cotton white gown that Fredrik bought for me, which covers my legs and doesn't leave me exposed. He would never leave me exposed. He is kind to me. Most of the time.

His feet must be bare because I don't hear the bottoms of his dress shoes tapping against the concrete as he descends the steps. But I can hear the fabric of his dress pants touching as he moves down them, and I see his shadow cast against the wall growing larger. My heart begins to thrum against my ribcage to the composition of desire and fear. Because when it comes to him, the two always come hand in hand.

"Cassia." His voice is deep and sensual, like water moving over rocks, all-consuming, yet delicate. "I've asked you not to sit on the floor."

He steps out of the shadow and into the light before me, his tall height towering over me, casting its own shadow in the small space that separates us. I always feel controlled by his shadow, as if it's another entity in and of itself, another part of him which watches me when his back is turned.

"I'm sorry," I say looking up at him. "I just like it here."

He offers his hand to me and hesitantly I reach up and take it, placing my small fingers into his large ones. His hand collapses around mine as he carefully pulls me to my feet, the chain secured to my shackle clanging in the quiet. My slim gown tumbles down to just above my ankles when I stand up all the way. Fredrik looks me over with the sweep of his dark blue eyes, like he always does, searching for imperfections on my clothing or on my skin. I don't know why he does this. It's not as if I'm an object of fascination in which he feels some obsessive compulsive need to retain perfection of. He told me once when I asked, that he was making sure no one had tried to hurt me while he was gone. Greta would never hurt me. She's like a mother to me. I think Fredrik should have more confidence in her.

Fredrik walks with me toward the bed on the other side of the room, turning me around by the shoulders when we get there and guiding me to sit. Only after my bottom presses against the soft mattress, does he take a seat on the armless chair next to the bed beside me, where he always sits when he comes here.

"I've missed you," I say softly, placing my hands within my lap. "I was worried something had happened to you."

"Nothing will ever happen to me," he says in an unemotional voice. "Not unless I let it."

I smile softly and drop my gaze momentarily.

"Has Greta treated you well?" he asks, verifying further that he doesn't fully trust her.

Nodding once, I look up and meet his eyes. A shiver runs down my spine when I look into the depths of them. I'll never understand how any man can turn a woman's insides into warm mush with just a look.

"She always treats me with kindness," I say, honestly. "I like her very much."

Fredrik nods.

He sits up straight and crosses one leg over the other at the knee, lacing his strong fingers together within his lap. He's wearing a long-sleeved shirt with little black buttons down the center and the sleeves rolled up to his elbows. His feet are bare, just as I suspected, his legs covered by long black dress pants that drop over his ankles. He has strong, manly feet. Large feet. Just like his hands. I don't know why I'm always drawn to look at them, such a seemingly unimportant part of a man's body, but I'm always compelled. It's as if every inch of him was made to perfection and deserves to be admired. Even his flaws are perfect to me; the deep, but thin scar that runs three inches from behind his earlobe and around the back of his head, the larger scar along his abs that dips down into the left side of his rigid oblique. The tiny mole on the back of his neck, just at the top of his spine. They are all perfect. Or perhaps I'm just besotted for the first time in my life, and I don't know any better. All women experience nature's trickery at least once. Whether it's with the man next door, or the actor one dreams about but knows she'll never have.

Mine turned out to be my captor.

I straighten my back somewhat so that I don't appear to be slouching. My fingers fumble restlessly in my lap. Fredrik looks at me—he never took his eyes off me to begin with—and I know what's coming next. The part of his visits that I dread. I sigh and break eye contact, staring toward the wall far behind him and letting it blur out of focus.

"Have you remembered anything?" he asks softly.

I swallow down my nervousness and interlock my fingers together tightly so that I don't look so afraid.

Shaking my head gently, I answer, "No. Nothing new, anyway."

I can feel his gaze on me, seeking my attention. I yield to it and look at him.

"I've told you before, Cassia, that even if you think you're repeating yourself, that I want you to tell me what you remembered, what you saw while I was gone."

I swallow again and glance down at my hands.

"Just the fire," I say. "I was daydreaming. Yesterday. And the flames licking the ceiling bled through my memory, just like last time."

"Was she there?" he asks and it hurts my heart.

It always hurts my heart when he asks about that woman.

I nod slowly, reluctantly. "Yes."

He remains quiet and incredibly still, waiting for me to go on, to tell him everything I saw down to the last detail. But I don't want to this time. I want him to lay next to me and hold me in his arms like he did not long ago. I had never felt so safe. I want to feel like that again. Right now. Not because of my enigmatic fear of Fredrik, but because of the fear I feel when I see that woman's face in my memory. A woman with jet-black hair and sinister dark eyes. A woman I always tell Fredrik that I do not know, that I can't remember, but the truth is that I don't *want* to remember. And the more he presses me, tries to help me regain the memories of my life before the fire, the closer I get to knowing what she did to me. As much as I fear her without even knowing her, I know she must've done something horrible, unspeakable.

I would rather leave my past far behind if it means that to know it again, it would haunt me for the rest of my life.

But worse than that, I fear more than anything that once I remember and I give Fredrik the answers that he seeks, he'll find her and forget all about me.

"Tell me, Cassia…tell me what you remember."

I look beyond him, past his tousled dark hair and deep blue eyes, past the attractive scruff of his face that I often feel prickling against my cheeks even when he isn't touching me, and I let the memory blur into focus.

*The Fire...*

*The screaming in the apartment building wakes me. I shoot up from the bed, my face drenched in sweat, my lungs beginning to burn from the smoke filling the tiny room. It takes me a moment to realize what's happening and still it's not even the smoke that makes it all apparent. It's the screams. I realize that if I was the only person in the building, I never would've woken up at all. I look down at the bed and imagine myself lying there, curled within the white striped sheet, flames engulfing the mattress, licking the walls and the headboard and slithering toward my long blond hair spread out against the pillow, fast, like a desert snake moving in a sideward motion over the top of the sand.*

*I don't remember standing from the bed. How did I get here? I ask myself.*

*The screams in the hall are getting louder. I hear crashing and pounding just outside the door, but it's not my door that someone is beating on. And the crashing noise I can't make out, but I think it's the ceiling caving in. I see from underneath the door the lights flicker in the hallway and then go out.*

*The screams cease and I feel my heart in my throat.*

*Then as if time skips, I'm not standing in front of the bed anymore. I'm climbing out the window and making my way down the fire escape.*

*I slip and everything goes black.*

*Quiet.*

*Though I still hear my breath expelling from my nostrils unevenly as if my sinuses are clogged. The sound of my heartbeat*

*I hear and feel in my head, racing, beating violently through the veins in my temples.*

*But everything else around me is quiet; the sirens and horns fading quickly into the background.*

*Then I hear a voice. A woman's voice. At first it sounds distant as though she's talking to me from behind a wall, or across the length of a giant field. But her voice is getting closer.*

*"I told you I'd find you," the voice says with a hint of cruelty, mockery, satisfaction.*

*I try to open my eyes but the lids are too heavy. The tips of my fingers scratch against a hard, coarse surface. I move one hand around, pressing my palm fully against the surface, trying to decipher what it is and why I'm lying face down on it. My body solidifies and I recoil into myself as I begin to cough, my cheek scraping roughly against the hard material that is beginning to feel like concrete or asphalt. I taste the smoke in my lungs, I feel it burning my esophagus and the back of my throat and my nostrils.*

*I cough again violently and try to catch my breath as my body goes still. I sniffle once feeling the drainage behind my eyes and it burns like a hot poker is being shoved into my nostrils. I cry out in pain and then lie still, trying to breathe only through my mouth. My lips are dry and cracked and bleeding, and they too taste like smoke.*

*Tears seep from my eyes and my body shudders against the cool, hard surface like a quivering ball of muscle and bone. I think I'm going to die here. Wherever here is.*

*I'm freezing.*

*"You should've known better, Cassia," the voice says and it sounds like she's right behind me.*

*Determined to place a face with the voice, I try desperately to pry my lids apart, but like everything else inside of me, my eyes are burning.*

"Who are you?" I ask weakly and my voice cracks. I need water. I need something to wet my mouth. Anything...

She laughs quietly and the cruelty in it frightens me to my bitter core. I feel heat on the side of my face, the side not pressed against the hard surface. And then I hear her voice again and I know that she's right there, hovering over me with her mouth near mine, tracing a path from my earlobe to the corner of my lips.

I feel her lips on mine, so warm and soft and tender. My body is cold, so cold, and her lips so warm that I don't have it in me to protest. I feel her tongue slip into my mouth and gently tangle with mine. My eyelids, heavy before, now slam shut and leave me absolutely no control over them anymore.

"You'll always belong to me, Cassia," the woman whispers onto my mouth. "You owe me."

The coolness of her hand grazes the skin on my stomach and she slides her hand into the front of my thick cotton pajama pants. I feel her fingers hook inside of me harshly, painfully, and my eyes spring open to see her face looking back at me with malice and menace, her dark eyes swirling in the blue hue of the night sky, her slim outline illuminated by the streetlamp several feet behind her. Her hair is jet-black, cut short around her oval-shaped face, each side following the curvature of her jawline. She is beautiful. She is evil.

I'm afraid.

And then in a whirlwind the vociferous sounds of the frantic city catch up to my ears again. I begin to choke, coughing so terribly that I think my lungs are going to come up with the black-tinged saliva I expel into my hands. I roll over onto my back and stare upward at a starless black sky, rolling with winter clouds and brisk with winter wind. My body shakes so harshly that it feels like my bones are going to shatter like glass if I can't control it. My head falls back to the side and I see a pile of boxes. The leg of a couch. A black trash bag with a hole ripped in the bottom and some kind of fabric *pushing through it. A cracked mirror with a weathered wooden frame. A red milk crate full of random things: old beat up boxes of food, a bottle of antifreeze, a crushed soda can.*

*The woman is gone. I thought I heard her tall black boots crunching in the snow behind me when I went into the last coughing fit.*

*My body aches. I think my leg is broken. It's a wonder how I didn't feel it before. I grit my teeth and screw my eyes shut tight as the pain sears through me. I hear more voices approaching. Cops. Firemen. No...it's an EMT.*

*My eyes open and close from pain and exhaustion, but I try to fight the sleep. I want to see what's going on around me. I want to see if the woman is still close by. While the paramedics are tending to me, I don't pay them any attention, not even when they ask me questions looking to see how alert I am. But I look beyond them, toward the street filled with red and blue flashing lights that bounce off the nearby buildings. A crowd has gathered on the other side, all bundled in thick winter coats, pointing upward with their gloved hands at the building still engulfed in flames behind me.*

*But there is one tall dark figure amongst the crowd that appears out of place. He stands with his hands in the pockets of his long black coat. He is calm, unaffected by the chaos in the streets.*

*He is you.*

*You look at me instead, across the street and through moving bodies and vehicles that pass by and temporarily block our path. Your eyes pierce through me like...like nothing I've ever felt before. All I know is that my stomach feels hot and that I'm afraid, yet I still want to look back at you.*

*I-I don't know why, but...but my heart is breaking. Tears sting the backs of my eyes and my chest feels like it's falling in on itself, like a star burning up its last breath before it collapses into a black hole.*

*And then I wake up in your home and I barely remember my name much less anything else about me.*

# FIVE

*Cassia*

—

Fredrik reaches out his hand and wipes the tears from underneath my eyes. I gently coil my fingers around his strong wrist and I shut my eyes softly to savor his touch.

"She said that you owed her." Fredrik's voice pulls me back into the moment and my eyelids carefully break apart again.

His hand falls away. He places it back within his lap.

I look at for a long moment and then back up at his eyes.

"What?" I'm confused.

Fredrik tilts his head slightly to one side.

"You didn't say that before," he explains. "That the woman told you just before she left that you owed her. It's a new memory."

I blink, a little surprised, and nod as the realization sets in.

"Yes," I say. "She did say that. But I don't know what it means." I lower my head with regret and even shame. I want to give him whatever he needs or wants from me. I have since shortly after he brought me here many months ago. Even if it means that I'll lose him to that woman, I love him enough that I would let him go if it's what he wanted.

I don't know why I love him. I don't know how it's possible to love a man who keeps a woman chained in a basement. But then again, there are so many things I don't understand because I can't *remember* anything. So much doesn't make sense. Actually, *nothing* makes sense. I feel trapped in someone else's life. Out of place in the world, and as it goes on all around me, I stay put in the same place trying to recall a life I had before that doesn't seem to want to be found.

"Cassia," Fredrik says kindly and I raise my tear-filled eyes to him. He sighs regretfully. "If you can't make progress on your own, you know what I'll have to do."

My hands begin to shake within my lap, my bottom lip begins to tremble.

I shake my head. "No, Fredrik, please—"

He leans toward me in one swift motion, punishment in his eyes. I ground the palms of my hands against the mattress on both sides of me and push myself backward against the wall.

"I-I'm sorry," I say, fear lacing my voice.

"Do not call me by my name," he demands. "I can't have you doing that." He lowers his eyes and I can tell by that look of pain hidden behind them that his own rule burdens him in some way.

Fredrik stands from the chair and takes a seat on the edge of the bed closer to me.

"Come here," he says gently, holding out his hand.

I take it with only slight hesitation because even as much as I fear him, I still want to be with him.

He guides me next to him and I lay my upper body in his lap, my cheek pressed softly against his firm thigh. His large hand strokes my blond hair. His touch is gentle and kind and euphoric, but I know too what else those hands are capable of. I've seen the things he does to people. Terrible, nightmarish things. The very things he is threatening me with now.

"I can't bear to watch again," I say. "Please…don't make me watch."

His fingers continue to comb through my hair, leaving shivers to dance along the length of my spine.

"But you'll have to," he says in a calm, relaxing voice, "because I don't see any other way. Your memories only seem to be triggered by traumatic experiences. You wouldn't know what you know now about the fire if it wasn't for making you watch."

I move my head against his lap so that I can look up at him. His fingers fall from my hair and he brushes the backs of them down the side of my cheek.

"Tell me about her," I say in a powdery voice, trying not to force him away like I did the last time I insisted such a forbidden thing. "What did Seraphina do to you? Why do you want to find her so badly?"

He shoots up from the bed, leaving me to fall against the mattress.

"I've told you—"

I shoot up after him, stopping him mid-sentence, intent on making him understand, to make him talk to me once and for all. The chain around my ankle clanks loudly as I force myself across the few feet to stand in front of him.

"YOU TELL ME!" I scream at him, more tears pouring from the corners of my eyes. "*PLEASE!* I DESERVE TO KNOW!" I cry out. "You've kept me down here for a year. Took me away from… from whatever life I had before the fire. I may not remember it, but it was *mine*." I point at my chest; my voice and I know my expression, strained by pain and desperation. "You believe I know this woman well enough that I can lead you to her, that somehow I can help you find her. And I'm willing to do that…" my voice begins to soften. I only want to make him understand, not show defiance.

He shakes his head, though not as if telling me no, but it seems more like he's convincing *himself* not to tell me. Something he has done time and time again in all these months that I've been his prisoner. His willing prisoner.

I lower my voice to a whisper and clasp my thin fingers about his wrists. "Please, Fredrik," I say and he doesn't reprimand me for calling him by his name. I look deeply into his hardened, con-flicted eyes that refuse to look back at me. "Maybe if I knew more about her...I could remember. I might begin to understand who she was to me, how I knew her and"—I try to force his gaze but it's unshakable—"and what it is that I owe her."

This has been the one thing I've tried time and time again to make him understand, but he always cuts me off. He would rather make me watch him torture people to death to trigger my memo-ries than to do something as simple as tell me more about this woman who I apparently used to know before I lost my memory in that fire last year.

"*Please.*" It's my last desperate attempt. My chest is heaving with long deep breaths. My heart is aching with hopelessness.

He looks down into my eyes from his tall height and I can't read him. So much confliction. So much regret and anger and emotions I'm not sure I ever want to know. There's a beast that lives inside this man that I have seen, but I never want to meet it again. Not face to face like others have met it. I feel in the deepest part of me that he holds that beast down for my sake. Because he doesn't want to hurt me. But I also feel that it's only a matter of time before it controls the man I know and love. And every time he looks at me, he inches that much closer to succumbing to the beast and letting it take control.

I feel like I know, because it's what my heart tells me, that one day I *will* die by his hands.

I step toward him and soften my eyes as I reach my hand up and touch it to the side of his face. I smile warmly and push up on my toes, placing my lips against his.

He gazes deeply into my eyes when I pull away, and still, there's so much going on inside of him that I can read nothing.

*Fredrik*

—

I step back and away from Cassia, resolved to end this before it begins. I can't let her do this to me. Not again. I won't let her. Seraphina is important to me and I'll stop at nothing to find her, my ex-wife, the only woman I've ever known who I could be the real and true Fredrik Gustavsson with and not have to hide. The one woman who was so much like me that it was fate we were brought together.

Seraphina is the epitome of darkness. And I need her back.

She and I have unfinished business.

"Fredrik…" Cassia says and I raise my eyes to her. Hers are so innocent and pure, so…vulnerable. I want to take her. Now. To press her tight pink flesh against the wall and ravage her little body violently from the inside out. I want to mark her with my blade and lick the blood from her wounds, the way I used to do to Seraphina.

I force the need away, rounding my chin. Because I can't. I can't do that to Cassia. I *won't* do that to Cassia.

I force myself to walk away.

"Fredrik...please...don't go. Not yet. Please!" she calls out after me.

I hear the chain wrapped around her ankle hitting the floor as she tries to catch up to me, but it stops hard when I step out of her walking range and head toward the basement steps.

I hear her crying. I hate to hear her cry. Goddammit...I hate to hear her cry!

Slowly, I turn to face her, and she looks back at me with the same light brown doe-eyes that I have come to admire...that I've become a victim of.

I'll need to kill tonight. Just so that I can wash this threatening feeling from my dark heart.

"I'll be back in four hours," I say impassively, coldly even. "And you will watch."

I leave her standing there, drowning in her own tears, as I ascend the steps and out of the basement.

# SIX

*Fredrik*

———

If Dorian Flynn wasn't part of our new Order, and my assigned partner, he'd be the one I killed tonight. I hate this guy. I might just kill him anyway.

"Tha fuck is this bitch talkin' about?" Dorian asks, staring down into a magazine with some famous couple posing with a baby on the front. He flicks the center of it with his middle finger, making a short snapping noise and then drops the magazine on the table between us. "Don't you ever read this shit?"

"No," I answer simply, uninterested, and bring my mug of coffee to my lips.

I continue to watch out the tall glass window of the coffee shop for signs of my next interrogation—short bald man with a death wish long overdue.

"Well, you should," he says, looking at the magazine again. "This is what society has become. An overpopulated flock of loud-mouth, zero talent celebrities who get paid to fondle America's nutsack with bullshit drama." He shakes his head and presses his back against his chair. "Y'know, I could make a goddamn killing on pickin' these motherfuckers off. Hell, I think even Faust would be up for it."

I really don't care much about what Dorian is going on about, but I know that if I don't respond with something soon, he'll notice and might never shut up.

"Those people, as moronic as they may be," I say looking across the square table at him, "aren't hits. At least not yet."

Dorian shrugs and reaches out to close the magazine with two of his fingers. "Well, for the record, I want the first one that is."

I nod and look back out the window. "I'll let Victor know." And then I add with a smirk, "Seems to me they're fondling your nutsack just fine. The fact that you care about any of it at all proves that."

Dorian grins. He crosses his arms, covered by a dark brown leather jacket, over his chest. He has short dark blond hair, clean-cut though spiked up in the front and on the top. He's not as tall as I am at 6'3, must be about 6', with bright blue eyes that he often covers with sunglasses. He's been killing people for eight years now (he told me this when we first met, as casually as he might tell me he's been working in real estate for eight years) and I admit, he's good at only twenty-six years old. But a lot like Niklas Fleischer, Victor Faust's brother, Dorian is undisciplined and sometimes reckless. Though, I also admit that it seems to work for him.

He shakes his head, smiling across at me. "I'd like to bag one of those bitches. It's true. You got me." He puts up his hands, palms forward, and then drops them back onto the table. "But only to see the look on her face when I kick her out of my bed after I'm done with her. Knock her off her pedestal a little."

My left brow rises. "Oh, I see."

He nods. "Yeah, I could fuck a woman like that all day long, but at the end of the day, I'm looking for a nice, quiet, respectable girl to bring home to my folks, y'know."

"I thought your folks were dead?" I take another sip of my coffee.

Dorian shrugs and stretches his arms behind him high above his head. "Yeah, they are, but you get the picture."

"Sure I do," I say, though I still wish he'd shut up already. "But somehow I just don't see you settling down."

The spot between Dorian's eyes hardens as he rears his chin back. "I didn't say anything about settling down."

"Well, nice, quiet and respectable usually means settling down," I point out.

He throws his head back and laughs lightly. "Maybe in your world," he says. "Then again, you're kind of sadistic and I highly doubt that a nice, quiet, respectable girl would get too close to you for you to find out."

No, but I happen to have one in my basement. Granted, I have to keep her shackled inside the room so she doesn't run away or try to kill me, but Cassia is the kindest, most respectable girl I've ever met. And I've met a lot of women. Broken a lot of women.

A short, stubby bald man wearing a waist-length thick coat steps outside of a black sedan that just pulled into the parking lot. Its headlights are on, beaming at us through the tall window, and the motor remains running. Puffs of exhaust pour out of the rear stimulated by the frigid December air. Snow is thick on the outskirts of the parking lot where a snowplow made its rounds this morning, shoving mounds of it off the parking lot and out of the way.

"It's James Woodard," I say quietly, keeping my eyes on him from the tall window.

Dorian turns his head to look as the target leaves the running car and heads to his own car parked three spaces over.

I glance at my Rolex. "Same time. Just like last week."

"He's consistent," Dorian says.

"Yeah, fortunately for us that's his first mistake."

I stand up and remove my black coat from the back of the wooden chair and slip my arms into it. I zip it up to my throat. Dorian follows suit. We wait until the drop-off car is completely out of the parking lot before we head outside into the winter air. James Woodard glances at us once as we approach my car on the other end of the lot, but neither of us make eye contact. Woodard passes us off as any other customer leaving the coffee shop. He's not a smart man and it's a wonder why he was ever employed by any organization like mine to do even the simplest of tasks.

His stupidity is one reason we have to get rid of him. That, along with his selling information of our new Order to another black market organization. It isn't much and none of it's true. Victor has been suspicious of Woodard since he took over Woodard's Order last month. He has been feeding Woodard false information on us ever since. Just to see if he'd sell it. And he did. Twice. It just so happens that the man in the black sedan who just dropped him off was the buyer *and* one of our guys.

But where *I* come in, is interrogating him to find out if he's been selling that information to anyone else. And to find out if anyone else is involved. It's a perfect night to torture a man. And I have two hours left to make it back to my house with Woodard.

I told Cassia four hours, and I always keep my promises.

Dorian and I hop inside my car and the engine purrs to life. Woodard pulls out of the parking lot first, and already knowing which direction he'll be going, I wait about thirty seconds before I put my car into reverse and set out to follow him.

"What a fucking idiot," Dorian says with laughter. "How long did Victor say Woodard was employed under Norton?"

THE SWAN AND THE JACKAL

"Two years," I answer while pulling out of the parking lot and heading east.

"Shit," Dorian laughs again, "I'm surprised he lasted two *days*."

"Yeah, I have to agree with you on that one." I keep my eyes trained on the dark road, retaining the speed limit and trying to keep Woodard's car in my sights.

"You don't agree with me on much, do you?" Dorian asks, glancing over at me briefly. Not that he cares, really, but he's not so arrogant that he doesn't at least *try* to get along with others.

"No, I do agree with you on a lot," I admit. "It's just taking me some time to adjust to your guns-blazing methods."

This time his laughter fills the car.

"Are you *serious*?" he asks with humor and disbelief. "You're fucking scary, man. All I do is shoot people. You're one step away from a full-fledged serial killer. Talk about adjusting."

He says I'm scary, but I doubt he's at all afraid of me, or much of anything for that matter. He's too cocky and reckless to be afraid.

"I take it you'll be sitting this one out then?" I ask as my head falls to the right and I grin over at him.

Dorian smiles and nods. "Yeah, man, he's all yours. No arguments here."

That's good, because there's much more to tonight's interrogation than what a typical one entails.

And my audience will be limited to one.

We follow Woodard to a house he's been staying in since Victor killed his employer and took over their operations. Woodard also has a house over in Roland Park, the one he thinks he's led us to believe he spends most of his time at. Further proof this man is a lowlife piece of shit because he has a wife and two daughters he leaves in that Roland Park house, unprotected and oblivious to what he's involved in and how much danger they're in, while he hides out in the rental.

I think of killing him tonight as my good deed for the month, because his wife and daughters will probably live longer if he's dead.

After Woodard pulls into the driveway and kills the engine, he locks himself inside the house. Dorian and I park on the street in the cover of shadows cast by a thick of trees. One light glows from the window on the downstairs floor. I make my way to the front door while Dorian heads around back. I hear his boots crunching in the snow as he rounds the corner. After a few minutes, giving Dorian time to position himself at the back door and scope out the house through the windows, I raise my knuckles to the red-painted door and knock three times.

The curtain covering a tall, slim glass window running down the side along the length of the door frame, moves as Woodard tries to get a glimpse of me. The porch light flips on and I smile looking right at the peephole in the door, knowing that he's looking back at me through it.

Still with a smile on my face, I raise two fingers and wave.

"Who the hell are you?" he asks nervously, his voice muffled by the thick block of wood between us.

He knows who I am, or rather, he knows why I'm here. There's no way he's opening that door freely.

"Open the door, James," I call out in a singsong voice. "We have something to discuss."

"G-Go away!" His voice is trembling. "I don't know you and—I-I'll call the cops if you don't get off my property!" He says this with a sudden burst of confidence as if he actually believes the police are going to be able to help him.

But too soon the confidence fades when I don't move from my spot in front of the door and the smile on my face doesn't lose its potency. I stand with my hands clasped together in front of me.

Suddenly I hear a rhythmic beeping noise, as though Woodard is punching in numbers on an alarm keypad next to the front door.

BACK DOOR OPEN, I hear a robotic voice say when he tries to set the alarm.

Then I hear a scuffle inside, a loud *bang* against the door and something similar to glass shattering against the floor inside.

"No! Please! I-I…please!" Woodard calls out with a straining voice as if something, Dorian's arm perhaps, is pressed around his throat.

"Sit down and shut the fuck up," I hear Dorian say, and I picture him waving that gun of his in front of Woodard's face.

Everything goes quiet and then the porch light flips off, bathing me in darkness again. A second later, I hear the locks on the front door clicking and then it opens.

Woodard has been shoved into an oversized lounge chair in the front room.

"I-I don't know who you are or—"

"Sure you know who we are," I say, stepping around a broken vase and toward him.

I pull the ottoman away from his legs and take a seat on it directly in front of him, resting my arms on my thighs at the elbows, my hands dangling between my legs.

Woodard is shaking, the extra chin jiggling in the dim light cast by the lamp on the table next to him. He's wearing a navy and tan checkered long-sleeve with the top three buttons left undone and a white flannel shirt underneath. He reeks of cheap cologne and permanent markers.

Reaching up one pudgy hand, Woodard presses the tip of his finger in the center of his glasses and pushes them back over the bridge of his nose.

"Look, seriously, I really don't know why you're here," he says rather pathetically, his dark, beady eyes jerking between me and

Dorian. "I don't work for Norton anymore. Someone else took over. I just do what I'm told."

I smirk and glance behind him at nothing in particular. Already I can't seem to get the image of him in my chair, out of my head.

"So you *do* know why we're here," I mock him, cocking my head to one side. "Trust me, my friend, you'd do better to be honest up front."

I hope he's not honest up front. I want him to deny everything so I can get to work on him.

Woodard glances at Dorian.

"Tell me who you are," he says, more pleading than a demand, and then he looks back at me. There appears to be realization in his eyes. "I-I remember you. Both of you. Y-You were at the coffee shop. You followed me from there, didn't you?"

"Does that really matter?" I ask and cock my head to the other side.

I stand from the ottoman and straighten my coat.

"Search the house," I tell Dorian. "I'll send a cleaner to dispose of everything after you're done."

"Wait...what are you doing?" Woodard asks nervously from the chair.

I remove a syringe from my coat pocket and pull the protective cap off the tip of the needle.

"No...w-wait a goddamn minute! Y-You haven't even asked me anything! You haven't given me a chance to talk!"

*I don't* want *you to talk.*

Dorian's eyebrows crease as he looks at me questioningly.

"Let's see what he has to say first," Dorian speaks up, waving his gun at Woodard who keeps looking at the barrel apprehensively, worried it's going to go off. "There's a lot of shit to go through, Gustavsson. If the guy is willing to talk, I'm all for listening."

"Yeah…" Woodard agrees, hoping I'll do the same, his eyes jerking back and forth between us.

Suddenly he looks as though he was slapped in the face. His beady eyes grow wider and his breathing begins to elevate.

He points a shaky, pudgy finger at me.

"Gustavsson? Y-You're Fredrik Gustavsson…t-the one they call The Specialist?" His big head begins to shake side to side, over and over. "No…I-I'll tell you anything you want to know. But I don't have anything to hide. If I'd known who you worked for—shit, if I'd known who *you* were—I'd have let you in at the door. No questions asked. I'd have made you fucking soup!"

"There's nothing to tell," I say, though I'm pulling straws here. "We already know what you've been selling and to whom. There's no coming back from that." I just need him to shut the fuck up. I need to interrogate and kill him. I need Cassia to see it. "Stand up."

Woodard looks to Dorian for help, seeing as how he was the one of us willing to give him more time. Lucky for Woodard, Dorian doesn't like paperwork, and this big house full of files he'll have to sift through when I leave is the only thing keeping Woodard alive right now. In any other case, Dorian would've blown his brains against that hideous tapestry curtain behind him already.

"Five minutes," Dorian suggests. "Come on, man, you know I'm all about taking them out quick, but he's ready to talk."

Woodard nods furiously, his hands gripping the edges of the chair arms, his double chin moving like Jell-O.

I sigh heavily and drop my hands at my sides, the syringe filled with a cocktail that would've put Woodard to sleep long enough to get him back to my house quietly, dangles from my fingertips.

"Three minutes," I say.

"O-OK…three minutes," Woodard stutters. "I'm not a traitor."

"So you're a liar," Dorian says from beside me.

"No." Woodard shakes his head. "I *did* sell information to Marion Callahan, the guy who dropped me off in the parking lot. But—"

"Sounds like a traitor to me," Dorian adds and then raises his gun, pointed right at Woodard.

I reach out and place my hand on the cold steel, lowering it. The last thing I need is for Dorian to kill my victim and leave me with no one to put in my chair. Or the gun to go off that close to my ear and make me go deaf.

"Clock's ticking," I say to Woodard.

He puts up his hands momentarily and then drops them on the tops of his legs covered by khaki pants.

"I wanted to prove to the new bossman that I'm worth keeping," Woodard says. "Because I knew I was on my way out the first day Norton was killed and you guys took over. Look at me. I'm not necessarily considered an asset at first glance. And I couldn't get a face-to-face meeting with the new boss." He sighs. Already, I'm feeling a wave of disappointment beginning to wash over me. "Marion Callahan approached me outside my house, where my wife and daughters sleep for Christ's sake, and told me that if I could get him information on the new boss and his operations, they'd secure me a top level position in their outfit. N-Not as a killer, of course"—he smiles squeamishly—"I'm useless in the field. Never killed anyone in my life—w-well, once, but it was an accident."

"Two minutes," I remind him.

He nods and goes on:

"I met with Callahan twice and gave him two flash drives. Bogus information. Nothing on those drives is real. False names. False locations. Hell, I even made up details of a mission that never happened."

"Why would you do that?" I ask.

As much as I need to deal with Cassia, I equally need to deal with this. It is my job, after all, and I could never bring myself to give Victor Faust less than one hundred percent of my effort.

"Because I looked into Callahan," Woodard says. "I know my way around computers and information. I have backdoor access to FBI, CIA, Interpol—shit, I can get information on anyone from *any* database. But Callahan, he wasn't in any databases. None. I took his fingerprints from the business card he gave me. I ran him against everything for two weeks. Nothing."

"Well, that's not entirely unusual," I point out. "Given his profession."

Woodard stands from the chair, so deep in thought that he probably doesn't even notice. I let him. Dorian does, too, but keeps his gun at the ready down at his side. Woodard begins to pace, stopping every few seconds to look back at us, gesturing his hands intensely as he explains.

"Come on," he says as if we should know better, "there's always *some* kind of record, even if it's hidden on a Girl Scouts application. *No one* is a ghost. Not like this guy."

"So then he's using a fake name and his prints have never been recorded," Dorian says, getting as impatient as I was moments ago. "So fucking what. That doesn't prove anything other than he's good if there's no record of him."

Woodard smiles chillingly. "Not if he's a Boss."

That gets our attention.

Dorian and I look at each other briefly.

"Do you have any proof?" I ask.

"No," Woodard says. "But think about it, the ones at the top of the food chain, they're the most protected. They have no ties to anyone other than their right-hand men and their gatekeepers. They trust no one and they kill at the first sign of betrayal or suspicion. It's why the bosses are harder to find." Woodard points at me, still smiling darkly. "Have you ever *seen* Vonnegut?" he asks and it surprises me that he knows anything about my former employer, or that he was my employer at all.

"No," I answer. "Not face-to-face."

A grin spreads across Woodard's heavily cracked lips.

"Do you even know his first name?"

I don't answer, but I imagine the confused look on my face does that for me.

"That's what I thought," Woodard says.

He's feeling much more confident now about this whole situation. I, on the other hand, have surpassed the feeling of anxiousness about getting back to Cassia in time, and am now more concerned about the things Woodard is telling us.

Dorian shoves the barrel of his gun into Woodard's chest and forces him back into the chair.

"What the fuck are you trying to pull?" Dorian demands. "Marion Callahan has been reporting your stubby ass up the chain of command. Our boss knows what you did. If Callahan was the leader of another organization, why would he be messing with you at all? Why not just go to the source and take out our boss if he's such a ghost?"

"Because Callahan can't *get* to our boss," I say, pulling Dorian by the shoulder to move him away from Woodard. "He's trying to get in the old fashioned way, by working his way *up* that chain of command, gaining trust by pretending to weed out traitors."

"OK, but since when do bosses go out in the field and get their hands dirty like that?" Dorian brings up a good point. "Why risk himself by putting himself out there? Why not just get one of his men to do it?"

"Because the best place to hide is in plain sight," I say. "And if it was me and I wanted to take out another leader, I'd probably do it myself, too."

Woodard nods at me as if telling me he couldn't have said it better.

Even Victor Faust is guilty of this, wanting to be the one to take out the leaders. It's like another badge on his shirt, a trophy, and completely understandable. When Victor sent me to France to get the key to the deposit box in New York from François Moreau, he didn't send me there to kill their leader, Sébastien Fournier. He insisted that he'd be the one to take Fournier out.

"There's one thing to prove before anything you've said can be taken into consideration." I sit down on the ottoman in front of Woodard again, making sure he has a good view of the needle dangling from my fingers in between my knees. "The information on those drives that you sold to Marion Callahan."

Woodard's chin jiggles again as he nods rapidly.

"It can be verified," he says putting up his hands in surrender. "I swear it."

I glance at Dorian still standing on my left. "Looks like you'll be babysitting tonight," I say and he looks instantly argumentative. "I'm going to get in contact with our employer after I leave here and tell him everything that was said here tonight."

"Fuckin' A, man, you can't be serious," Dorian contends, waving his gun hand out beside him. "I can't fucking stay here. It smells like cough drops and..." he wrinkles his whole face, "... cheese."

I get up from the ottoman and dig in my pocket for the protective cap, slipping it back on the needle.

"If his story doesn't check out," I say as I start to walk past Dorian, "then you can shoot him," I add with my hand on his shoulder.

Despite knowing I'll never hear the end of this from Dorian later, I leave him there with James Woodard and set out to do what I have to do. First I call Victor and tell him everything about our visit with Woodard. He instructs me to wait until I receive word about what to do next, which thankfully got me out of doing anything else about it for the rest of the night.

Now I can focus on Cassia.

My teeth are on edge, my throat is dry, my head is spinning with scenarios, all of which begin with a brutal interrogation and end with Cassia remembering more of her past and more about Seraphina. But I've waited too long as it is. I have no one to take back to interrogate.

Feeling defeated and angry about how wrong this night has gone, I slam both hands against the steering wheel. The back of my neck is sweating. I've been grinding my teeth so abrasively on the drive back that my jaw hurts.

Just when I think it's over and that I'll have to wait another week or two before I get another interrogation job, I accept in my mind that returning to my old ways is all I have left.

And so I make a sharp U-turn in the split in the road and head east to find a man I've had on my backup list for times just like these, when I have no other choice.

# SEVEN

*Cassia*

———

The man's screams fill my ears with terror, like hands reaching for me out of an inferno and it burns too hotly for me to pull them out. All I can do is cover my ears with the palms of my hands and hope to deafen them. I don't want to look, but my subconscious forces my eyes open every few seconds as if a part of me can't resist. I sit on the floor, curled in the fetal position with my back against the wall. My favorite corner. The one farthest away from the enormous television screen protected behind a thick piece of Plexiglass. The television feeds live video of the other side of the basement, the side that has been closed off by a brick wall, and a single wooden door so thin that I don't really need the volume up on the television in order to hear the sounds coming from the other room.

"Please…please…I can't…I can't take anymore," the man says from the ominous chair that often haunts my dreams. "I've told you everything! I can't tell you what I don't know!" Blood spews from the man's swollen and busted lips. Fredrik beat him before he started pulling out his teeth.

Why did Fredrik *beat* him? He never resorts to that.

I'm frightened.

Have I angered him?

I swallow what's left of the saliva in my mouth and shut my eyes as tears seep between my lids and down my chapped cheeks. My arms are wrapped around my bent knees, pressed tightly against my chest. I'm shaking all over. Every inch of me trembles so terribly that I feel like I'm going to fall apart. I rock myself back and forth, weeping.

And then I begin to sing. I don't know this song, but it feels so familiar. I know the words, yet I'm not sure *how* I know them.

With my hands pressed over my ears, I sing louder as the man's screams amplify.

I sing louder...

*Fredrik*

I stop abruptly, the bloody pliers suspended in my hand just above the head of Dante Furlong, heroin dealer from the West Side. Even his blood stinks, not like normal blood which smells metallic and harsh. Is it possible to smell the evil in someone like a canine might scent a tumor?

I wonder if *my* blood smells as disgusting as his.

His wide eyes look up at me, partly petrified, partly questioning. He knows the beautiful voice is what made me stop, is what saved him from further suffering. But for how long, he wonders. It's what *I'd* wonder if I was the one in the chair.

"W-What is that?" he asks with a lisp, unable to set his tongue right in his mouth now that his front teeth are missing. "Where is that coming from?"

His long dirty fingers grip the ends of the chair arms, still trying to break his hands free from the leather restraints tight around his wrists. But at this point I doubt he realizes he's doing it anymore. It has become instinct, a way to deaden the pain, and his body doesn't want to let go just yet.

I look out ahead where the video camera is hidden in the wall, knowing that Cassia is looking back at me through the flatscreen in her room just on the other side of the brick.

Suddenly she stops singing *Where the Boys Are* by Connie Francis. Just when I was beginning to get lost in her voice, she stops and forces my mind back into the moment.

It's for the better.

I get back to work.

"Fuck! No! *Please!* You crazy motherfu—" The rest of Dante's words come out in garbled, choking sounds.

I twist the pliers back and forth to the sound of bone crunching in my ears. The tooth pops out and I drop it in the silver tray next to me with the other six.

Dante chokes on the blood draining into the back of his throat. His body shakes violently like a fish dropped on the shore just inches from the water. His beady pale blue eyes open and close from exhaustion and pain. But he hasn't felt pain yet. I'll pull out his fingernails next.

"I-I'll stop selling!" he spats. "I fucking swear it! I won't sell anymore." His mangled words begin to roll out amid sobs. His curly black hair, covered in filth and oil, glistens under the bright floodlight clamped on an IV stand at the back of the chair.

I hover over Dante and look into his eyes.

"You're a liar," I say in a calm, dark voice. "You're a fucking liar. A shit stain in a pair of underwear. Men like you never stop. You'll beg and plead in the face of pain, but the second I let you out of here, you'll be selling heroin to little boys in abandoned houses."

"Little b-boys? Man, I-I don't sell to little boys!"

I grab his blood and spit-covered chin vigorously with my latex-glove-covered hand, wrenching it still, digging my fingertips into his unshaven cheeks. "How many little boys have you given drugs to for a blowjob? Huh?" I squeeze his face harder.

"W-W-What tha' fuck are y-you t-talking about, man?!"

"HOW MANY?!"

I dig my fingers into his cheeks so deeply I can feel the outline of his lower jaw. He struggles in my grasp, his head secured to the chair by a leather strap like the ones on his wrists, ankles and torso, it fights to move side to side. But I hold him immobile.

"HOW *MANY*?!" I glare into his terrified face.

He tries to speak and I loosen my grip on his jaw enough to let him.

"I-I-I don't k-know! A few. I don't *know*! But they weren't children! Teenagers, maybe! But not little b-boys! I swear on my life I'll never sell again! I-I won't sell again!"

Without blinking, I bury the pliers inside his mouth and work on the next tooth. His body goes rigid in the chair, his filthy fingers curling in on themselves, his thighs covered by faded blue jeans hardening like blocks of cement. His eyes screw shut so tightly that a hundred deep crevices form around the corners of them.

Cassia starts singing Connie Francis again.

I try desperately to ignore it, pulling harder on Dante's teeth. One by one, I rip them out mercilessly as if the more aggressive I become the more of her voice I'll be able to block out. I'm never this sloppy, this angry. I pride myself on keeping full composure in the face of my victims, not allowing them to see that anything is bothering me. But Dante must know. He has to know probably just by the look in my eyes as I stand over him, that she's getting to me.

I choke back my tears.

I step away from him, the pliers dropping from my fingers onto the concrete beside my shoes. My breathing is heavy, deep. The tears are burning the backs of my eyes.

*Why is she doing this to me? How could I have ever let her do this to me?*

I bring my arm up and wipe my tears from my face with the back of my shirt sleeve. Tiny smears of blood stain the white fabric when I pull it away.

I'm never this sloppy!

The singing stops when Dante's pain stops. It's a pattern now, I realize. She was singing to block out his screams.

I hurt her.

And I hate myself for it.

But what's worse, I hate myself for giving a shit.

I snap the latex gloves off my hands, making sure not to get any of the blood on my fingers, and drop them on the floor by the pliers. And then I storm through the door into her side of the basement to find her sitting on the floor in the corner, crying into the palms of her hands.

# EIGHT

*Fredrik*

———

I walk past her and head into the restroom not far from her bed. It's a clean and cozy room just like the rest of Cassia's side of the basement. With ivory walls and a fancy marble counter and marble tile flooring. Greta keeps it clean for her. Every day she comes down here and scrubs the toilet and washes out the sink and shower. She replenishes Cassia's toiletries and makes certain that she has fresh towels. Everything in Cassia's space is immaculate.

That is until I brace my hands on the edge of the counter and leave bloodstains on the white marble. I don't know how I managed to get blood on my hands after being so careful.

I can't think straight!

I turn the bronze knob on the faucet and water gushes into my hands. Using more soap from the pump bottle than what's necessary, I scrub them hard and vigorously like a surgeon would scrub his hands before performing surgery. I want them to be clean, but I'm doing it mostly for a distraction. I don't want to face her. I don't want to see Cassia crying.

But the singing…she's never done that before. She has to have remembered something, and as much as I need to know what it is, I still don't want to face her.

With the water still blasting I brace my hands on the edge of the counter again, sigh heavily and drop my head in between my shoulders.

*Get it together, Fredrik,* I think to myself. *Get it together. It's all about Seraphina. Remember that.*

I never wanted it to go this far.

When I took Cassia from the shelter the night of the fire—she refused to be taken to the hospital—I never in my wildest imagination thought that what happened, *could.*

And here I am today, nearly a year later, and not only have I not found Seraphina, but I've developed feelings of remorse and sympathy for the very woman I need to help me draw Seraphina out of hiding.

I can't do this.

I've never felt so conflicted about anything in my life before this. I've ruined this woman, Cassia, this sweet and innocent and almost child-like woman who wouldn't kill a spider if it was crawling across her leg. All for the sake of finding my beloved Seraphina. I've been using this poor girl to draw Seraphina out like drawing venom from a snake bite. And I hate myself for it.

But it's the only way.

*Cassia* is the *only* way.

Opening my eyes, I see that I'm white-knuckling the counter, all of my fingers clamped down hard against it.

I raise my eyes to the small oval mirror in front of me.

Tiny flecks of blood are sprinkled about my unshaven face. Disgusted, I fill my hands with water and splash myself, two, three, four times before I'm satisfied. I reach out and pull the hand towel from the rod hanging on the wall and dry off. There's blood on my shirt, I notice, and I strip it off quickly.

How could I have been so careless?

When I finally shut the faucets off, I can hear Cassia crying again without the water to drown it out. And it sears through me.

Goddammit, I was never cut out for this. Not *this*. Feeling pain and sorrow for someone, *anyone,* and letting it control me. With Seraphina, I never had to *feel* it. Not like this. So goddamn unpleasant. We were alike, she and I, like two damaged souls cut from the same sadistic cloth. We *thrived* on pain. We got off on it. Whether it was our own pain, or the pain of someone willing to let us enjoy theirs.

"What do I do?" I ask myself aloud, looking into the mirror. "Fight it like I have been the past year? Or do I give in to it?"

I shake my head no. *No. No.* And pull my fist back and slam it into the mirror. Shards crack and fall into the sink, breaking into even smaller pieces, but leaving my skin unbroken. And when I look back into the mirror, all I see are pieces of myself that are missing. Not the glass, but of myself.

I've never been whole, not since the day I was born to a mother who left me wrapped in a shirt beside a public toilet.

I step out of the restroom and look first at the television screen mounted behind the Plexiglass. Dante is still struggling in the chair. He seems more alert now that I'm not in there with him. He's scanning the dark, dank room—the only part of this old house I never restored—for a way out, or something to use in which he can free himself. He has no idea that I'm watching. But he's not going anywhere. Houdini couldn't get out of those restraints.

"Please, Fredrik, please turn it off," Cassia says with a whimper.

I don't hesitate, despite something in the back of my mind— the dark, malevolent part—telling me to leave it alone. That she needs to see it, to hear it, to smell his pungent blood through the cracks in the wooden door that separates the rooms.

I walk over to the television and take the remote down from a shelf on the wall next to it, pressing my finger on the Power button. Cassia winds her frail fingers through the top of her hair, her face buried behind her knees.

"I'm sorry," I say standing over her. "I—"

"Lemme out'o 'ere! Omeone 'elp!" Dante cries out in garbled, choppy words.

Glancing back down at Cassia, her fingers begin to tighten in her hair as if she's trying to pull it out, inflicting pain on herself to block out Dante's cries.

"Fuck!" I march back across the room toward the wooden door and swing it open, slamming it against the wall.

The whites of Dante's eyes grow stark underneath the floodlight. Blood, more black than red, covers his face, pouring down his chin and soaking into his t-shirt. His face is swelling; his lips red and purple and puffy.

"Be quiet," I snap.

"M'beggin' oou! On't hurz me 'ny'ore!"

One of three syringes ready and waiting on the tall silver tray behind the chair is within my fingers in seconds. Holding it up to the light, I gently push on the silver plunger, releasing some of the heroin from the tip of the needle.

"W-What are 'ou 'oing?" His head struggles to see me behind him; fear of the unknown saturating every syllable.

"I. Said. Be. *Quiet*." I push the words through my teeth.

After quickly checking the placement and tension of the thin blue tourniquet wrapped around his upper arm, I jab the needle into his vein and pump the contents into him.

Scrubbing my hands all over again in Cassia's restroom, I find myself drifting off in deep thought as I stare at the broken mirror.

Dante is no longer screaming, but Cassia is still crying, albeit not as loudly as before. But her cries, no matter how hard or soft, make me ache just the same.

"Let me see your face," I say to Cassia gently, crouching beside her on the floor.

I reach out and fit my fingers underneath her chin, carefully raising her face from the confines of her legs.

"I won't hurt you," I say. "You know that. You should know that by now."

She shakes her blond head as her soft brown eyes look up into my blue ones. "You've hurt me before," she says, tears straining her voice. "You put me in that chair when you first brought me here. Who's to say you won't do it again?"

"*I'm* to say I won't do it again."

I sit down fully on the floor in front of her, my knees bent, my arms resting atop them at the wrists.

"I will never hurt you," I say, though I've told her this many times since that night. "Things were different then. I thought you…" I stop myself. I have to be careful the way I talk to her and with the things I say. "Cassia, I thought you knew more than you were telling me. But I know the truth now."

My heart utterly melts when she scoots across the short distance and moves to sit between my legs. My body instinctively allows her in, conforming to hers as my bare arms wrap around her small form. Her long delicate fingers curl about my bicep and she presses her head in the warm hollow where my shoulder and chest muscles meet. My eyes shut softly and a small breath emits from my parted lips as I feel her body against mine. I cup her head in my large hand and savor the softness of her hair pushing between my fingers and brushing my chest like a blanket of silk. My heart thrums inside of me, the first sign of an inevitable betrayal, the one where I become a man who I despise. A man who is weak and defenseless at the mercy of emotions that I learned long ago to reject.

I wish Seraphina would've let me fucking burn in that fire six years ago.

"You were singing," I whisper onto her hair. "Connie Francis. Why were you singing, Cassia?"

She shakes her head.

"I don't know. I'm sorry."

My arms tighten gently around her.

"It's OK," I say in a quiet voice.

After a pause, I ask carefully, "Do you remember anything?"

Cassia raises her head from my arm and turns at an angle to look into my eyes.

"Fredrik," she says as softly as I had spoken. "Can I speak freely? Can I tell you whatever I'm feeling?"

Confused, and even troubled by her question, I'm not sure at first that I want to let her.

"Yes," I say, against my better judgment.

Cassia turns around fully between my legs so that we're sitting face-to-face, her white gown pulled down over her bent knees, her hands resting on the tops of her delicate feet. I don't know how my hands found their way at each side of her neck, with my fingers splayed carefully to touch the edges of her jaw, but there they are, like two traitors setting out on their own, independent and defiant of the rest of me. I don't argue with them.

Her eyes soften and so does my dark heart.

I feel like I want to kiss her. But I don't. I can't. That'll only make me want to do other things to her and I've been down that road with Cassia before.

It's a very dangerous road.

"What is it?" I urge her, brushing my fingers against her jawline.

She reaches up and carefully hooks her hands about my wrists, peering into my eyes.

"The things that you do to those men," she says with words kind and understanding. "I want to know why, because my heart tells me that your darkness was born from darkness. It's not just a job like you've told me before. It's more than that, Fredrik."

My hands drop from her neck and fall atop my bent knees again, dangling at the wrists. I shake my head. In the eleven months and nineteen days that I've kept her here, she's never asked this question, never pried into my life before Seraphina. Her curiosities have always been—understandably so—only about Seraphina, the very reason that Cassia is here. I guess I never thought that after spending so long with someone that they eventually begin to see through all of the things you think you're hiding from them so well.

Cassia pushes herself closer when I thought she couldn't get any closer and urges me to look at her. Her right hand moves toward my face to console me, but I stop it, holding it at the wrist and pushing it back down.

"The only one of us who should be talking about our past, is you," I tell her.

Her doe-like eyes fall under a shroud of disappointment.

But she's not going to give up so easily.

"You've asked so much of me, Fredrik," she says with such kindness, "but when I ask anything of you, you turn me away. I only want to know this *one* thing. I don't care anymore about Seraphina, or the history you have with her. I don't even care what *I* have to do with it." Her soft hand ends up touching the side of my face anyway, and I'm not sure how she slipped it past my barrier. "All I care about anymore is you, Fredrik." She peers deeply into my eyes and ensnares my gaze, her face full of heartbreak and longing. "What are your demons trying so hard to kill?"

I push her hand away more forcibly this time.

"Do you remember anything?" I ask, disregarding her question altogether.

"Stop," she says with more intensity than I expected. "You're going to give me this. Before you leave me alone down here another night, you're *going* to tell me."

The desperation in her eyes bores into me. I look away, only to look right back at her.

"*Please…*" she says.

A lump moves down my throat and settles somewhere in my chest. All ten of my fingers spear through the top of my dark, messy hair and I let out a miserable sigh of defeat.

I never talk about my past to anyone. Ever. I try not to think about it, but on some days that is as futile as trying not to breathe. It wasn't until I met Seraphina eight years ago that I learned to control it, that I became a much different man from the one who hunted shit stains like Dante Furlong, tortured and sometimes murdered them every other night, never feeling the satisfaction that I longed to feel with every kill. I was like a drug addict, always looking for a fix but never really satisfied enough to stop. Never satisfied at all, because I only wanted to do it more and more.

Seraphina helped me control the perpetual urges. She showed me how to release the darkness within me with quieter, cleaner methods so that I didn't leave a trail of bodies and evidence behind. But the biggest impact that Seraphina had on my life was making me feel like I *had* one. Because before her, I was just a speck of dust floating around in oblivion. I didn't know the meaning of happiness, or understand the thrill of pleasure or the hunger for excitement. I was just a shell of a man who knew only darkness and death, who only felt the emotions of anger, and hatred, and rage and vengeance.

But Seraphina, she was my dark angel, who came into my life and showed me that there was so much more to living than I ever understood. Ever since she left me in that field the night she set my house ablaze, I've been slowly but surely succumbing to my old life again, and I need to find her before I fall too far.

If I haven't already.

Seraphina is the only person I've ever talked to about my past. If I do this with Cassia, I fear I might open doors that need to stay shut, for both our sakes.

But…I can't deny her.

I feel like I owe her after all I've put her through. And since it isn't anything about Seraphina, which I can't tell Cassia no matter how hard she pries, I resolve with myself to tell her what she wants to know.

Gazing into Cassia's eyes, I search them for a moment, rapt by her strange feelings for me, and briefly wonder why she even cares. And then my gaze falls on the wall behind her, in the corner where she's always sitting when I come down here.

Finally a fragment of a memory spills reluctantly from my lips.

*Twenty-three years ago…*

*Dust swirled up before me when the heavy door to the chamber room groaned opened. A dull gray light filtered inside the room from the hallway onto the stone floor. It hurt my eyes. My filthy hands came up mechanically to rub them only to push dirt behind my eyelids. I winced and shut them tight as tears—brought on only by the aggravation—drained warmly from the corners.*

*Boots tapped against the stones. Olaf's boots. I knew the sound of his just as I knew those of all the men who ran this place. It became mandatory to know, like that of every other part of my* surroundings at all times. The smell of the guard's body odor who watched this chamber room from dawn to noon. The squeaking noise the guard's cigarette lighter made who guarded the chamber from noon to dinner. The swishing of guard number three's long trench coat that always sounded like the rustling of a plastic garbage bag. These things were vital that I know because I was going to escape this place no matter what, and I needed to memorize every aspect of my environment.

I looked up from the edge of my elevated cot made of old wire and worn springs to see Olaf standing over me. My eyes still burned from the dirt I smeared in them. The other boys in the room were also sitting on their cots just as I was. Quiet. Scared. Each of them fearing that Olaf was here for them for punishment, and not for advancement like I was being treated to on this day.

"Come now," he said with the subtle backward tilt of his head, "I'll show you to your new quarters."

It had been a day to look forward to, when Olaf, after six months of confinement, believed I had learned my lesson and would never try to escape again. I was caught just outside the tall brick wall that surrounded the massive property. My only friend, Eduard, who spoke only French, was with me. He was shot in the head next to me—his sentence for fleeing. I was left alive and Eduard's death had been my final warning.

Olaf had always had a soft spot for me. He showed that by taking me away from the violent men and from the brutal beatings they inflicted on me. And he continued to show it by having me sleep in his quarters on some nights, sometimes on a cot on the floor next to his bed, while other times he insisted I sleep with him in his bed. I did not want to, but it would've been foolish to protest.

I stood from the cot and kept my eyes on the floor, my small, boyish hands folded together down in front of me. I smelled of urine and I was embarrassed. I had been wetting myself in my sleep the whole six months I had been imprisoned in this room. They did terrible things to the boys here. Unspeakable things.

Following Olaf past the tall iron door, my eyes finally began to adjust to the light in the hallway. The humid air stank of mold and garbage. I heard the pattering and squeaking of overfed rats scuttling down the hall in front and behind me. In this section of Olaf's estate, the rats were fed better than the boys were.

Olaf was wearing cologne and this frightened me. He was also dressed in a suit, although his pants were an inch too short and he wasn't wearing anything as distinguished as a tie. But the suit was a stark difference from the navy pants and wool sweaters he often wore. Olaf only wore suits and cologne for special occasions. And his special occasions almost always entailed teaching me the greatest of lessons, which I was always the most afraid to learn.

I dared not speak unless spoken to as he guided me down the long, dusty hallway and outside the building. I walked alongside him obediently toward the old, yet more immaculate building I had lived in with Olaf before I attempted escape. The sun was shining brightly overhead as my bare feet went over the prickly grass. The warmth on my skin was a godsend. The clean air filling my lungs. The sweet smell of the white flowers with bell-shaped petals that grew alongside the building.

But it was gone all too quickly, as well as the sunlight, when we stepped through another door and I was bathed in a harsh orange light in the foyer and the acrid smell of incense and cigars.

Willa, in her average height and average frame, greeted us wearing a long gray dress that fell just above her ankles, and a pair of flat black shoes over thin white ankle socks. Her arms were covered by the sleeves of a white button-up top that she wore underneath the dress, the collar fixed neatly around her neck with a little four-leaf clover broach pinned to the left side. I liked Willa. She was the only person other than the boys who were imprisoned here like I was, who I didn't want to see die a painful and horrific death.

*Willa was young, but older than me by at least five years. A kind and beautiful girl of about fifteen or sixteen. She was taken by Eskill at a young age, the same as I was. But she would never be sold and was treated kindly by the other men for the most part. I never knew why.*

*But Willa, also like me, put on a very different face in front of the men.*

*And as always when I saw her, I went along with it.*

*"Vhy geev me the runt?" Willa snapped in a heavily broken accent, her pretty natural pink-colored lips curling with censure as she looked down at me through harsh, but beautiful green eyes. "Vhy must you always geev me ze hopeless ones?"*

*"Because you are the only one here, my dear Willa, who can make the hopeless ones at least* appear *worthy." Olaf smiled. I wouldn't dare look at his face, but I could tell there was a smile on it without having to see.*

*My body jerked forward and I nearly lost my footing as Willa's hand yanked on my elbow. And then I saw stars when she slapped me hard across the face with her free hand, and finally my wobbly legs came out from underneath me. My bare knees scraped against the wood floor, but I kept myself from falling further, bracing my free hand against it to hold up my frail weight.*

*"Geet up!" Willa pulled me to my feet.*

*"Willa," I heard Olaf say in a forewarning tone, "I've told you, not in the face. Now go. Get him cleaned up."*

*"Yes, sir," Willa said, curtsied and then turned on her heels with my elbow still clutched in her hand.*

*She walked me up the winding staircase to the second floor. Passing other servants in matching gray dresses, Willa grabbed me by the back of my dark, filthy hair and wound her fingers aggressively through it, pushing me along in front of her cruelly.*

*"I said valk straight, boy!" she growled behind me.*

When the door to her quarters was opened, she gave me a hard shove and I fell through the doorway onto my hands and knees.

The lock on the door clicked behind me and then Willa was sitting on the floor next to me, pulling me into her lap and rocking me against her chest.

"I'm so sorry, Freedrik!" she cried into my hair. "You vill forgive me?"

Tears soaked my cheeks, streaking through a layer of dirt I could feel on my face. But I wasn't crying because of the way she treated me. I was just glad to see her again.

"I'll always forgive you, Willa."

I felt her lips on the top of my head and it sent a rush of warmth through my body.

"Ve must get you ready quickly," she said, helping me to my feet again. "I don't want Olaf to have any reason to put you back in confinement."

"I'm afraid, Willa."

"I know, Freedrik. I know."

She kissed me lightly on the cheek and wasted no time getting me into the bath. She was always so careful with me, just as she was with all of the boys who were placed in her care. And she never violated me. She cleaned every part of my body with a caring touch, but never in violation. I never wanted to leave her room whenever I was there, but I would always be whisked away soon after, to avoid suspicion and to make certain that Willa maintained her place as head servant.

After I was bathed and dressed in a clean white t-shirt and a pair of khaki pants, Willa hugged me goodbye as the kind and loving young girl, before taking me back out into the hall as the girl with the iron fist.

Minutes later she was gone and I was back in the company of Olaf, who seemed to be waiting eagerly for me in his too-small suit and headache inducing cologne.

"Before I take you to your new quarters," Olaf said walking beside me with his hands resting folded on his backside, "there is something you need to see."

I didn't like the sound of that. Already my legs felt shaky, my stomach queasy and tied up in knots. I inhaled a deep breath and remained silent with my eyes facing forward.

"Do you remember when I punished you long ago for forgetting to brush your teeth?" he asked.

I nod. "Yes, sir."

How could I forget? He brushed them for me in such a violent manner that the toothbrush had been shoved into the back of my throat numerous times, and he scrubbed my gums so hard that they bled for three days afterward.

We turned left at the end of the hall and came upon a door.

I heard screaming inside and my legs began to shake more noticeably.

Olaf placed his weathered hand on the lever-style handle and said, "This is what will happen to you if your teeth become damaged, or diseased, or grow in crookedly after the old ones have fallen out. You've been lucky so far to be blessed with good teeth. Let's hope it stays that way. You will become a young man soon, in your prime, and how your body begins to take shape now will be with you forever. If any part of it isn't satisfactory, you'll face extensive cosmetic corrections, or, depending on how well you are fancied by myself or another Master, you could be disposed of."

My heart sank and my knees began to buckle, but I straightened up quickly.

He pushed open the door and the screams escaped the room in a whirlwind as if they had been waiting on the other side of that door to be set free. I wanted to cover my ears with my hands, but I knew better than to try. I knew to remain standing with my back *straight, my eyes lowered and my arms either down at my sides or placed on my backside like Olaf was standing. I opted for folding my hands together behind me so that I could at least dig my fingers into one another as a way to cope and distract from the screams. They echoed vociferously through the moderately-sized room with high vaulted ceilings. I could smell blood. Bitter and stout, as clearly as if my face had been shoved in a pool of it. I had always had an unfortunate strong sense of smell that I often thought of as a curse. Especially in times like these.*

*Olaf guided me into another room adjacent to the main room where a boy, older than me and probably Willa's age, was strapped to a strange-looking chair that allowed his legs to stretch out in front of him elevated evenly with the rest of his body. His blond head was strapped against a headrest by a thick piece of leather, like his torso and his ankles and his arms, which were laying out straight against the chair arms and bound at the wrists.*

*The boy thrashed about in the chair, though he could hardly move. Blood spilled out over his chin, crimson and sticky. His hair was drenched in sweat. His eyes were wide and frightened.*

*I wanted to throw up. I wanted to run out of that room as fast as I could, to hide in Willa's room and hope to never be found but by her so that she could hold me against her breasts and comfort me.*

*But I could do nothing.*

*A man with curly gray hair, wearing a white lab coat, stood over the boy with a pair of pliers in his hand, covered in blood. He didn't even wear gloves. I got a dark feeling from that man, even worse than the one I got from Olaf. This man liked blood. The smell of it. The mesmerizing crimson color of it. The thickness of it. The taste of it. But most of all, I could sense that he loved drawing it, in any way possible. This man frightened me more than Olaf ever could.*

*"Is this the little jackal?" the man asked.*

*"Yes, this is Fredrik."*

*"Good, good," the man said and caught my eyes with a spine-chilling smile.*

*I didn't want to look at him, and I wasn't supposed to, but I couldn't help it. Thankfully he didn't feel any need to have me reprimanded for the mistake. No, this man was beyond beatings and punishment. His mind danced in Death's realm too much to be bothered with such petty things.*

*He turned back to the frightened teenaged boy strapped in the chair and inserted the pliers into his mouth. The boy grunted and tried to scream while attempting to bite down on the pliers at the same time. But the man grabbed his lower jaw with the other hand and forced his mouth open.*

*My hands were shaking on my backside. Bile churned violently in my stomach. I started to look away until I remembered promptly that if Olaf noticed, he'd punish me.*

*The pliers wrenched back and forth, side to side, and a blood-curdling sound of bone crunching almost made me faint. My knees began to buckle again, but this time I wasn't able to control them and I felt Olaf's hand around my elbow, catching me before I hit the floor.*

*I gathered my composure quickly and stood up straight, my breathing heavy and rapid, my hands trembling now down at my sides.*

*The man jerked the tooth from the boy's bleeding mouth and dropped it on the floor.*

*And then he went to work on another one.*

*By the fifth tooth, I could no longer stand up on my own.*

I can't look at Cassia. My chest is heavy with the memory, a weight so oppressive and unforgiving that I'm still surprised every day of my life that it hasn't killed me yet. I still have the nightmares. I still wake up in a feverish sweat, so tormented by the faces—those evil, those incapacitated—that I believe I'm living it all over again. And in my reality, it makes my need that much greater. It makes my addiction that much more dangerous. All-consuming.

I will never stop. I can never stop.

The past has shaped me, molded me into a monster. A monster with a persecuted heart and a dead soul.

# NINE

*Cassia*

———

I can't speak, not because I don't know what to say, but because I don't know where to start.

My heart is breaking into a million pieces.

Fredrik pushes my hands away carefully when I try to cup his face within my palms.

"No pity," he says. "Is that understood?"

"How can you *say* that?" I gaze deeply into his eyes filled with absolutely nothing—mine filled with heartbreak. "Fredrik—"

"No," he says resolutely and rises to his feet, leaving me on the floor. "You have to understand, Cassia, it doesn't hurt me to talk about it. I don't cry myself to sleep at night thinking about my childhood. It does something *else* to me. It puts me in a much darker place." His beautiful blue eyes peer down into mine with a chilling darkness. "I neither deserve nor *want* pity."

I stand from the floor, the chain around my ankle shuffling as I approach him.

"Did that man ever put you in that chair?" I ask quietly from behind now that his back is to me. "Did he pull out your teeth?"

Fredrik's shoulders rise and fall with a heavy, silent breath.

He turns around to face me, his tall height and gorgeous features as always make my heart flutter and my stomach harden when he looks at me like that, like he's hungry for something. It's the darkness within him, the part of him that takes over and compels him to control me, to ravage me in ways that, although I can't remember, I know that no other man ever has.

"No," he answers. "It never came to that with me. But many of the other boys, they weren't so fortunate." He looks away, his bare arms defined by hard muscles crossed over his hairless chest. "*Other* things were done to me. I would've preferred the teeth pulling."

"What kinds of things?" My chest clenches uncomfortably just thinking about it. I step a little closer, being careful not to invade his space too quickly because I'm unsure of his mindset.

"Why do you want to know, Cassia?" He turns around fully now so that he can face me. He appears suspicious. "What are you trying to pull?"

Shaking my head repeatedly I say, "Is *that* what you believe? That I'm trying to *manipulate* you?" While I can understand why he'd have suspicions, it still troubles me to know that he even remotely believes that.

I step right up to him and close that last bit of space between us, resentment in my eyes. "Is that what you *truly* believe, Fredrik? That I would use something as horrific as your past against you for my own benefit?"

"If I were in your position," he says cocking his head to one side, "it's what *I'd* do."

Hurt by his admission, my eyes fall away from his.

"Do you remember anything?" he asks, all too soon going back to the inevitable.

And I don't have the energy to fight it anymore.

"No." I shake my head. "I don't remember anything."

The chain is dragged noisily across the floor as I walk away from him and go back toward my corner.

"Cassia," Fredrik calls out softly, "please don't sit on the floor. I'm asking you."

I do anyway.

Curling up in the corner with my back pressed against the wall, I pull my knees covered by my long gown toward my chest and wrap my arms around them. And I stare out at nothing, defeat consuming me.

"Why am I not enough?" I ask listlessly.

I feel Fredrik's eyes on me without having to look up at him.

He says nothing.

"Why do you love that woman so much?" I go on. "I may not know anything about her because you refuse to tell me, but I know in my heart that she must be evil. She's done something terrible to you, something unforgivable, yet you still love her. I can tell."

"You aren't seeing the whole picture, Cassia."

He walks over and stands above me. I still don't look up at him. My gaze remains fixed out ahead; something white, probably the dresser, slowly blurs into focus.

"And I'll never see the whole picture if you won't tell me." I choke back my tears. I don't want him to see me cry anymore. "But why am I not enough? Tell me why you love her, a woman who doesn't seem to want to be found, yet…I'm *here* and you refuse me."

"I love no one," he says and I know he's lying. "And neither do you."

Stung by his accusation, I finally look up at him. But I can't speak. I'm too hurt to speak. I wonder how any man can be *so* damaged that he doesn't see love, *real* love, when it's right in front of him.

"I'll ask you one more time," he says. "Is there anything you want to tell me about what you remember?"

"No," I lie. "I remember nothing." I glare up at him for a tense moment, the tears finally seeping from my eyes, and then my gaze drops toward the floor and Fredrik leaves me sitting here as he makes his way toward the concrete steps.

"Are you going to kill that man in there?" I ask without looking at him.

He stops for a moment, but then proceeds up the stairs without another word.

# TEN

*Fredrik*

———

Today is the first day in a long time that I've left Cassia alone in Greta's care and am relieved to be away from her. She is dangerous to me and I can't let her get under my skin. I may be a devil in my own right, but I'm still human, and I feel remorse and compassion for Cassia, among other things, that are a recipe for pain and regret.

Seraphina is my priority. She's all that should matter to me because in the end—

No, I can't think about that right now. Not here.

"Fredrik?" Izabel Seyfried says from her seat. Her voice snaps me back into the moment. "Are you still alive in there?" She waves her hand in front of my face, grinning at me with bright green eyes framed by long auburn hair that lays over both shoulders.

Izabel has become quite an asset—and quite the killer—to our growing organization. She's like a sister to me, a stubborn, feisty, bloodthirsty vengeance-seeker, but a sister, nonetheless. And I have no room to talk. She and I are more alike than I care to admit.

I let out a heavy sigh and lay both arms against the elongated table. Between them are photos of two targets in Washington State. The same photos are on the table in front of Izabel, Niklas on the other side of the table directly across from her, Dorian across from me, and next to him, of all people who stink of permanent markers and cheese, James Woodard.

It turns out that Woodard was telling the truth about Marion Callahan, the man he was selling false information to, which in turn almost got him killed.

Victor sits at the head of the table where he always sits, between Izabel and Niklas. I'm of higher rank than Izabel and would normally sit to Victor's left, but seeing as she's the one sleeping with him and might cut me if I argue with her about it, I don't mind so much the demotion in seating arrangements.

The room is dimly lit with dark, dingy walls and a single exposed light bulb set in the high ceiling. There are no windows and the entire place reeks of mold and water damaged walls. It's but one of dozens of bases scattered all over the United States that we use to conduct business and hold meetings just like this one.

I crack a smile at Izabel, hoping to deter her from digging deeper into my head.

"That's a fake smile if I've never seen one," she says, calling me out. "Seriously, what's goin' on with you?"

"I just haven't had much sleep the past few days." I refrain from looking her in the eyes. If anyone at this table can detect a lie other than myself, it's Izabel. She is, after all, a master of manipulation and deceit.

"If you need to sit this mission out," Victor speaks up, "you're free to do so, and you'll only be contacted if an interrogation is needed."

"No," I say right away because I want to be as far away from Cassia as I can be. "I'm good to go. I'll get some shuteye on the flight out." I glance back down at the photos of a man and a woman taken outside of restaurants, convenience stores, and one of the man coming out of a daycare center, which is disturbing on so many levels. "Besides, I have a feeling that this woman, if we don't get to the man before her, won't give him up."

"What makes you think that?" Izabel asks with curiosity.

I glance at the fair-haired woman in the photo standing outside a restaurant, carrying a fountain drink in one hand and a small purse in the other.

"I don't know exactly," I say peering down at the target, "but she's got that look. They'll likely need me. She won't be easy to break."

Woodard's chair legs scrape annoyingly against the floor as he adjusts his seating position. All eyes shift to him. He smiles dopily across the table at me and reaches a hand up to push his glasses over the bridge of his nose with the tip of his pudgy finger.

"I suppose you've been interrogating people long enough to see these kinds of things," he says with admiration that makes me uncomfortable. "I really admire your work. I-I mean, not that I'm a sadistic freak with a hard-on for that kind of stuff, b-but I just mean how you're able to break *anyone*." His smile gets bigger, revealing his lightly yellowed teeth. "It's impressive."

Dorian, sitting next to him, tries to suppress a smile. Niklas, on the other side of Dorian, raises a brow and grins at me.

"Sounds like someone *does* have a hard-on for you Gustavsson," Niklas jests.

"Damn, man," Dorian says looking over at Woodard, "could you be more obvious?"

"H-Hey, I'm just giving credit where credit is due," Woodard tries to cover himself. "I've heard things about The Specialist for years." He points at me now as if something jumped in his mind. "I've always wanted to ask you, why do they call you the Jackal?"

THE SWAN AND THE JACKAL

My teeth crash together behind my closed lips.

I turn to Victor.

"Why is he here, exactly?" I ask.

"You should probably shut the fuck up," Dorian tells Woodard.

"Y'know, that's actually a good question, about what he's doing here," Izabel says to Victor. "I still don't think it's a good idea letting him see your face. We don't even *know* him."

"And I don't like him," Niklas adds and Woodard appears quietly offended.

I've noticed the entire time we've been in this meeting that Niklas' hand often twitches over the pack of Marlboro reds on the table in front of him. I'm mildly surprised he hasn't said, *Fuck it*, and lit one up already, but he has more respect for his brother and leader, Victor Faust. At least until the nicotine eventually wins out.

Victor sits quietly and seemingly unperturbed by everyone talking around him, but when they realize they should let him speak, the table gets quiet and all eyes shift his way.

"Woodard is here because I *want* him to see my face," Victor announces. He steeples his hands in front of him. "Marion Callahan is unaware that we're onto him. I'll be using Woodard to feed Callahan information that I want him to have. But it's nothing any of you should concern yourself with. Seattle is your priority. I'll handle this situation with Callahan while you're gone."

Izabel's auburn head snaps around.

"I don't like that, Victor," she says demandingly. "Sending all of us away while you—"

"I've been doing this longer than anyone in this room," Victor cuts in, retaining his unruffled composure. "No disrespect, Izabel, but I'm very capable of taking care of myself."

Izabel's nose crinkles on one side. I pretend not to have noticed. Obviously, Victor isn't pleased with her 'lover's worries' being thrown on the table like that for all of us to see. Victor is all business when business is being conducted. Izabel, although she knows this, still hasn't quite grasped it yet. She may never.

Relationships are quite fucking ridiculous.

"Hey, I'm trustworthy," Woodard speaks out offensively. "Don't be so quick to—"A scraping noise pierces the air as Woodard nearly falls out of his chair when Izabel leans across the table in her tight black pants and buries the tip of her knife in the wood in front of him. His dark, beady eyes grow wide in the sockets and his double chin rears back.

"Nobody asked you," Izabel growls. She pulls the knife from the table and slowly slides back into her seat.

Woodard, as stiff as a statue, moves only his eyes to look at Victor.

Victor shrugs. "Don't look at *me*," he says nonchalantly. "If she wants to kill you, I won't stop her. So perhaps you should mind your tongue."

Woodard slinks against the back of his seat and drops his short arms from the table placing his hands in his lap.

Dorian and Niklas can't stop grinning. I just shake my head.

"As I was saying," Victor goes on, "I'll be dealing with Callahan on my own. If he's an order leader, *I'll* be the one taking him out. This will be Woodard's chance to prove to me that he's an asset to us. And if he doesn't, I'll kill him myself."

Woodard's throat moves nervously as he swallows.

I take the opportunity to further the discussion on *our* mission, sliding the photo of the man coming out of the daycare center, into the center of the table.

I tap it with my finger. "The guy allegedly molested a five-year-old girl," I point out. "What's he doing anywhere near a daycare center, much less leaving one?"

"He wasn't convicted of the crime," Victor says. His steepled hands fall away from the table as he rests his back comfortably in the chair. "Guilt could not be proven."

"Lemme guess," Dorian says, leaning forward and folding his hands together on the table, "parents of the five-year-old girl are the clients. Fuck yeah. I like their style. Nothing I wouldn't do if some greasy motherfucker touched *my* daughter." He pauses and then adds, "Well, actually I'd kill the piece of shit myself."

Niklas pulls a cigarette from the pack and slides it between his lips, but doesn't light it. He leans back in his chair, interlocking his hands together behind his head. "What about the woman?" he asks.

"She's the girlfriend," Victor says and then looks at me. "And the reason he's coming out of a daycare center is because he just dropped off their eighteen-month-old daughter."

A series of deep sighs moves lightly around the table.

"I don't like this already," Izabel says. She leans against the back of her chair and crosses one leg over the other, afterward her arms.

"Are both parents targets?" I ask.

"No," Victor says. "Just the man. His name is Paul Fortright. The girlfriend, Kelly Bennings."

"OK, but why do all four of us need to take care of this?" Dorian asks. "I'm pretty sure any one of us can handle this *one* guy."

"And you could," Victor says. "But we're not the only organization that the client employed to get the job done. The one to pull it off first is the one that gets paid."

Niklas' face spreads into a grin. "A competition. That's my kind of work."

"Hmmm"—Dorian rubs the underside of his chin with the edge of his index finger, in thought—"so because the stakes are so high, does this mean we kill whoever gets in our way? Rival operatives included?"

"*Especially* rival operatives," Victor confirms. "The payday is twenty thousand—not a lot—but the money isn't why I took on this job."

"You took it because of the rival organization," Izabel assumes. "It's the perfect opportunity to draw them from the shadows."

"Precisely," Victor says.

"What happened to *recruiting* members of other organizations?" Dorian asks. "Don't we need numbers?"

"We *have* numbers," I speak out and Victor nods, confirming that I'm on the right track. "And if recruiting is the only thing we demonstrate, other rival organizations will begin to fear us less, leaving only the leaders and their right hand men and women looking over their shoulders."

"Yes," Victor says. "It's time we start taking entire groups out and sending a message. In the past year after taking over the black market orders that we have, we've come across too many who have no loyalty. They'll sell out their leaders and their entire organization at the drop of a few thousand dollars. I want future recruits to *want* to work for us, not because of how much they're paid, and not only because of loyalty, but because they know we are the most dangerous and the most intolerant."

All heads around the table, including Woodard's, nod simultaneously in agreement.

Victor stands from the chair and straightens his suit jacket.

"There is a kill preference," he says, "though ours is different from our rivals. It's how the clients will know which of us got there first." He pushes his chair underneath the table and stands behind it. "A single shot to the back of the head," he adds.

"Well, that counts me out," Izabel says disappointed. "I'd love to kill me some child molester."

"Sorry, Izzy," Niklas taunts, knowing she hates his nickname for her, "but you're not the best shot at the Round Table."

"Shut the fuck up, Niklas," she snaps. "I could always practice on you."

Niklas smirks and places the unlit cigarette between his lips again.

Victor's eyes shut momentarily, appearing as though he has suddenly acquired a mild headache.

Then he looks over at me.

"The offer stands," he says. "You can be notified if you're needed. They may have no problem finding Paul Fortright without the girlfriend. She's just a backup plan that likely won't be utilized."

I shake my head. "I'll go just in case," I say and stand up as well. "Besides, I'll feel better about already being there if I'm needed, especially if we have competition."

Victor nods, accepting my decision and probably agreeing with it. It strikes me somewhat odd that he would leave this decision up to me with so much at stake. That's not like Victor Faust. While although he's not a selfish, tyrant leader and he takes our well-being into careful consideration at all times, it's still not like him to allow me such freedom on a job like this.

"All the information you need," Victor says, looking at each of us in turn, "is in the envelope. Keep me updated on all events. I'll see you in no more than three days."

Everyone else stands from the table, all except for Woodard who isn't sure what to do. His beady eyes dart around at all of us, taking in what's expected of him by watching, and finally he follows suit.

"James Woodard," Victor says and jerks his head back lightly, "come with me."

Woodard swallows nervously again and stumbles around his chair as he walks away from the table. That guy's going to have to grow a pair soon if he expects to survive with us, even if all he's destined to do is sit behind a computer screen and be our eyes and ears over the information waves.

By midday, I'm on a plane to Seattle and although normally I would be able to think of nothing but the anticipation of a possible interrogation, Cassia is all that's on my mind.

# ELEVEN

*Cassia*

———

Greta retrieves my empty dinner dishes and sets them aside on the bottom step of the concrete staircase. She's a wonderful cook. A wonderful person who has treated me with nothing but kindness since Fredrik introduced us. I think she worries more about me than I worry about myself.

"Would you like dessert?" she asks. "There's a fruit bowl upstairs in the fridge. I made it just how you like it, with honey and coconut."

I lay on the bed on my side, my hands fitted between my knees, the soft memory foam pillow crushed against my cheek. The chain around my ankle dangling over the side of the bed.

I smile at Greta. "No thank you."

She approaches me with that motherly look she always gives when she's about try to get me to open up to her. The bed moves gently as she sits down beside me. She brings my favorite blue and white tapestry quilt up from the end of the bed and drapes it over my exposed legs. The palm of her hand pats me lightly on the hip before sliding away.

"I didn't tell Fredrik," I say in almost a whisper.

"You didn't tell him what?" Her voice is soft and kind.

Staring out ahead of me, I let the memory move across my eyes again before finally telling Greta.

"That I remember I used to love Connie Francis," I say and suddenly my face breaks into a warm smile the more I picture the pieces of my old life. I laugh gently under my breath. "And my friend who lived across the hall—I think her name was Lanie—she thought it was funny I listened to that old stuff." I adjust my head so that I can see Greta next to me. A bright smile has etched deep lines around her mouth and drawn out crow's feet in the corners of her eyes.

She pats my hip again.

"I love Connie Francis," she says, beaming. "She's one of my favorites. Do you remember what made you start listening to her?"

My gaze falls out ahead again. "No, I don't remember that much. But I can't help but think it's more than that. Maybe I didn't just listen to her music, but that I might've…"—I blush inwardly at the thought—"That I might've performed it somewhere. I don't know. It's ridiculous, I'm sure."

"Hey, maybe not," Greta says, "I don't see any reason why that couldn't be true. Surely you can sing."

"What makes you think *that*?" I ask smiling in an unbelieving manner.

Greta shrugs. "Oh I don't know. Just a hunch I guess. Maybe you'll sing one of her songs for me someday."

"Oh no, I couldn't do that," I say and feel my cheeks warm with a blush.

I hear the central heat hum to life amid the sudden silence between us and then the warm air filtering through the two vents in the ceiling.

"Why didn't you tell him?" she asks quietly.

The smile fades from my face as I stare out ahead, thinking only of Fredrik now.

"Because I wanted him to tell me more about his life. And he did. But it wasn't enough." I pause and sigh deeply. "I wanted him to tell me about Seraphina. *Anything* about her. I think he owes me that."

"Did you ask him again?"

Shaking my head against the pillow I say, "No. In fact, I even told him I didn't *care* to know about her anymore. I guess I had hoped he might have a change of heart if I…it was stupid of me. I just don't understand his…*obsession* with that woman. And I don't like it."

"Cassia?" Greta's voice is careful and motherly. "I don't mean to question your heart, but why do you care so much for him? A man who took you from your life, who keeps you chained in a basement. I guess I just have a hard time understanding your mindset." She lays her hand on my hip again but this time doesn't move it away. "I understand Stockholm syndrome. And for a long time I thought that you were a classic case, but…"

I feel her eyes on me and I look over at her. When she doesn't continue right away, I raise my body from the bed and sit upright, looking directly at her with a feeling of impatience in the pit of my stomach.

Another moment of quiet passes between us.

"But Fredrik employed me only a week after he brought you here," she finally goes on, "and you weren't afraid of him, Cassia. Even with Stockholm syndrome, there's usually still a lot of fear that early after a kidnapping. You showed absolutely none. At least not toward Fredrik."

"What do you mean?" I peer in at her with curiosity and determination. "I was afraid of *you*?"

She nods. "At first yes. Cassia, you were so traumatized when I first met you. You talked in your sleep. You mentioned Seraphina's name." She looks away from me and I get the feeling she's deciding whether or not to tell me anymore, as though she's already said too much.

"What is it, Greta? What are you not telling me?"

Her bony shoulders rise and fall underneath her light pink button-up top. Her weathered hands move restlessly within her lap.

"Don't tell Fredrik that I said these things to you. Because I've never told him any of this."

I shake my head, eyes wide with anticipation, my heart pounding in my fingertips as I eagerly await her words.

"I believe you were very close to Seraphina," she says and it wrenches my stomach. "I don't know how close, but you know her and you know her well. And you're terrified of her. I think it's why you're not afraid of Fredrik, or of being imprisoned here." As her words, which I feel deep inside of me to be true, are sinking into my mind like missing puzzle pieces, she asks, "You don't want to leave here, do you, Cassia?"

Absently, I shake my head, my mind still trying to accept all of these things she's saying to me.

"No," I admit, "I'm *afraid* to leave this place. I feel safe here. I don't know why, but I do."

Greta nods and then pats the top of my bare foot pulled up onto the bed.

"But why wouldn't he want me to know these things?"

"I'm not sure," she says distantly, "but I think in a way...he doesn't really want you to remember. Fredrik has something with Seraphina that he needs to settle. I know this. I've seen that look in a man's eyes before. Nothing is going to stop him from finding that woman and taking care of whatever it is he needs to take care of. But…Fredrik also has another look that I've seen in a man before."

She stops.

"What look, Greta?" I lean toward her, eager for her to say it. I place my hand on hers. "Tell me. What look?"

Her lined blue eyes appear conflicted as if she still isn't quite sure of it herself.

"The one when a man knows he's going to have to give something up that he doesn't want to, for something else."

"I don't understand."

And truly I don't. For a fleeting moment, I thought maybe she meant that Fredrik was falling in love with me, and that he knew he'd have to let me go once he found Seraphina because she is the love of his life. But I quickly realized that I was wrong as something dark and sad appeared in her eyes and has been lingering there since, making me believe that the truth is something far more terrible.

"I'm not sure, but I think that's why maybe he doesn't want you to remember," she goes on. "As if in the beginning, you were just a means to an end, but now things are different. Very different."

She forces a smile and stands up from the bed.

"Honestly, I don't know, Cassia. All I do know is that I don't like it that he keeps you down here. But I've never seen him hurt you. It's very evident to me that he's protecting you. He knows what Seraphina is capable of and if he didn't keep you here, you might be dead. But at the same time he needs you to find her. He's protecting you, but he's using you, too."

My hands have been shaking lightly and I'm only now realizing it. I cross my legs Indian-style on the bed strategically so as not to hurt my bound ankle, and I fold my hands together in my lap to steady them.

"She tried to kill me the night Fredrik took me from the shelter," I say distantly. "I know in my heart she set the building on fire. But I got away by climbing down the fire escape. I vaguely remember falling a short distance and hitting my head. I remember seeing her. She even spoke to me. But she couldn't kill me there because I was out in the open." I run my hands through the top of my hair, feeling mentally exhausted by all of this.

I stop. "I hate thinking about this stuff."

Greta changes the atmosphere in the room with that big smile of hers and a look of excitement in her eyes.

"I've got an idea," she says, holding up a bony index finger.

She leaves me sitting on the bed and moves her way across the room toward the staircase. "I'll be right back," she says just before she heads up.

A few minutes later the giant television on the wall across from me comes to life. I feel the smile flee my face in an instant and a metaphorical fist collapses around my stomach. My breath hitches and my hands begin to shake and all I want to do is curl myself up neatly into my favorite corner. All of this is the initial reaction to whenever that television comes on because of the things that Fredrik sometimes forces me to watch. But reluctantly my body begins to calm, and instead of seeking out the corner, I get up from the bed and walk toward the television instead, the chain around my ankle shuffling nosily on my way.

The screen freezes on what looks like a web page. A few seconds later light from the hallway on the upper floor spills out on the steps as Greta opens the door and descends them. She's carrying some kind of flat electronic device on the palm of her hand with a brightly lit screen that illuminates the colors and lines in her face amid the surrounding darkness of the staircase now that the door has been closed.

"Fredrik uses this thing sometimes," she says looking down at the screen somewhat uncertain about her ability to use it properly. "He told me never to touch it, so let's keep this between us, OK?"

I bring my hand to my mouth and press my thumb and index finger together making a zipping motion horizontally across my lips. "Not a word," I say with a smile.

Greta moves her finger over the device and the television screen changes. She types in 'Connie Francis' in the YouTube search box and a row of videos appears. Immediately, I know what Greta's intentions are, and instead of making me nervous like it did before, my chest tingles with excitement and spreads outward through all of my limbs like a rush of heat.

I practically squeal when she clicks on *Fallin'*, and I have no idea why.

Greta's smile widens when she looks at me.

"I won't take no for an answer," she says and I know exactly what she wants me to do.

"Let's have some fun for a change," she adds, setting the device on the bottom step just after hitting play.

And as if I've performed this song time and time again like a professional, the second the music starts playing loudly through the speakers in the ceiling, my body and mind fall right into it without hesitation.

*Fredrik*

——

Music begins to stream loudly from my pants pocket and every pair of eyes, including Kelly Bennings', who we apprehended less than an hour ago, turns my way.

Dorian looks at me with a curiously raised brow.

"Really?" he mocks. "*That's* your ringtone?" Laughter ensues.

A knot lodges in the center of my throat. That's not a ringtone, but I can't tell anyone here that. And all I can think about is what the hell is going on back in Baltimore and how I managed to begin an interrogation without turning my phone to silent beforehand.

Izabel, trying to keep a straight face and doing a horrible job, walks up to me and glances momentarily down at my pocket with the humorous skirting of her eyes.

She cracks a smile and purses her lips. "I knew you were a man of class, Fredrik," she teases me, "but I didn't know you were *that* classy."

I'm glad Niklas isn't inside the warehouse to add to their banter.

Dorian bursts into laughter as the song—and Cassia's stunning voice matching it—carries on like a beacon in my pocket, alerting everyone to my dark secret and precisely where to find it.

"Better answer that, man," Dorian chimes in. "Might be your boyfriend."

I *really* want to torture that guy. Just for fun.

"What the fuck is going on?" Kelly says from the wooden chair we tied her wrists and ankles to just moments ago. "Who *are* you fucking people?!" she shrieks. "*Answer* me!"

Everyone ignores her just as we've been doing since we kidnapped her from the parking lot of a grocery store and stuffed her in the trunk of our loaner car.

I feel Izabel's hand rest on my arm and I look over at her. She's no longer smiling, maybe because even after their jokes, I've shown no indication of finding any of it smile-worthy. She tilts her head gently and looks at me in a concerned manner.

"Why don't you take a break," she suggests, nodding toward the door that leads outside. "Answer that call and deal with whatever you need to. This can wait a little longer."

Really it can't, but it's going to have to.

"Yeah!" Kelly calls out. "Take all the time you need, honey! It can wait all night!" Clearly she wants to put whatever's about to happen to her on hold for as long as possible.

Dorian moves from behind Kelly's chair and joins Izabel and me.

"Are you all right?" he asks, finally realizing that I'm not in the mood for his shit.

I don't answer, mostly because his and Izabel's words all sound stifled in the back of my head, and the only thing I can hear clearly is Cassia's voice.

Izabel catches my eyes again and her hand falls hesitantly from my arm.

"I'll be back in a few minutes," I say as I slip my twitching hand down into my pocket and grab my phone.

Izabel nods with acceptance and I turn and head across the frigid warehouse toward a side door, shutting it securely behind me once I'm outside.

I can't get the phone out of my pocket fast enough and I fumble it, nearly dropping it. It's freezing outside and my dress shirt sleeves are still rolled up to my elbows since preparing to interrogate Kelly on the whereabouts of her boyfriend, Paul Fortright.

Peering down at the screen, I begin to watch the live video feed that Greta must've accidently activated from my iPad.

Suddenly I don't feel the cold anymore, or understand that I'm standing outside in thirty-degree weather. I forget that I'm over a thousand miles away from my house and that I have an important, time-constrained interrogation to do on the other side of those tall steel walls. I don't care about anything in this moment except what I'm seeing.

*She must've remembered...she must've remembered something.*

With my heart in my throat, I watch the tiny screen in the palm of my hand, focusing so hard that I don't recall blinking. I think I've stopped breathing.

Cassia dances around in the center of the room, singing the song word for word and right on key. If I didn't know better I'd think she *was* Connie Francis.

I swallow hard and watch the screen until my eyes hurt.

#  TWELVE

*Cassia*

———

I dance around Greta, moving my hips in time with the music, clapping my hands while belting out the lyrics as if I had written them myself. It all feels so natural, so...*familiar*, but I'm having too much fun with Greta to worry about any of that right now.

And Greta isn't so bad at dancing 50s-style herself, easily keeping up with me. We start clapping together along with the music at the right times and it's like we're sharing a small stage...*in a classy bar tucked away in a big city that serves only the finest of wines... and I'm dressed in a skin-tight black dress that hugs my body down to my calves...with tall high-heeled black shoes...perfume...cigars...the sound of ice in the bottom of whiskey glasses, the tall mirrors lining the walls on either side of me, candles burning in deep, bubble-shaped amber candle holders in the center of every table in the audience, the sleek black piano on the stage to my left...the woman with short jet-black hair on the stage beside me to my right...*

The memory blinks out of my mind as Greta's voice shouts over the music. "Your voice is beautiful, Cassia!" she says as the song goes into its last few notes.

I'm giddy. Absolutely giddy. So much so that I can't stop smiling and my face feels like it's stiffened permanently in the same beaming position.

When the song ends, still high on the moment, I point at the device on the step and say, "Duffy. *Mercy*. Look that one up!"

And Greta does just that, and after I sing that one as if I'd done it a hundred times, she finds every other song I ask her to find, until eventually we go right back to *Fallin'* by Connie Francis because it's my favorite. I dance and sing until my throat is dry and I'm too out of breath to carry on another note.

I fall against my large bed with my arms out at my sides as if I were flying, and I look up at the ceiling still with a smile on my face as I try to catch my breath. My heart is beating so fast, I can feel it pumping through every vein right down into the tips of my fingers and toes.

Almost nothing in the world could take this moment away from me.

But that memory…I can't get it out of my head. And the more I think about it, the more I begin to see, and the darker the light over my eyes becomes. Instinctively I reach up and wipe the corners of them as tears burn their way to the surface.

"Cassia?" Greta speaks softly beside me. "Is something wrong?"

My head falls to the side and I force a smile, wiping at my face again at the tears that managed to escape.

"No, Greta, I'm fine. Everything's fine." I sniffle and smile a little warmer at her.

I wonder if she believes me, or if she can see right through the pain I now harbor.

*Fredrik*

———

"You've got to be kidding me," Niklas says walking up. "You stopped an interrogation to use your cell phone?" He shakes his head, cigarette smoke mixed with cold breath streaming in large puffs from his lips. The hot ember of the cigarette burns between his fingers down at his side. "Unless it was Victor on the phone."

Running my finger over the screen, I shut down the live video feed and then turn the phone to vibrate before dropping it back into my pants pocket.

I shake my head. "No, it wasn't Victor—it was unexpected." What a worthless excuse. I know Niklas is right. And I agree with him.

He just stares at me for an uncomfortable moment and then jerks his head back. "Shouldn't we get back to the mouthy bitch in the chair?"

"Yeah," I say nodding and follow him inside.

"Dorian," Niklas calls out as we approach, "you're up! It's cold as shit out there." His voice echoes through the empty warehouse.

Niklas, Dorian and Izabel earlier agreed to take turns watching the building outside, depending on how long this interrogation might take.

Dorian shrugs on his black bomber jacket and zips it up to his throat. He walks past me and says, "I hope you got everything squared away," and pats me on the shoulder, but his concern is laced with typical Dorian mockery.

Then he looks at Niklas. "I'd rather be outside on watch, anyway." He glances at Kelly secured to the chair with a look of hatred and defiance twisting her already unsightly features. "Kind of tired of that ugly bitch fucking me with her eyes. Damn, I feel like I need a goddamn shower." He shudders and then the shadows of the building swallow him up as he passes underneath a low section of ceiling and heads outside.

Wasting no more time, I walk straight over to Kelly Bennings, intent on getting this over with as soon as possible. Before, I wanted to stay away from Cassia, but now things have changed. They've changed significantly.

I just hope I can function during this interrogation, because already I feel off balance and profoundly distracted.

"I don't know what the fuck you people are doing," Kelly snaps as I step up closer, "but this isn't supposed to be happening!" She tightens her arms and legs against the ropes securing her to the chair and jerks her body roughly against the metal. The legs bounce against the cement floor. Her disheveled dishwater-brown hair falls down around her bony jaw structure and rests on her shoulders.

I pull up an extra chair and set it in front of her.

"You're here to give me information," I say calmly as I take a seat, crossing one leg over the other. "As long as you cooperate, and as long as you tell the truth, no one will hurt you."

For a brief moment she looks confused, her big bug-eyes bouncing around at the three of us, but when her eyes fall on me again, she smiles, of all things.

I find that very interesting. She's doesn't fear us.

"What the hell do you want to know?" she asks with a growing smirk stretching her thin, unpainted lips.

"The current location of your boyfriend, Paul Fortright," I say.

Her face falls. "Why? What do you want with him?"

"That doesn't matter," I say. "And you're not the one asking the questions."

"B-But I-I don't…want you to hurt him," she stutters, her eyes constantly darting between me, Niklas and Izabel. "Just tell me what this is about."

I don't have time for this.

I jump up from my chair and pull Izabel's knife from the sheath around her thigh, and in a flash, bury the blade into the top of Kelly's hand. Her bloodcurdling screams fill the warehouse, traveling from wall to ceiling like an injured banshee.

"Fredrik!" Niklas calls out. "What the fuck?!"

I feel Izabel's widened eyes on me, but she hasn't worked up yet what to say.

I sit back down in the chair as casually as I had before, and this time I lean forward with my legs spread, draping my hands between them.

"Where is Paul Fortright?" I cock my head to one side.

Tears stream down Kelly's reddened cheeks, but they're not so much tears of pain as they are of anger.

If she could kill me right now, she'd do it with a smile on her face.

"He's at his fuckin' friend's house!" she spats irately. "Watching goddamn pay-per-view wrestling!"

I glance at Izabel momentarily and she's looking back at me with shock and confusion in her bright green eyes.

Niklas says nothing else, though I can tell by the vibe he's putting off that it's only a matter of time.

"And where is your daughter?" I ask Kelly.

"My *daughter?*" A glimmer of true fear crosses her face. "W-W-Why do you want to know about my daughter?"

"No one will harm your daughter," I assure her. "But if you answer one more question with a question of your own, I'll put Izabel's other knife"—I glance down at the undamaged hand—"in your *other* hand."

"She's *with* him! But please don't hurt her! Please! This isn't supposed to be happening!" She begins to cry. "WHY IS THIS HAPPENING?!"

I stand from the chair again and Izabel intuitively reaches for the knife sheathed to her other thigh, collapsing her hand around the hilt.

"What the fuck are you doing, Gustavsson?" Niklas asks. "Have you lost your damn mind?"

"Yeah, seriously, Fredrik," Izabel says, still with her hand on her knife, afraid I might try to take it from her.

"Come with me," I say calmly and don't give them the opportunity to ask what for as I head back toward the side door that leads outside.

"FUCKING BASTARD!" Kelly screams from behind.

We step out into the cold air and join Dorian who stands leaning his back against the steel wall of the building. He pushes himself from it and stands upright when he sees us, instantly on alert.

"What's going on?" Dorian asks.

"That's what *I* want to know," Niklas says.

Izabel stands directly in front of me, looking at me with a desperate need for answers.

"This isn't like you, Fredrik," she says. "You didn't even give her a chance to tell you anything."

"What did he do?" Dorian cuts in and then looks directly at me as desperate for answers almost as much as Izabel. "What did you do, man? Oh shit, did you kill her already?"

"No," Niklas chimes in, crossing his arms to keep warm, "but I'm starting to wonder if it's a good idea to let him go back in there because he just might." He looks at me coldly. "She's not the target."

"She's in on it," I say and silence ensues for an intense moment. I go on as they're all looking at me, waiting for answers.

"There was something off about her the moment we tied her to the chair. She's not afraid of us."

"She does seem a bit defiant," Izabel adds.

"She didn't put much effort into worrying about the boyfriend when I asked for his location, either. Because it was an act."

"And she gave him up too easily," Izabel says.

I nod.

"He stuck a goddamn knife in her hand," Niklas argues. "I'd say that's an easy way to make someone talk."

"I got her to talk, didn't I?" I point out.

Niklas thinks on that a moment and shrugs his shoulders underneath his black leather jacket. "Yeah, I guess I can't argue with that. But damn, Izabel's right; you're not yourself tonight."

That's an understatement. This is the first time that I've *ever* in my thirty-five years of life been too preoccupied by other things to be able to carry out an interrogation, and I've no desire to even begin the torture. That is *very* unlike me.

"OK," Niklas speaks up, "what are you thinking? We need to do something other than stand out here and try to figure out life's mysteries. Let's go back in there and find out where this friend of Paul Fortright lives so we can find him before the other organization does, and *finish* this mission."

"Did you hear what I said?" I gesture my hands in front of me. "She's *in* on it. She kept saying '*This wasn't supposed to happen*', because she was in on setting up the hit on the boyfriend."

"Shit, he's right," Izabel says with widening eyes and parting lips. She turns to Niklas. "The client is the father of the girl Paul

Fortright supposedly molested. I saw the file. He's a single father. His wife died last year in a car accident."

"So what," Niklas says, growing more impatient. "None of this matters."

"It matters if Paul Fortright is an innocent man and Kelly Bennings and this client are somehow working together to off Fortright. Think about it. Fortright was never convicted of molestation. Now there's a hit placed on him. Any other time I'd find that normal. Kill the guilty guy who got off on a clerical error. But there's more to this than that and I *know* it."

"He's right," Izabel says, looking to Niklas for agreement because he outranks all of us. "That woman's shit stinks worse than any of ours."

Niklas shakes his head and sighs with aggravation.

"We came here to do a job," he says. "Not play detective and superhero games."

He pushes his way past us, clearing a path between Izabel and me, heading back toward the door.

"We're not a black market order, Niklas," I call out to him. "If we kill Paul Fortright and he's just an innocent man who the guilty want to kill just to get him out of their way, it'll *make* us one."

"He's right, Niklas," Izabel says softly from behind, "and I don't want that on my conscience."

Niklas stops in front of the tall silver door before opening it. His shoulders rise and fall and cold breath streams from his mouth as he turns around.

He reaches inside his jacket pocket and retrieves his cell phone.

"Dorian," Niklas says, "head inside and stay with Bennings for now. Make sure the skanky bitch doesn't find a way out of that chair. And don't let her onto what we discussed."

"Sounds good to me." Dorian, likely just wanting to get out of the cold, goes back inside the building without question.

Niklas talks to Victor for several minutes, explaining to him everything that's happened. And by the time he gets off the phone, it's apparent just by listening to Niklas speaking to Victor that our mission has changed drastically. It was never about the money to begin with. The payday this job offered was a drop in the bucket compared to what Victor normally accepts.

Niklas puts his phone away in his pocket.

"We'll use Paul Fortright to lure the other organization," he begins, "and then we'll take them out."

"What about Fortright?" Izabel asks. "Not to mention that crazy bitch in there, and their daughter?"

"For now we continue to play the game," Niklas says, lighting up another cigarette. "We'll get the location of the house and let her believe we're going to kill him and bring their daughter to her."

He stops and looks at both of us with intent. "But we're not to interfere in their drama bullshit. Victor wants us to take out the other operatives, leave Fortright alive for now and that's it. Hell, we're not even sure if this is even legit. You both could be delusional."

"I resent that," Izabel snaps.

"Of course you do, Izzy." He smirks and takes a long pull from his cigarette, the hot ember glowing orange around his face. "But I don't give a fuck."

Izabel's jaw clenches and if looks could kill Niklas would be a bloody pulp by now.

Suddenly my phone buzzes against my leg and my heart winds up dead center in my throat. My first thought was that it's Greta calling me about Cassia, but when I look down at the screen I'm surprised to see that it's not.

"It's Victor," I say out loud, though more to myself.

I answer quickly as Niklas and Izabel listen in, as curious as I am.

"I want you to sit the rest of this mission out," Victor says into the phone. "Go back to Baltimore and we'll touch base in about a week."

Confused and slightly concerned about his reasons, it takes me a moment to put my words together.

"I'm capable of finishing this," I say. "Yes, I was quick to stab Bennings, but it got the result I wanted."

"That's what concerns me," Victor says. "You're not yourself. You weren't yourself at the meeting yesterday, and we can't afford mistakes. Take the time off and clear your head. It's not an option."

I sigh deeply and give in. As much as I do want to stay here and finish what I started, I want even more to go back to Cassia and find out what she's remembered.

"OK," I say into the phone, "I'll head back now."

Two and half hours later and my flight is finally ready to depart Seattle.

I sit on the plane the entire time, playing the video of Cassia singing in the basement, over and over again, with my ear buds pressed into my ears so as not to disturb the people sitting around me.

Cassia knows something. She *remembers*. She *has* to remember. I can taste Seraphina in my mouth she's so close. Finally after six years of relentless searching I'll be with her again.

# THIRTEEN

*Fredrik*

———

I haven't slept in almost twenty-four hours, but I'm wide awake when I arrive back at my house in Baltimore just after ten a.m. the following day. Greta's old beige Honda Civic is parked in the driveway. I pull in beside her and kill the engine.

I'm incredibly nervous, a feeling so foreign to me that at first I don't know what to do with it.

Carrying my black leather travel bag in one hand, I head up the red brick driveway and feel like I can't get to the front door fast enough. The door is locked and while I'm scrambling to get the right key, I'm expecting Greta to open the door as she normally does when she knows I'm on my way back. But this time, I realize, she isn't aware of my early return.

Finally I get the door open and head inside quietly.

The house smells of eggs and biscuits and sausage. It's spotless as usual, not a speck of dust left on anything or even evidence of the breakfast she cooked other than the aroma lingering in the air. I set my bag carefully on the floor in the living room wanting to avoid letting them onto my presence. I move into the kitchen, stepping around the spot in the floor that always creaks when walking over it and head for the bar. My iPad is right where I left it before I went to Seattle, and in the same horizontal position as though Greta made sure to place it exactly as it was and hoped I wouldn't notice. I unlock the screen and move my finger over the app, opening the live feed from the basement.

They're sitting on Cassia's bed talking. Seemingly harmless. Turning the volume up just slightly, I listen in on their conversation for several minutes. Nothing of significance. Greta is telling Cassia about her daughter and their trip to Monte Carlo last year. Cassia smiles so beautifully, so innocently, and it affects me in the worst of ways. I push down the pain and guilt that I feel for keeping her imprisoned for so long, keeping her from living life and seeing the world like I know she must dream about seeing it. That brightness in her brown eyes is unmistakable as she listens to Greta talk about Monte Carlo. She's envisioning herself there. And rather than dwelling on the truth of her predicament, she just smiles and accepts it, instead.

I'm a fucking bastard.

With my palms pressed against the countertop, I drop my head slightly between my rigid shoulders and let out a long and miserable breath, shutting my eyes softly.

But when I open them again, I notice something that shocks me back into an upright position. My eyes grow wide with panic. Once I manage to shake off the paralyzing numbness my body has fallen victim to, I dash down the hallway toward the basement door, flinging it open and then taking the concrete steps two at a time until I make it to the bottom.

Greta and Cassia both jump at the sight of me, Cassia flinging herself against the wall on the other side of the bed.

I march over and snatch Cassia up into my arms.

"Why did you take it off?!" I shout at Greta, my voice and my face filled with reprimand.

Greta shoots to her feet while Cassia presses her head harshly against my chest. I hold her with one arm around the back of her waist and the other underneath the bends of her legs.

I glance briefly at Cassia's ankle where her shackle is supposed to be, and then back at Greta who's about five seconds away from meeting her maker.

"Please Fredrik," Cassia cries into my chest, "don't blame Greta. I begged her to remove it. It was hurting." She fits her small hand around the side of my neck to hold on to me. I nearly wilt by her touch.

I shake it off fast and set Cassia back down on the bed.

"Bring it to me," I demand Greta.

Greta, afraid to speak, scurries over and takes the chain into her hand. Crouching down on the floor in front of Cassia, I slide her thin yellow gown up her soft legs, grazing her skin with my fingertips and it reacts to my touch as tiny goose bumps appear.

"I'm so sorry, Mr. Gustavsson." Greta holds the shackle out to me. "I wouldn't have let her escape. But I was concerned about her ankle. I cleaned it like you always asked me to."

"I've told you never to remove it. *Never.*" With my hands on Cassia's warm thighs, I turn my head slowly, indignantly, and look up at Greta standing over me. "If she didn't like you so much…" I grind my jaw and look away.

Calming myself, I give Cassia all of my attention again, sliding her leg in my free hand downward until I make it to her ankle. And then I stop and drop the shackle on the floor instead of putting it back on. Letting out a heavy sigh, I drop my gaze to my shoes, feeling even guiltier than I felt when I had been upstairs watching her from the live feed. I look back down at Cassia's injured ankle. Blood has been drawn where the metal scraped against the back of her foot, just above her heel. And there are little blisters in a horizontal pattern on the inside of her ankle, just below the ankle bone. Her skin is yellowed by bruising, and red and inflamed around the cuts and blisters. Something clear glistens all over her skin, probably antibiotic ointment that Greta put on after cleaning it.

"Shit," I say under my breath.

I rise into a stand and pick Cassia up from the bed, wrapping my arms around her small form. She latches her legs around my waist and her arms around my neck. Her body trembles against mine, though I know she's only scared for Greta and not for herself.

"We'll discuss this in the morning," I say, turning to Greta who's looking back at me with fear at rest in her features. "Be here at your usual time."

"Yes, sir." She bows her head and moves quickly toward the staircase.

The moment I hear the basement door close, I tighten my arms around Cassia's body and shut my eyes to savor the moment.

"Please don't hurt Greta," she whispers in a teary voice into the side of my neck.

I swallow hard.

"I'm not going to hurt her," I whisper back, and cup the back of her soft blond head within the palm of my free hand.

The feeling of her bare thighs tightening around my waist makes me hard. The warmth between her legs on my stomach. I try to ignore it, pushing my need to be with her far into the back of my mind. But it's so difficult. Painful and torturous.

Cassia is my punishment. I know she is. For all of the horrific things I've done to people in all these years, I've known for the past year that she must've been sent as my punishment. And my undoing. I'd much rather be strapped to my own chair and my teeth be pulled out of my head, or needles be shoved underneath my fingernails or my skin be peeled from my muscles, than to suffer *this* kind of torture. I would rather die. Just kill me and get it over with. The pain of being near her and knowing that I can't give in to my feelings for her, is the worst kind of pain I've ever felt.

And the only other thing I want more in this world than to find Seraphina, is for this pain to go away.

"I should be here more," I say softly into her hair. "My job has been more demanding than usual. I never meant to neglect you."

Cassia raises her head from my shoulder and peers deeply into my eyes as I hold her propped around my waist with her bottom in my hands.

*This isn't right.*

*I should stand her up.*

I ignore my inner voice and stare back into her eyes, fighting eternally with my conscience.

The softness of Cassia's fingertips trails down the sides of my face and then her lips fall on the corners of my mouth. One and then the other.

*I should stop her*

*I should drop her on the bed and leave her be.*

I do neither.

Instead, I hold her tighter and shut my eyes softly, seeking her lips with my own, though still reluctant to taste them. Because I know what it will do to me.

Before I let myself kiss her, I pull away and carry her toward the bathroom. I drag my hands gently across the bare flesh of her thighs as I set her down on the countertop.

I snap out of the forbidden thoughts again and pull her ankle into my hand.

"This looks bad," I say. "I'm sorry for letting it get that way."

"Greta took care of it," she says kindly.

"Yes, but it shouldn't have gone that far." I step over to the tall shelf on the wall and open the cabinet, which is also usually locked, but isn't. I take down some peroxide in a spray bottle and a clean wash cloth. "I'll be here every day for the next week, at least," I go on, spraying her ankle with the peroxide. "But I think it's better that way."

It still bothers me that I've been given a 'leave of absence' because I'm obviously too distracted to carry out my duties, but it's for the best just the same.

"Fredrik?"

"Yeah?" I don't look up at her, but continue cleaning her wounds though they've already been cleaned recently.

There is a bout of momentary silence and finally Cassia speaks up in a quiet voice. "I…well, I don't want you to leave me again. Why can't you stay here with me? Or, take me with you when you leave?"

I raise my eyes from my work and look into hers. She smiles softly, but I also see desperation in her delicate features.

"That's not possible." I look back down at her ankle.

Her mood shifts and I can sense that her smile has fallen.

"I wouldn't run away," she says; the desperation taking precedence in her voice. "I want to be here with you. I *want* to stay with you. You have to believe that."

I drop her ankle more harshly than I intended and the back of her heel bumps against the cabinet door underneath the counter.

"Why do you feel that way?" I lash out, my eyebrows hardening in my forehead. "Cassia, look what I've done to you. How can you say or believe these things yourself? You've got to stop this—it's making it harder on *me*!" I didn't mean to say that last part, but by the time I realized it, the words had already fled my lips.

Cassia just looks at me, confusion and curiosity in her eyes.

"Harder on you why?"

I turn my back to her and walk back over to the cabinet and put the peroxide away.

"Because, Cassia, it can never happen. Nothing more than what has already happened between us, can *ever* happen." I can't look at her.

"Because of Seraphina," she says.

I nod. "Yes. Because of Seraphina." I hate the truth. I hate myself because of the truth.

This is the ultimate punishment.

"But I'm in love with you," she says quietly from behind and my heart collapses inside my chest with a crushing force.

"Don't say that!" I swing around at her. "You're not in love with me, Cassia! You don't even know what you're saying!"

Tears glisten in the corners of her eyes and all I want to do is crush her against me and never let her go. But I can't and I won't. Her brown doe-like eyes look up at me with such pain that I can hardly bear the consequences. Her plump lips tremble around the edges. Her long blond hair lays like silk over her petite bare shoulders, stopping just below her breasts that are somewhat visible through the thin satin fabric of the yellow gown she wears. I wonder why she never dresses in the regular clothes I bought for her. But I only wonder for a brief moment.

I try to avert my eyes until she says, "That woman has such a hold on your heart that it can't breathe. She's the reason your heart is dark. Look what she's done to you. Look what she's doing to you every day of your life." My hands have compressed into fists down at my sides. "Why won't you *look* at me?" Her voice begins to rise with desperation.

I look up and my eyes fall on hers.

"Seraphina is evil," she says. "And look what she's doing to you." A trace of anger laces her words.

But it's not the anger that attracts my attention, it's something cryptic that lies beneath it.

"What are you saying, Cassia?"

She shakes her head gently and her gaze falls toward the floor.

"Cassia?" I say in a cautionary tone. "Is there something you want to tell me?"

"No," she says after a long pause.

"You're lying."

She looks up. Pain and resentment and love resides in her eyes.

I step closer.

"What have you remembered?"

"Nothing."

"Tell me the truth!" My fingers dig into the palms of my hands. "What have you remembered?!"

"Nothing!"

She slaps her hands against the countertop.

"Goddammit! I don't remember anything!"

"You're lying!"

My hands fly to her upper arms and I shake her so hard her head bobs back and forth on her neck.

"Tell me the truth, Cassia!"

The side of my face stings when she frees one arm and slaps me so hard across the cheek that I hear a ringing in my ears. I grab her wrists into my hands and shove her against the wall where the mirror used to be, pressing my body between her opened thighs. Her feet raise up onto the counter. Her eyes expand as largely as they can, her pouty mouth lies halfway open as her breath expels rapidly from her lips. I can feel her heart beating in her wrists secured beneath my tightening fingers.

Leaning forward even farther, my eyes bore into hers, my lips are inches from her own. "You're going to tell me what you remember, Cassia, or I swear to fucking God I'll put you in that chair." My voice is calm, but harsh and unforgiving.

"Fuck you," she says and it's more surprising than the slap was across my face.

I pull back just inches and look at her. Tears pour from the corners of her eyes. It's not defiance I see in her, but pure, unadulterated pain.

"I remember," she says, trembling. "I remember everything about Seraphina. How I know her. Why she wants me dead. I remember." She sniffles. It's tearing me up inside to see her this way. But I can't let her get to me. Not now of all the times she's done it since I've had possession of her.

"Tell. Me. What. You. Know."

She shakes her head and my hands tighten around her wrists pressed against the wall behind her head.

"I won't tell you anything until you tell me *everything*."

Gritting my teeth, I hold my position with her body against the wall for mere seconds before finally letting go. I take a step backward. My mind is thick with merciless thoughts. A dark, soulless haze momentarily covers my vision and all I see in front of me is who I *wish* she was. Seraphina. The other half of my soul. The only other person in this world who can control me, who can control my urges, my violent, murderous tendencies. Because if she were here, I could fuck her. I could take my anger and guilt and pain and vengeance out on her and she would *love* me for it. Because Seraphina never wanted me to be gentle. She *wanted* me to hurt her. She wanted me to make her bleed. She wanted to feel it when I released my darkest side because she was only ever at peace with herself when someone darker than her was in control. I was the only person darker than Seraphina. Together, we could not be broken.

I need her now.

I need her now because Cassia *can* be broken. And I don't want to hurt Cassia. I could never live with myself if I allowed my demons to ravage her like I ravaged Seraphina.

Sometime during my soulless haze, Cassia managed to slide off the counter and now she stands in front of me.

*How did I get here?*

I look up to find that I've already stepped out of the bathroom, but I never remember walking through the doorway.

"Fredrik," Cassia's voice is soft and pleading and concerned.

I put up both hands, creating a wall between us. She stops and looks upon me with hurt in her eyes.

"I'll ask you one more time," I say calmly and avoiding eye contact. "Tell me what you remember."

"I'm sorry," she says gently and not at all out of anger, "but I meant what I said. You owe me that much. I don't care what you do to me. I don't care if you put me in that chair again." I feel her presence as she steps up closer, but I take another step back. "Do what you have to."

A last desperate attempt consumes me and I swing the rest of the way around at her. "I can't tell you!" I lean over into her face, but she stands her ground rather than shrinking away from me as I halfway expected her to do. "Why are you making this so hard, Cassia?" My voice begins to calm, reduced from anger to pleading. "I can't talk to you about Seraphina. Not you, of all people in this fucking world! Why can't you *understand* that?!"

Cassia reaches up and wipes the tears from her eyes. Then very slowly, as if it's the last thing she wants, she turns on her heels and walks toward the corner I often find her in.

She sits down, pressing her back against the wall and pulling her knees toward her chest with her gown stretched over them.

Then she looks up at me and says one last time, "Do what you have to do."

Wanting to put my fist through a wall, I storm over to the shackle and chain, taking it up into my hand and approach her with it. Crouching down beside her, I take her uninjured ankle and lock the shackle around it. She doesn't look at me much less fight me.

I make my way to the staircase and stop only long enough to hear her say, "I'll forgive you, Fredrik. For whatever you have to do to me," and I swallow down the pain her words caused and leave her sitting there.

I can't torture her. Maybe she knows it. Maybe she's playing me for a fool, using reverse psychology on me. I don't know, but I can't do that to her.

But I *will* do something.

Before this day is over, she'll tell me what she remembers.

I'll get it out of her. One way or another.

# FOURTEEN

*Fredrik*

———

I spend the rest of the day ignoring Cassia, and only checking in on her every so often by way of the video feed streaming from her room. I've thought of everything and the only idea that comes to mind is forcing her to watch another interrogation. Forcing her to watch me kill a man. For a while, it was what I intended to do. Instead of making her watch from one side of the basement, I was going to tie her to a chair *in* the interrogation room with me and let her see it up close and personal. Let her witness the horrific torture that she can barely stand to see through a television screen. Smell the fresh blood as it's drawn, the sweat.

But there's only one problem: I don't have anyone to torture. No one left like Dante Furlong who I know deserves to be put through that. The closest 'backup' I have is four hours from here and I can't leave Cassia alone in the basement for that long.

Feeling utterly defeated, and angry, and resentful toward Cassia for keeping the one thing from me that I need, I shoot up from the sofa, accidently knocking my portable tray with my dinner over onto the floor. Reaching up with both hands, I drag them through the top of my dark hair, clenching my teeth and biting back the roar sitting behind my tongue.

My arms fall to my sides and I look up at the ceiling, letting the defeat do what it wants with me.

But then suddenly a thought flickers in my mind and all is right in the world again. I take the iPad from the sofa beside me and switch on the camera in my bedroom. In a split screen, Cassia looks up instantly when she hears the television in her room come on. She stares at the live feed of my empty bedroom for a moment, curious, confused, and nervous.

If I can't scare or torture the information out of her, I'll draw it out in an equally cruel way.

I slip my feet down into my dress shoes and then my arms into the sleeves of my suit jacket, afterward shrugging my long coat on. As I walk briskly through the kitchen I swipe my keys from the counter and leave the house.

—

It's not usually my style, picking a woman up from a noisy bar like this one that smells of ash trays and cheap whiskey. The place is loud with drunk voices and some kind of classic rock continuously streams from the speakers of a juke box. I typically hunt in quieter places where wine is served and I can hear myself think. But this isn't a typical night and I don't have time to hunt in my usual places.

I'm out of place, dressed in an Armani suit and shiny black shoes and an eight thousand dollar watch. It's all drawing attention, but that only makes it easier for me.

It doesn't take long after I'm seated at the bar with my shoes propped on the stool's spindle to find the woman I want. Dark hair that streams past her shoulders. Her eyes are brown, I can tell even from this far across the room. She's petite, wearing a loose-fitting black skirt that stops just above her knees, and a pair of black women's cowboy boots on her feet. A long-sleeved black top that buttons down the front covers her upper body, but the top few buttons have been left undone revealing her cleavage. A long silver chain necklace is draped around her dainty, cream-colored throat with a pendant dangling on the end that dips below her breasts.

She's single. At least for tonight she is. I can tell by the way the two men standing next to her by the pool table are eyeing her and her friend. The way both women smile and blush when the men say how beautiful they are and how much they'd like to take them home tonight. I can't actually hear what they're saying, but whatever their exact words, it all translates to the same thing.

The dark-haired woman, the one I want, has already made eye contact with me once.

This will be easy.

I sit hunched over the bar with my arms resting on the bar top, a small glass of whiskey in my right hand. I run the tips of my fingers up and down the artistic indentions in the side of the glass to appear distracted. My long black coat is draped on the back of the stool behind me. I left the suit jacket on, unbuttoned, and my white dress shirt untucked from my slacks.

Finally I take a small drink, letting the rim of the glass linger near my lips afterward. I glance over again and sure enough the woman sees me as if she's been waiting for me to look.

Far too easy.

She smiles inwardly and then looks at her light-haired friend. Words are passed between them, but I get the feeling they're not close, probably just met tonight because the other woman seems more interested in the two men than their conversation. Soon, all four of them are looking my way, the two men with disappointment on their faces.

The dark-haired woman takes her small black purse up from the table in the corner and tucks it underneath her arm.

She walks toward me, swishing her shapely hips gently underneath her skirt.

"Hi," she says shyly as she steps up, but I get the feeling there's little shy about her. Perhaps she's pretending to be the shy type, but I already sense that it's not in her nature to turn a man like me away, one who she knows deep down inside of her somewhere is the kind of man who embodies sexual control.

"Good evening," I return with a faint smile.

She blushes.

I stand halfway from my stool and gesture at the empty one next to me, indicating for her to sit down. She does, propping her boot on the spindle to push herself onto the seat. She sets her little purse on the bar.

She smells good, like perfumed powder lightly dusting her skin. Her hair has been freshly washed and even though she has been drinking, I can still faintly smell traces of her minty toothpaste.

I gesture for the bartender who comes over and waits.

"Would you like a drink?" I ask the woman.

She smiles and her brown eyes appear to twinkle.

"Sure, thanks," she says. "Rum & Coke."

As the bartender goes to make her drink, I take another sip of mine and push the glass out of my way. I turn around on the stool to face her, leaving my right elbow on the bar.

"It's not often men like you come in here," she says.

The bartender places her glass down and then leaves us alone again.

"Men like me?" I inquire casually.

She nods with a blush growing in her cheeks.

"Well, yeah," she says, fingering the indentions in her glass as I had been doing. "A businessman of sorts by the looks of it. With an accent at that." She glances at my watch peeking from beneath my jacket sleeve. "And men don't usually come in here wearing Rolex's."

Interesting. She actually knows a Rolex when she sees one and doesn't even need to get a closer look. Gold digger? Wealthy herself? She could be a lot of different things, but one thing she isn't is demure, and she has a deep relationship with money. But she's far from being vulnerable. No, this one is good at a game of her own. She could easily fool a man into *thinking* she's vulnerable. But I'm not a man who is easily fooled. I just wonder if she's good enough to realize that.

"Gwen," she introduces herself. "What brings you to a place like this? Needed to drown your sorrows? Trouble with the wife?" She glances at my bare ring finger.

"Fredrik," I introduce with a dark, faint smile. "Fortunately I have no sorrows to drown. And certainly no wife."

She grins and takes another sip. Then she slides the glass out of the way with the tips of her long slender fingers, afterward propping her elbow on the bar top. She crosses her legs and stealthily pulls the ends of her dress over the top of her knee by tugging the fabric in her lap with her free hand. She has sexy knees attached to long flexible legs.

Gwen is a very confident woman hiding behind the guise of a shy Jane. She's a hunter, like me. And she's used to getting her way. She's used to men who drool at the sight of her, who can't get past staring at her breasts long enough to see that they're being played.

Tonight will be interesting for her, if not an eye-opener.

If this were any other night and finding my ex-wife wasn't a priority, I might want to hunt this woman a little longer. Take my time. Feel her out to figure out her game. I'd play it just because I can, and because she's not so unlike me and would probably enjoy it, too.

"What is that?" she asks. "The accent."

Her eyes seem to light up with the possibilities, as though the thought of sleeping with a man with an accent excites her.

I incline toward her, closing the space between us and inhale her scent. My gaze scans the curvature of her neck and the plumpness of her mauve-colored lips. "Swedish," I answer and let my eyes fall on hers. I lean in closer so that she can feel the heat of my breath on the side of her neck. "I should tell you, Gwen"—her body leans into mine eagerly—"I never waste time with the mating ritual, getting to know one another before we fuck by offering little spoonfuls of personal information to break the ice." I sense her body tense up and her breathing begins to deepen, but she makes no effort to pull away from me. "If you want to leave with me, then let's go. I can promise you one thing."

I pull away and look at her, waiting for her answer. Her eyes are wide and that plump mouth of hers sits partially agape. She's no longer the confident, game-playing woman she was when she walked over here. She's stunned for probably the first time in her life.

She hesitates for a long contemplative moment and finally asks, "What can you promise me, exactly?" Then she laughs nervously and adds, "That you won't kill me and throw my body in a dumpster?" She seems only slightly concerned about that prospect.

I smile and curl my fingers around my glass before bringing it to my lips and taking a drink. "No, I won't do that," I say and set the glass back down. "But I *will* have my way with you—that is if you can handle it. I won't lie to you, I'm not gentle."

She bites down tenderly on the corner of her bottom lip.

Gwen pauses and then turns slowly on the stool, facing forward. She takes another small drink and sets the glass down letting her fingertips linger on the wet rim. I've seen that look of excitement and conflict in a woman before. It's unmistakable, the look of a woman who wants to taste the darkness no matter the risks. Her cream-colored skin is flush with heat. Her long slender fingers continue to dance around the rim of the glass in a slow, repetitive movement. The inner ridge of her bottom lip stays moist as the tip of her wet tongue carefully traces it.

Quietly reading her thoughts, which are as loud as the music playing in the background, I oblige and drop my right arm from the bar, slipping my hand between her thighs and carefully breaking them apart. Without looking at me—and without objection—her body relents and her legs come uncrossed on the stool.

Like the rest of the bar, the area is dark, only the orange and red glow from various bar lights humming against the walls. The shadow plays against Gwen's profile, accentuating the way her throat moves every few seconds when she swallows. And when my fingers slip behind the elastic of her thin panties in the bend of her leg, the shadow reveals her mouth parting even more with anticipation.

Grazing her little bead of sex, Gwen gasps lightly and both of her hands collapse around her glass on the bar, her fingers loose, but restless. Her legs part farther, giving me—*begging* me—more access.

I slide my middle finger inside of her and feel her tighten around me, wanting to hold me there. Her eyes close softly. Her back has straightened like a proper English girl. Her shoulders are slightly stiff, her breasts heaving between them with every pleasure-filled breath she takes, but tries to contain for the sake of being in public. And only when she feels the sensation of my finger sliding carefully out of her does she turn her head to look at me again. Placing my hand over the top of my glass, I let my middle finger fall between the others and dip into the whiskey before taking a drink. I set the glass down, afterward placing the tip of my wet finger into my mouth and tasting her.

She just stares at me. Lustful. Conflicted. Confused.

Then I stand from the stool and remove my long coat from the back of it, sliding my arms down into the sleeves. Gwen watches me quietly, intensely, still fighting with the angel on her shoulder which lost to the devil on the other side the moment I touched her.

I drop a fifty-dollar bill on the bar beside my glass.

And then I walk away.

I don't look back as I make my way to the front exit, passing occupied tables and busy waitresses and pushing myself through thick wisps of cigarette smoke.

As casually as I had gone in, I walk back outside into the frigid air, pulling my coat together in the front as the wind brushes bitingly against my face. Before I step off the sidewalk and into the parking lot, I hear the music and the voices from inside the bar funnel from the front door as Gwen steps from it behind me.

"I'll take my chances with the dumpster," I hear her say and I grin with my back turned.

I turn to face her, my hands buried in my pockets. She's wearing a long coat, too, with a faux fur-lined hood draped around her dark hair where loose strands push against her face by the wind.

She is quite beautiful.

"I'm glad to hear that," I say matter-of-factly.

She smiles, breaking a little of the sexual tension for the sake of conversation. "You're really…blunt."

I shrug and gently purse my lips.

"I guess I am." I smile faint and close-lipped, offering my hand to her.

She smiles back and places her fingers into mine.

# FIFTEEN

*Fredrik*

———

We're at my house after a ten minute drive. Gwen talks a lot. Maybe she's just nervous after getting into a car late at night with a man she doesn't know, but I couldn't care less what she has to say or what she might be thinking. I brought her here for one thing and it isn't conversation.

"Wow, this is a nice house," she says when she steps through the doorway. "From the outside, I never expected it to look so… expensive." She looks back at me with dollar signs in her eyes as I pull her coat off from behind. "Not that the outside looks bad, it's just…well, very different." She smiles.

I don't respond to the mating ritual. Already this is beginning to feel like the start of a dating relationship—even if it's just with my money. And I don't date. In fact, I don't do 'normal'. This is very awkward for me.

I wish she'd just stop talking.

I needed a house under the radar to make it more difficult to be found by The Order. So I chose an old, small brick house and redesigned the inside to fit my expensive lifestyle. But the large basement, it got the most treatment. I wanted Cassia to feel safe in my home…despite the imprisonment.

I pull both of my coats off and break apart the buttons of my dress shirt. Gwen watches me with vaguely concealed lust in her eyes, and a little concern, which won't go away until she's sure I only brought her here for sex.

"How long have you lived here?"

*Kill me now.*

"Take off your boots," I say, just to derail the pointless chit-chat.

"Huh?"

I tilt my head slightly to one side.

"I said take off your boots." My standard expression never falters.

Gwen's eyes grow a little wider. She bites down on her bottom lip again.

I pull my shirt off and drape it over the back of the nearby leather chair.

Finally to ease her fears and get this night underway, I lean in toward her mouth and say, "I won't force you to stay"—I graze her lips and slip my hand up the bottom of her skirt. She gasps—"but if you're *going* to stay, you're going to do whatever I tell you to do. Is that understood?" My middle finger presses between her nether lips over the top of her wet panties. A small moan vibrates from her lips into mine as I slip my tongue into her mouth. Breathing in deeply, I kiss her with predatory intent and when I pull away, it takes a moment longer than it should for her to open her eyes again.

"Now take off your boots," I repeat.

She steps out of them without reluctance this time, and then her close-lipped mouth turns up at the corners seductively as she waits for my next command. But what I really want her to do is to tell me to go fuck myself. I want her to be defiant and aggressive, just like Seraphina often was. I want her to hit me, but still want me to despoil her with lust and violence. That's the kind of sex I need tonight, but I know I can't have it because only Seraphina can give it to me the way I crave it.

But, this isn't about me. This is *all* for Cassia.

I reach out with both hands and finger the buttons on Gwen's shirt, slipping it off once the last button is undone. Her generously-sized breasts are practically busting out of her black, lacy bra. The chain she wears lies neatly between them. I reach behind her and clasp my fingers around the back, unfastening it on the first try. Her eyes are looking into mine, but I'm not ready to return the gesture. She needs to earn it.

Her bra falls around her bare feet with her top and she stands before me halfway naked. Almost all traces of nervousness gone, leaving only anticipation and desire. She appears demure with her eyes lowered in a submissive fashion.

That frustrates me, but I ignore it.

Fitting my fingers behind the elastic of her skirt, I slide the material slowly over her hips and down her thighs. The fabric pools around her feet. Once she's fully naked, I wind my fingers within the back of her hair, jerking her head back, shocking her into full submission. Her eyes grow wider, unsure, even a little afraid. But she says nothing and I walk her toward my bedroom down the hall, flipping the overhead light on as I pass the switch by the door so that Cassia can see everything without shadows and darkness impeding her view.

I shove Gwen to her knees on the carpeted floor where she doesn't dare move. I can sense every part of her body already opened up to me, desperate to feel me inside of her. She's played this game before. She knows how to be the submissive. She likes it. And any other time I'd accommodate that desire and enjoy it myself, because I am a man of control. But the truth is that I've never respected a woman completely submissive to me. I like a woman to put up a fight, not to bark when I tell her to bark, or suck without argument when I put my cock in her mouth.

Not even Cassia, as soft and fragile as she is, who I know would do anything for me, would subject herself to that. And it only makes me care about her that much more.

*Cassia…*

I look toward the small camera hidden on the dresser across the room. I wonder if she's looking back at me.

Why do I hope that she's not?

I shake it off quickly when I feel Gwen's hand moving between my legs over the top of my pants. She looks up at me suggestively—and quite surprised—her almond-shaped eyes softened by willingness, heated by hunger.

If only Seraphina was here to be in on this. She was the only one who could ever make a submissive girl exciting to me.

I wrench the back of Gwen's hair in my fist again and pull her to her feet.

"I'd rather you on your knees on the bed."

Letting go of her hair once she's standing, she does exactly as I tell her, just barely looking over her shoulder at me, telling me with her eyes that it's OK, that she wants this the way *I* want it. Only, this *isn't* the way I want it and I continue to pretend.

Gwen crawls onto the edge of the bed and I step behind her, placing my hand against the small of her back and pressing her body forward to raise her ass in the air. My dick twitches when I touch her with the back of my middle finger, sliding it lengthwise between her wet nether lips. Two smacks zip through the air when I slap each of her butt cheeks hard enough to make her whimper.

"Don't move," I tell her as I step over to the nightstand, sliding out of my pants on the way.

After shutting the nightstand drawer, the condom wrapper is on the floor seconds later and I'm behind Gwen again.

"What was that?" Gwen raises her face from the mattress, her eyebrows drawing inward as she concentrates to hear the cry that I pretend not to have heard.

But I *did* hear it. Cassia's side of the basement is directly beneath my room, precisely where I'm standing.

Suddenly I feel more of an urge to check the video feed from her room on my cell phone, than to continue what I was doing.

"A condom," I say, pretending.

She turns her neck at an angle so that she can see me. "No, I thought I heard something…like crying."

"I didn't hear anything," I say. "Might've been the TV in the basement."

Gwen accepts my answer and presses her cheek against the bed again.

I try to ignore my thoughts of Cassia, grabbing Gwen's thighs firmly in my hands and pressing myself against her. But I *can't* ignore her and I become irate with myself, digging my fingertips into Gwen's flesh.

"Oww! Jesus! That fucking *hurt*…" She sounds angry. But just a little.

Was that *defiance*?

Suddenly I feel like I might get the violent sex that I need, after all.

Then I hear Cassia screaming my name and although faint and muffled through the floor, it rips through me like a hot poker burning a hole through my chest.

I don't think Gwen heard it that time because when she looks back at me again, it seems only out of curiosity. She wonders why

I've stepped away from her, why I'm not already inside of her by now.

She's as confused as I am.

I look at the hidden camera again, wishing that I could see her through it just as she can see me.

"Are we gonna' do this, or—"

"You need to leave," I cut in.

She blinks, stunned, and then turns around on the bed.

"You're kidding, right?"

"Do I look like I'm kidding?"

She blinks several more times as if trying to reset her brain because maybe she didn't hear me right, and presses the palms of her hands against the edge of the mattress. Her arms and shoulders become rigid as she lets her body slouch in between them.

She cocks her head to one side and grins.

"Is this part of your game?" she asks teasingly and then cocks her head to the other side. "I'll play whatever game you want me to play, baby."

Concerned for Cassia, I'm growing more impatient and intolerant by the second. Reaching out, I take Gwen by the elbow and pull her from the bed.

"Just fucking leave, all right?"

She's speechless. And pissed. And humiliated. Her mouth falls open partway, her eyes draw inward harshly and it looks like I just slapped her across the face.

"I'll call you a cab," I say, but she puts her hand up in front of her, indicating she doesn't need or want my help.

"No thanks, asshole," she snaps, stomping naked across the room toward the bedroom door. "I'll call *myself* one and wait for it at the gas station on the corner." A few minutes later, after Gwen has gotten dressed in the living room and found her purse, the house shakes as the front door slams shut.

I'm numb. Completely numb inside and out. I haven't moved from the spot in my bedroom since Gwen stormed out of the house. My chest aches for Cassia.

*What is* happening *to me?*

Shuffling around inside my pants pocket for my cell phone, I grab it and pull it free, dropping my pants back on the floor. I open the feed to Cassia's room to see her curled up in the fetal position on her bed—not in the corner—crying softly into her delicate hands. And I watch her for a moment, still trying to sort through the disarray that my mind has become.

My heart aches. *Everything* aches. But this time I don't fight it because I don't have it in me anymore.

I toss the condom in the trash beside the dresser and step into my black boxers before rushing into the basement to fix what I broke.

# SIXTEEN

*Fredrik*

———

Taking the steps one at a time, I make my way slowly into the basement with a boulder sitting in the pit of my stomach. The concrete is cold against the bottoms of my bare feet, the air getting cooler as a winter storm begins to bear down on the East coast. I make a mental note to be sure to turn the heat up significantly when I go back upstairs so that Cassia stays comfortable down here.

But all of these random thoughts are just my way of shoving the inevitable moment I know is sure to leave me reeling into the back of my mind for as long as I can before I'm forced to confront it.

When I step off the last step, I can't help but glance over at the television behind the protective glass to see the view from my bedroom. That boulder in my stomach starts to burn painfully when I picture what Cassia just saw. When I picture what I almost did. When I realize how much of a bastard I really am that I was going to make her watch.

I turn the television off.

"Cassia?" I speak up softly.

She doesn't respond right away. She lies on her side with her back to me, her body covered only by the thin material of her nightgown. I feel a desperate urge to go over and cover her with the blanket so that she doesn't get cold. But I don't. Not yet. I'm unsure if she even wants me there. And I'm unsure why that even matters to me. What *she* wants. When did what Cassia wants first become my priority? I want to say 'just moments ago', but that would be a form of denial and I think I've been in denial for far too long. Cassia has been my priority for a very long time, since shortly after I brought her here. And I'm only just now allowing myself to believe it.

"Stay away from me," I hear her say in a small, wounded voice.

Compelled by her rejection, I move toward her instead of away.

"I didn't want to hurt you," I say, stepping up closer to her bed. "I never wanted to—"

Cassia rolls over and springs to her feet so quickly that I barely have time to react.

"I said stay away from me!" she shrieks, tears shooting from her anguished eyes. "I hate you! Bastard, I *hate* you!" I'm directly in front of her in a flash with her small fists pummeling my chest.

I let her hit me as hard and for as long as she wants, taking blow after stinging blow deservingly. Sobs rattle her entire body, her eyes are clenched shut so tightly that I wonder how tears can continue to seep through her lids at all. She screams at me, so vociferously and strained that I know it must be shredding her throat.

"I'm sorry," I say softly behind her screams, still trying to understand why I've even apologized. And it's in this moment that I realize the shackle isn't locked around her ankle.

Confused and panicking a little inside, I want to ask her how she got it unlocked, but I can't as it isn't the right time.

Her fists pound my chest some more, until finally I seize her small frame in my arms and crush her against my heart.

My hands are shaking.

*Why are my hands shaking?*

The backs of my eyes sting and burn. It feels like a fist has collapsed around my heart restricting the blood flow, and that hot boulder in my stomach has grown to encompass all of my chest, robbing me of my breath.

Sobbing into my body, at first Cassia tries to push me away, but I refuse to let her go. I want her here, now more than ever. Because it's where she belongs. Her fingernails dig into my chest muscles. Her cries break my heart over and over again. But I just hold onto her tighter until she relents and her body collapses into mine.

"I hate you," she cries, slowly letting go of anger and surrendering only to pain. "*I hate you…*"

I shut my eyes softly and press my lips into the top of her feather-soft blond hair.

I know she doesn't hate me. She *loves* me. She loves me more than she's ever loved anyone or anything in her whole life.

How can Fate be so fucking heartless and cruel? Was what Life did to me as a child not enough?

I squeeze her tighter.

"Cassia, I'm sorry."

"Why didn't you just put me in the chair?" she cries. "How could you *do* that to me?" Her fingertips press harder into my bare chest muscles. "Break my body! Break my will, Fredrik! But don't break my goddamn *heart!*"

"I'm sorry…"

It's all I can say.

It's hard to say anything else when you don't even understand your own feelings, your own reactions. When you've come to the realization that there's more to you than you ever wanted to believe. I feel like I've just been introduced to a man who looks exactly like me, yet is so very different on the inside that nothing makes sense anymore. I'm staring into a mirror at my doppelganger and all I want to do is kill him fucking dead so that I can feel normal again. So I can be in control again. So that I can go back to not caring about her again.

It's so much easier when you don't care.

"I couldn't do it," I whisper into her hair about Gwen.

I feel her tears warm and wet on my chest.

"I wish she was dead," Cassia says through gritted teeth. "I hope Seraphina is dead by the time you find her." She pushes away from me and I finally let her go.

Cassia takes several steps backward, her small fists clenched down at her sides, her angelic features twisted angrily, resentfully. I've never seen her like this before, so defiled by indignation, and it's a tragic thing to witness in one so kind and beautiful.

She locks eyes with me and there's something else in them I've never seen before. Fury? Retribution? I can't be sure. And then just when I intend to explore it further, it disappears from her face and is replaced again by pain and heartbreak.

Cassia falls on her bottom against the soft rug covering the floor. I move immediately to crouch in front of her, balancing myself on the front pads of my feet. She cries into her opened hands and I reach out to pull her into my arms again, but she refuses me, raising her brown eyes to mine full of defeat. Withdrawing my hands, I sit down fully against the rug with my legs splayed and my knees drawn up with my forearms resting atop them.

She says softly, "Why can't you love me back, Fredrik?" and every word is laced with sadness which breaks my heart into a million tiny shards of glass. "What is wrong with me that you can't love me back?"

I shake my head rejecting her self-depreciation and reach out to touch the side of her face. "*Nothing* is wrong with you. You're perfect in every way, Cassia." I brush the edge of my thumb against her jawbone. "Don't let my imperfections as a worthless human being make you feel like less of a person—you're a better person than I could *ever* be."

She stares back at me—her eyes welled up with tears—with enough heartbreak that if she wasn't so strong inside it would surely kill her.

"I don't care about your imperfections, Fredrik." Her hand falls atop mine still resting against the side of her cheek. "I just want to know why you can't love me."

My gaze strays.

"I can't love anyone," I say in a quiet voice.

"That's a lie," she says equally.

She moves in between my legs, keeping her knees bent and her gown covering them.

"That's a lie and you know it."

I look up even though I don't want to face her. Because she's right.

*Love is a wicked game,* I think to myself, remembering what Seraphina sang to me on stage one night in New York sometime after we met. *Wicked Game.* Because just like Cassia, Seraphina was once a singer. And as I recall Cassia admitting to remembering everything about Seraphina, I realize that right now in this moment with her, I don't care. I don't care to know what I've waited so long to find out.

I just don't care…

Cassia's soft lips touch mine, and my arms are around her little body before I realize what I'm doing. I grab her against me, pressing her thinly-covered breasts into my bare chest, my mouth collapsing about hers hungrily as I kiss her unlike I've ever kissed her before. Her warm tongue tangles with mine, her fingers press into the back of my neck, mine into the flesh of her bottom as I hoist her onto my lap. Pushing her gown up and out of the way, her bare thighs straddle my waist, and still without breaking the kiss I dig my fingers in deeper, moaning into her mouth with anticipation.

She bites down on my bottom lip, breaking the skin. The stinging pain sears through my mouth and travels down into my stomach, warming every part of me and making other parts ache and throb with need. I taste the blood in my mouth, and she just kisses me harder as if wanting to taste it herself, to share it with me.

Gripping her bottom vigorously, I force her hips toward mine, pushing my hardness against her until I can't stand it anymore and I race to get her panties off. I yank and pull blindly, our eyes closed, our lips still locked in a devouring kiss, until I finally get them off and her naked legs fall around my waist again.

She pulls back and looks into my eyes, her arms draped around the back of my neck. Her lips touch mine again lightly, one hand falling to find the waist of my boxers. Softly pushing her hips against mine, it drives me crazy feeling my cock pressed into her through a thin layer of fabric which feels like the difference between ecstasy and Hell. Moaning against her lips, I raise my ass from the floor enough to give her access to get them off. But impatience takes over and I grasp her around the waist with one hand to hold her steady while wrenching them off the rest of the way myself with the other.

Flesh on warm flesh, she presses herself into me, peering into my eyes with her mouth gently parted. I want to taste her lips again, but I study them instead, the plumpness of her bottom lip, the perfect little indention of the top, just below her nose. Her breath smells faintly of mint. The natural scent of her skin which always sends me into a brief high when I'm this close to her.

"I am yours. Always." she whispers onto my mouth and kisses me once, pressing the warm wetness between her legs against the aching stiffness between mine. "Even if you can't love me the way you love her, I'll always be yours."

I grab the back of her head in both of my hands and crush my lips against hers, stealing her breath away and replacing it with my own. I ache. Every part of me aches. For her. Only for her.

I need to kill someone to wash these feelings away, but in this moment I can't do anything but give in to them.

Grasping her firmly around her back, I push myself to my feet with her legs wrapped around my waist, carrying her to the bed where I fall between her thighs.

I gaze down into her eyes—*What am I doing?*—and secure her head with my hands on her cheeks. The warmth from her thighs I feel on either side of me, the softness of her flesh. So delicate. So innocent. *How can I do this to her? How can I do this to myself?*

"I'm sorry, Cassia," I whisper and lower my body onto hers. She never takes her eyes off of mine, her fingers dancing against one side of my unshaven face. "I'm sorry for everything I've done to you...and for what I'm about to do." I kiss her deep and hungrily, and slide my cock into her with careful, predatory intent.

The sweet sound of her whimpering as I enter her only makes me want to go deeper. Her thighs tremble at my sides, her fingers dig into the skin on my back. *Break the flesh, Cassia*, I say only to myself.

She does break the flesh and my body reacts in such a primal way that I can't help but hurt her as I force myself inside of her as deeply as I can go. Her neck arcs and her arms come up behind her, seeking the wall behind the bed. I can't bring myself to *ask* if I'm hurting her. I *want* to hurt her. I want to feel her breaking beneath me, to see the tears in her eyes, to hear the shuddering of her breath. I want to know that she wants the pain as much as I need to inflict it.

Tiny moans and whimpers move through her throat as I thrust into her. She's so small and tight that I feel like her first all over again.

*All over again...*

Almost losing control too soon, I force the feeling of ecstasy back for as long as I can, rotating my pelvis against hers to hit her sweet spot. She pushes her hips forward, her thighs tightening around my waist as if she could crush me with them. "Don't stop," she says breathily, "please don't stop." And I push harder until she breaks the skin on my back again with her fingernails and it sends me over the edge. I devour her lips as I empty myself inside of her, moaning intensely into her mouth. Her thighs strengthen as I feel her tighten and throb around my cock. She whimpers again, arcing her head back against the mattress, her breathing out of sequence as her body melts into oblivion beneath mine.

*What have I done?*

I gaze into her eyes, holding myself deep inside of her, and I brush her cheeks with the pads of my thumbs. Her eyes, filled with so much love and innocence, they only briefly detract my need to cut her back with my blade and lick the blood from her wounds. To bond with her the way I bonded with Seraphina.

I *want* to do it.

But I know that I can't. I've taken it too far with Cassia already. I can't allow myself to take her all the way, or then I would truly be the Devil.

I press my lips to her forehead. She smiles up at me softly.

*I'm no better than Seraphina...*

Intent on stopping this, I start to pull myself out of her, but her legs tighten around my waist as she holds me still.

"Don't go," she whispers, her fingertips touching my lips, her other hand winding carefully within my hair. "Please don't go."

She kisses me lightly.

I try to avert my eyes, because I'm ashamed for what I've done. It isn't the first time I've given in to Cassia like this, it's not the first time I've slept with her in the year she's been my prisoner. But it *is* the first time I've done it with something more in my heart than darkness.

"Cassia, I shouldn't have—"

She shakes her head softly against the mattress. "Please stay." Her smile fades and she suddenly appears dejected, but I feel like it's not an attempt to keep me here.

It's something else.

Her head falls to the side and she looks out at the room as silence descends between us. I wait patiently, though hanging onto her sudden change of mood with an *im*patient and conflicted heart. I feel like what's left of my world is about to be pulled from underneath me.

"I was ten-years-old when I met Seraphina," she says in a distant voice that seizes every fiber of my consciousness. "She was my best friend…until she murdered my parents and was sent away."

A tear moves from the corner of her eye and pools around her nose, resting in that little indention above her lip.

I swallow down her words and say nothing because there's nothing more to say. I know now that everything is lost and I'm never going to get it back.

# SEVENTEEN

*Cassia*

———

Fredrik carefully raises his warm body from mine and sits upright with his back against the wall. His legs are moved apart, arms propped on the tops of his bent knees. He tilts his head back. His beautiful, stubbly face appears crestfallen and defeated as he gazes out at the room.

I lift up and position myself between his legs, the side of my naked body lying against his chest. I can still feel him moderately hard as his manhood presses against my lower back. I love to sit between his legs. He makes me feel safe. And I melt into him when I feel his warm, solid arms wrap around me from behind.

"My mother and father were very loving people," I begin. "They would never hurt me. But Seraphina didn't like them. She said they were evil and that she wanted to help me get away from them."

I pause, attentive to Fredrik's heartbeat thrumming through the muscles in my back. I feel the breath from his nostrils warm against the top of my shoulder as he releases a long deep breath from his lungs.

# THE SWAN AND THE JACKAL

Still, he doesn't speak, but holds me very close to him, and I tell him what happened exactly the way I remember it.

*Twenty-three years ago...*

*I thought the girl who moved in next door was a little strange. I never saw her around her parents. I didn't even know there was a little girl living next door until months after they moved in. I was alone in the shed behind our house—I spent most of my time there because it was quiet—when I heard the girl singing in the backyard. I crept out of the rickety metal door, trying not to let my father know about my hiding place, and snuck around the side to peek through a slit between boards in the big wooden privacy fence that separated our backyards. She had jet-black hair cut just below her shoulders. And she wore a pair of pink shorts with a whimsical rainbow printed on the left thigh—I had a pair just like them and was intrigued by that otherwise insignificant detail.*

*She was sitting on the grass with a stuffed animal of sorts in her lap, tucked in between her crossed legs. Beside her was a thick coloring book. I thought that was strange, too, as we looked about the same age and I had already grown out of coloring books. She scribbled furiously across the paper with a crayon while she sang quietly to herself. She had a beautiful, melodious voice.*

*I pressed my face farther against the fence, trying to get a better glimpse of what she was coloring, but she was a little too far for me to make it out.*

*But then she sensed she was being watched and the singing stopped. Her head shot up and she just sat there for a moment, listening for sounds. I didn't move. I couldn't even breathe. I don't know why I was trying so hard to remain unseen because I really wanted to talk to her. Maybe a part of me—the part that knew how dangerous she was before the rest of me did—was afraid of her.*

147

*And then she saw me. I only moved an inch because my back was starting to cramp, but that slight movement was enough to give me away.*

She watched in my direction for a minute before rising to her feet and approaching me, the stuffed animal—a raggedy, dirty lamb, I noticed as she got closer—in one hand and a red crayon in the other. She left the coloring book on the grass.

"Hello," she said, tilting her head to one side as if to see clearer through the uneven gap in the boards. "What's your name?"

"Cassia Carrington," I answered. "What's yours?"

"Seraphina." She smiled toothily.

I smiled in return. I liked her instantly.

She sat down in the leaves next to the fence and I did the same and we talked for a few minutes.

"I haven't seen you at my school," I said.

"Nah, I'm home-schooled."

I watched her through the gap in the fence, only able to glimpse the dirty lamb in her lap and the tip of her index finger tracing around its little beady black eye.

"How old are you?" she asked.

"I'm ten."

"Me too," she said. "But my birthday is almost here, so I'll be eleven."

"I just had my birthday. My mom bought me a new bike."

"That makes me older than you," she said with an innocent air of authority in her voice that actually made me feel sheltered. "But I don't have a bike," she added sadly.

I never had any brothers or sisters and had always wanted one. It was hard being an only child, especially when I had no friends, either. At least not until Seraphina. And in ten minutes of talking to her, I felt like I not only finally had a friend, but that older sibling that I always wanted, too.

*It took me a moment to realize there had been something sad in her voice when she said she didn't have a bike.*

*"Hey, you could come over and ride mine whenever you want," I offered.*

*I heard her sigh. "Thanks," she said, paused and then added, "but my dad doesn't like for me to go to other people's houses."*

*"Oh." I flicked the end of a twig with my middle finger and it shot across the grass. "Well, maybe I could come to your house."*

*Seraphina was quiet for an even longer moment.*

*"They don't like that, either," she finally said, "but we can still be friends."*

*I wasn't sure how that would work out seeing as how a fence separated us and she wasn't allowed to have company or to go anywhere.*

*But we made it work.*

*Every day after I got home from school Seraphina snuck over into my shed through an opening in the fence that we made at the end of the backyard. I had used a hammer from the shed to loosen the nails on two boards so that we could slide them out of the way and easily put them back in place to make it appear that nothing had ever been moved.*

*Seraphina and I spent a lot of time in my shed, playing with Barbie dolls and stuffed animals. I even started coloring again and I found that I really liked it.*

*We were inseparable, like sisters. But as the weeks wore on, I began to see just how different we were, how different our parents were.*

*One afternoon, the rough voice of her father yelling her name from the back door, caused Seraphina's whole body to shake like she had been stuffed in a freezer. She ran out of the shed as fast as she could and scrambled on her hands and knees across the dirt and leaves and rocks toward the secret opening in the fence. I guess she* was afraid if she ran upright that her father would see her from the back porch.

I helped her get through the fence quickly and I closed it off after she was on the other side. Minutes later I heard Seraphina screaming from inside her house. I sat curled up inside the shed, shaking all over hearing her bloodcurdling cries rock through every bone in my body. I wet myself it scared me so bad. What sounded like a long strip of leather rang out through the air. Over and over again. And Seraphina screamed and screamed until she fell silent. But even still, I could hear the leather strap beating down on her.

I sat curled up in the corner of the shed, sobbing into my hands, tasting salt and snot and bile in the back of my throat. For a very brief but profound moment, I had hoped he'd killed her so she would never have to go through that again.

I didn't see Seraphina for a week after that, but then one day she was sitting on the grass in the backyard again, just like she was the day I met her.

"Seraphina?" I whispered quietly through the gap in the fence.

She wouldn't look over, but I could sense that she heard me.

"Seraphina? Are you OK?"

She barely turned her head, but even at such an angle I could see the pain in her face. She was dressed in pants and a long-sleeved shirt even though it was warm outside. I knew why. I could only wonder what the bruises looked like underneath her clothes.

We were both afraid for her to come over to my side of the fence, but we also both wanted her to. So after a few minutes, she finally snuck to the back of the yard and I helped her crawl through the opening.

"Did he find out?" I asked once we were hidden away safely inside the shed. "About you sneaking over here?"

She shook her dark head and lowered her eyes to the little lamb in her lap. "No," she said quietly, "he was mad because I left my clothes on my bedroom floor."

THE SWAN AND THE JACKAL

I thought that was the most terrible thing. The stupidest thing to get in trouble for. I just sat there staring at her with my mouth agape.

Seraphina hardly ever looked me in the eyes. She sat awkwardly, as if the bones in her back and bottom hurt too badly for her to sit with comfort. And I noticed she kept pulling at the crotch of her purple pants as if the material was aggravating her skin down there. It made me feel weird. Dark. I wanted to ask why she was itching, but I was too afraid. I didn't know why.

Seraphina raised her eyes to me.

"I have to go," she said suddenly and pushed herself—with difficulty—to her feet, the stuffed lamb secured in the bend of her arm. "I have to get back to my project."

"What project?" I asked with intense curiosity.

Seraphina smiled, which I thought too was odd in such a circumstance—had she already forgotten what happened to her? She offered her hand to me. I took it and she helped me to my feet.

"Just something I gotta do," she said. "I'll tell you about it soon."

And then she left, sneaking back through to her side of the fence without another word.


Fredrik has never held me so tight. His arms are wrapped around me so securely that if it were any tighter I wouldn't be able to breathe. I feel his lips on the top of my head, and his heart beating powerfully against my back.

I lift my head from his arm and turn it slightly at an angle so that I can see him. There is moisture in his eyes. I've never seen him this way before and it reminds me of the things he told me he went through when *he* was a boy.

I kiss the tops of his knuckles.

"I'm sorry...if this is bringing back bad memories," I say. "I can stop."

Fredrik shakes his head and wipes his eyes before the tears can fall. "No," he says softly, "don't apologize to me; this has nothing to do with me. Please…just tell me the story."

I kiss his knuckles again and reluctantly continue.

*Seraphina was different after that last time her father beat her, but it wasn't thanks to me or my mother. Because I tried to help Seraphina. I sat down with my mother one night when my dad was gone at the bar and I told her about what happened.*

*"But momma," I said, "he beat her so bad. I heard her screaming and it gives me nightmares."*

*My mother shook her head and stuck her fork in her mouth, taking in a bite of salad. "You should stay out of it, Cassia," she said, chewing on the leafy greens. "Don't you tell anyone else, either. Do you hear me? If you do, you'll be in a lot of trouble yourself." She pointed her fork at me. "Her daddy is some big shot government guy. Very dangerous. We don't get involved, do you understand?" She sipped down the last of her water.*

*I nodded nervously, and while although I couldn't understand why my mother—who was such a loving and smart woman—wouldn't want to call the police right away about what was happening next door, I knew too that she must've been afraid of Seraphina's father for good reason. And so I did as she said and kept my mouth shut.*

*This went on for three years.*

*By the time Seraphina and I turned thirteen—her a few months before me—Seraphina was a very different girl from the one I met on the grass holding the little lamb. She still took beatings from her father, but she didn't seem afraid of him anymore.*

*She even started coming to my house. Walked right out her front door one day, up my sidewalk and my front porch steps. I was shocked when I answered the door and saw her standing there. For a moment, I just stood there staring at her.*

"Aren't ya' gonna let me in?" she said with a grin.

She was no longer carrying the stuffed lamb by this time. Said she got rid of it. I found its remains in a heap of ash in my backyard.

Seraphina never did tell me everything about her 'project', but she did say that one day she was going to get away from her parents and that her project was her ticket. I had stopped asking her questions about it.

That afternoon, Seraphina spent the rest of the day at my house, tucked away in my room with me. We watched TV and talked about whatever. She bragged about stealing some of her mother's perfume and stuck her wrists under my nose so that I could smell it. I really liked that perfume. By nightfall, when I heard my father coming in from work, Seraphina got nervous. I could see it in her eyes, her posture, the way her back stiffened and her chest stopped moving as if her lungs forgot how to work. Like a lot of things I thought about Seraphina, I thought her reaction to my father coming home from work, was strange. Especially after it seemed she wasn't even afraid of her own father anymore. So why would she be afraid of mine?

"Cassia!" I heard my father call out, "Come eat dinner!"

Seraphina's eyes widened as she stared at my bedroom door.

"Just a minute, daddy!" I called out.

Turning back to Seraphina, I said with a jerk of my head toward the bedroom door, "Come on, I guess it's time for you to go home."

Seraphina shook her head and it seemed she didn't even blink.

"I'll go out the window," she said. "I don't want your parents telling mine that I was over here."

She was still afraid of her father, after all, but had only gotten better at hiding it, I realized.

I nodded. "OK," I said and walked over to my window, flipping the latch open and raising the glass.

"CASSIA!" my father shouted. "GET YOUR ASS IN HERE AND EAT!" I gasped sharply at his tone.

He was a good father—nothing like Seraphina's father—but intolerant to disobedience.

Seraphina had just started to climb out the window, but when she heard him the second time, she stopped and looked back at me with an enraged look in her big brown eyes.

I waved my hands at her, trying to hurry her up and shuffle her over the windowsill.

"Why is he talking to you like that?" she asked with narrowed eyes and anger in her voice.

I kept looking back and forth between her and the bedroom door, growing more nervous the longer she took. I didn't want to get grounded.

"He's always like this when he gets home from work," I said. "Now hurry up. I've gotta go."

A few more seconds of looking between me and the door, Seraphina finally slipped outside and ran through my backyard. I saw her slip through the secret hole in the fence instead of waltzing through her front door boldly as I expected her to after so boldly coming to mine earlier.

A week later I was sitting in the shed writing in my notebook that I kept as a journal, when Seraphina joined me. She had a spiteful and cunning look on her face, a grin that sent a chill up my back. Her eyes were dark and she looked upon me as though about to tell me something I knew was going to make me uncomfortable.

She plopped down on the concrete shed floor and kissed me on the cheek.

"Do you love me, Cassia?"

I smiled ridiculously. "Of course I do. You're like my sister."

She cocked her head to one side and folded her hands in the hollow of her lap.

"Remember that time you told me you wanted to go wherever I go? That you wanted us to be sisters forever, no matter what?"

*I nodded with an even brighter smile, because it was true. I did want to go wherever she went. She was my best friend. I wanted us to grow up and grow old together.*

*"Yeah, I remember."*

*She smiled and softened her eyes. "Good. Then tonight we're going to run away together."*

*My face fell and I tried to swallow the knot that had suddenly formed in my throat, but it was too dry.*

*"W-What do you mean, run away?" I felt guilty for even having the conversation.*

*Seraphina pulled me into a brief hug, afterward letting her hands brush down the length of my arms until her fingers found mine. She held my hands firmly and said, "I want to go to New York. I've got it all planned out. We can get on a bus—it's easy, they do it in the movies all the time and no one ever checks for identification unless they look like kids. But we don't look like kids"—she waved her finger back and forth between us—"I can easily pass for seventeen, and you, well I think you could too if you put on a little makeup."*

*I was shaking my head absently the whole time she was explaining her plan, but she just kept on talking with the excitement of it all ever-growing in her eyes.*

*"I want to be a singer," she said with the biggest smile of wonderment I had ever seen on her face. She gripped my hands tighter. "And Cassia, you could, too. We could both be singers. You sing even better than me!"*

*I blushed and lowered my gaze to our hands.*

*"I-I don't know, Seraphina." I looked toward the shed door, terrified my parents might've been listening in. "Running away won't be easy. My parents check in on me every night. First my mom. Then later my dad. They'd know I was missing before we made it to the bus station—and what about money? I don't have any money."*

*Seraphina grinned and leaned forward so she could reach around to her back pocket. There was a wad of cash in her hand when she brought it back around.*

*"Stole it from my mom's jewelry box," she said with a proud smirk and then placed the money into my hands. "This'll get us both to New York."*

*I looked down at the cash and then back up at her. I didn't want to tell her no, but at the same time, I was scared. I was scared of running away. Getting caught. Getting grounded for the rest of my life.*

*But I think most of all, I was scared of Seraphina.*

*"So are you going to leave with me?"*

*She sat there with her hands in her lap, her fingers coiling anxiously around one another. Her face was full of excitement and danger and risk and trouble—everything I always steered clear of. Everything I was afraid of.*

*But then finally I said, "But what if my parents wake up and see that I'm gone? What if they catch us before we get to New York?"*

*"They won't catch us," she said with such resolve that I couldn't help but believe her. "I'm going to take care of that before we leave."*

*Before Seraphina snuck out of my shed that afternoon and went back into her yard, I had agreed to go with her. And to trust in her, no matter what she had to do to help me get away.*

I'm lying down against the bed now with my head on Fredrik's thigh. I don't even recall when I shifted position, I've been so engrossed in the memory. It's been a year since I've remembered any of this, or anything about my life at all, so it's all quite a lot to take in.

Fredrik's hand moves softly through the top of my hair, sending shivers from the back of my neck and throughout my body. It feels like he's consoling me, but more than that, it feels like he's hurting and I don't want to go on. I know he had a terrible life and that he went through some horrific things when he was a boy, things that he will probably never tell me. But I know they were much worse than anything I ever went through.

"What did Seraphina do to your parents, Cassia?" he asks in a soft voice while spearing his fingers through my long locks.

I stare out at the television on the wall across the basement and let the scene from that night play out before me as if it were playing out on the dark screen.

And then I answer, "She stabbed my father in the throat while he was downstairs asleep in his favorite chair. And then she poured gasoline she took from the shed in my backyard all over the house and set the house on fire. My mother burned to death in her room."

A part of me misses them, but another part of me feels nothing because it was so long ago.

"I didn't go to New York with Seraphina," I say distantly, picturing Seraphina's face in my mind, the way I saw her when she was driven away in the police car. The way her face was pressed against the glass as she looked at me. "I told the police what she had done and they sent her away. She admitted everything. I never saw her again." My fingers grip the sheet beneath me on the mattress. "I never saw her again until a year ago when she found me in my apartment in New York and tried to kill me. I know she thinks she was helping me by killing my parents—I think she killed hers, too, before mine. But I betrayed her by giving her up. And now...she wants to get back at me for the life she lost."

Fredrik says nothing for a very long time and I grow concerned about what he must be thinking. Can he still love her now that he knows what she did? It was never my intention to make him stop loving her by telling him the truth, but I can't help but hope that maybe he will now be able to see reason.

"Fredrik?"

# EIGHTEEN

*Fredrik*

———

"Yes?" I answer her, though at this point, I'm not sure if I'll be able to force anymore of an answer than those three letters.

My life is over. Everything I ever thought I knew about Seraphina, about our life together, the love that we shared, it's all over. Because now I know that there's no way I can help her, there's no way I can bring her back to me. She's a danger to me, to herself and everyone around her. Even Cassia. *Most of all...* Cassia. Seraphina was disturbed when I met her eight years ago and when I fell in love with her. But I never knew the extent of her illness until now. I never knew that she suffered traumatic experiences as a child just as I did.

I never knew.

But she and I are very different despite our somewhat similar pasts. I don't kill innocent people. I, while although a sadistic bastard and torturer and killer, have limits and standards. I know when to stop. I feel guilt for my mistakes. But Seraphina, I know now, doesn't *understand* guilt or remorse.

How could I *ever* have been so wrong about her?!

How could I *ever* have been so blind?!

Love.

Seraphina was right all along. To be in love is to be dead already because eventually it kills us all.

Cassia raises her head from my leg and pushes her naked body up propped on one arm. She looks into my eyes.

"Talk to me," she says and kisses my cheek. "Are you OK?"

I force a very light smile around my eyes and I nod in answer.

Then she lowers her eyes and I feel sadness and worry consume her emotions. Reaching out my hand, I raise her chin with the tip of my finger.

"Now *you* talk to me," I tell her gently. "What's on your mind?"

She swallows nervously and looks up, her brown eyes soft with worry. "Will you still protect me from her when you finally find her?"

My heart is dead. Black. No more. But not for Cassia. It just barely beats for her, though for how long it can hold on, I'm unsure.

I lean over and press my lips against her forehead, cupping the back of her head in the palm of my hand, and I hold it there with my eyes shut tight.

I'm going to have to do the hardest thing I've ever done in my life soon. But for now, I will give Cassia whatever she wants from me.

"I will always protect you from her," I say, pulling away slowly. "Seraphina will never hurt you again. I will make sure of that."

Cassia gives me a warm, thankful look and lays her head back down on my lap.

We sit in silence for the longest time, me combing my fingers through her hair, until eventually she falls asleep. I move out from underneath her carefully so as not to wake her, and I cover her with the blanket after locking the shackle back around her uninjured ankle. I noticed the key was on the nightstand beside her bed all along and realized that I never brought it back up with me the last time I stormed out and left her alone. That was how she was able to get the shackle unlocked.

She never tried to escape, and I doubt that she ever will, but I can't take the chance.

I leave Cassia alone and go back upstairs where I sit on the sofa in my boxers, staring into the darkness thinking about all that transpired. And I remain this way until the light of a new day burns through the curtains and pools on the floor beside my bare feet.

—

"Fredrik, what is it?" Izabel says into the phone, detecting the urgency in my voice.

"I just need to talk to you," I say after finally breaking down and admitting to myself that I should talk to anyone at all. But if it's going to be anyone, it can only be Izabel. "Are you back from Seattle? When and where can you meet me?"

"Yes. I got back this morning. Niklas and Dorian stayed behind to finish up. The other order sent only two men—easy-peasy."

"OK, where can we meet?"

"Why don't I just come to your house?" she asks warily. "I can be there in two hours."

"No," I say walking to my front door to let Greta inside. "We need to talk somewhere else. Anywhere but here."

"Fredrik, you're really starting to worry me. First you—"

"Can you meet me in Druid Hill Park?" I cut in. "Same parking lot we met before the Vanderbilt hit last month? Two hours."

Izabel pauses.

"All right, I'll be there."

Running my finger over the screen, the call ends. Greta walks past me offering a rather skittish smile. She's always been afraid of me, but after unlocking Cassia from her bonds without my permission, she likely didn't want to come here today at all.

She sets her purse down on the kitchen counter, dropping her keys in the top of it afterward. She starts in on cleaning immediately, bending over to retrieve a spray bottle of kitchen cleaner from underneath the sink and avoiding eye contact with me at all costs.

Already dressed in a pair of jeans, a thick black sweater and my more laid back Converse shoes, I slip my arms down into my coat and prepare to leave.

"I'm going to be gone for a few hours," I say, adjusting the neck of my sweater around the inside of my coat. "Under no circumstances will you unlock Cassia from that chain. Is that understood?" Lastly, I pull a black knit beanie over my head.

Greta nods with little eye contact. "Yes, Mr. Gustavsson."

Swiping my keys from the counter, I hold them in one hand while double checking for my wallet in the back pocket of my jeans.

Greta sprays the countertop and begins wiping it down.

"By the way," I add, "Cassia might confide in you about the things she remembered."

Greta looks up from her work, surprised. "She *remembered*?"

"Apparently." I step up closer, seizing her nervous gaze. "But I don't want you talking to her about it. Not unless she brings it up herself. And even then, say little in return. Let her do the talking if she needs to, but that's as far as it goes. Do you understand?"

The confused look on Greta's heavily lined face deepens, but she agrees with another tense nod of acknowledgment.

"Will you be here for dinner?" she asks as I'm making my way to the front door.

I don't stop to answer and I step out into the cold winter air, heading straight for my car.

I stop for coffee and gas and then a newspaper, trying to find things to do to waste two hours. And to think. Mostly I think. How much do I tell Izabel? Not everything, but enough to—I'm regretting this meeting already. There's nothing that Izabel can even do but give me advice, and since when was I ever the type of man who needed advice? I've never confided in anyone in my life other than Seraphina, and Willa before her when I was just a boy under the thumb of evil men. But now…now I'm desperate and I'm closer to no one in this world more than Izabel Seyfried. Victor Faust may be my friend and someone I believe I can trust, but he's a man, and I've never been able to develop the type of bond with any man that I have with very few women.

My past with men forbids such bonds.

Two hours drag by endlessly and I spend the last half hour of it waiting in the parking lot of the park with the engine running to keep warm. The sky is gray and covered by thick winter clouds that will start dumping snow on everything at any moment.

*Note to self: When this is all over, move south.*

Izabel's black Mercedes pulls into the parking lot. She parks next to me.

"Shit, it's cold," she says shuddering while hopping in the passenger's side of my car and closing the door quickly.

I pass her a hot coffee in a cup with a lid.

"You know me so well." She smiles and her big green eyes brighten thankfully as she takes the cup into both hands to warm them. Pursing her lips she blows on the steam rising from the small opening in the lid and then takes a careful sip, hissing when the liquid burns her lips.

"So what's this all about?" She sets the cup in the cup holder in the console between us. Then she adjusts her long white coat, pulling it from underneath her bottom and then hides her keys away inside the pocket. Her long auburn hair is pulled into a silky ponytail at the back of her head.

I hesitate for a rather lengthy amount of time, dropping my hands from the bottom of the steering wheel and into my lap. My head falls back against the leather headrest.

"Well, before you say anything," she says quickly, "I want you to know that I did tell Victor I was meeting you here."

"I didn't expect you *not* to tell him." I smirk over at her and then jest, "What, you think I planned to kill you?"

Izabel laughs lightly and nudges me in the shoulder with a half-fist.

"I tell Victor everything, you know that," she says with a smile. "Besides, you wouldn't kill me."

I raise a brow and one side of my mouth. "Oh really? You must think you're special. Got news for yah, doll." Her whole face breaks into a grin. "OK, you *are* kind of special," I admit, but then point at her and narrow my eyes and say, "But don't let that shit go to your head. I'd still kill you."

She smiles, rolls her eyes and rests her head against the head-rest for a moment.

Then she says, "Is this your way of breaking the ice?" Her head falls to the side so she can look at me. "Because I get the feeling whatever it is you have to tell me is something serious."

"It is." I nod.

"Well," she says, looking forward at the windshield, "just remember the reason I told you about Victor."

"I know," I say. "Because you keep nothing from him."

She raises her head and back from the seat and turns around a little to face me.

"I admire you for that," I tell her. "That you're honest with him."

"I have to be. One, I love him. Two, if I'm not honest with him, he might kill me someday."

I smile. "I doubt Victor would ever kill you."

She looks at me in a sidelong glance. "You haven't been around him much lately. All that power." She laughs. "He scares me a little."

The smile in her eyes tells me that she's full of shit.

"Look, you're like a brother to me," she says getting serious again. "And if you ever asked me to keep anything *personal* about you a secret, I wouldn't tell Victor, or anyone else. But I just wanted to give you a heads-up before you start talking, so you can be *sure* that whatever you're about to say is something I should know, or not."

"I know," I say, "and I appreciate you looking out for me, but I'm only senseless on Wednesdays. I know what I'm doing."

"Umm, Fredrik"—she smirks and tilts her head thoughtfully—"this *is* Wednesday."

I sigh. "Yeah. I know."

The smile drops from her face in an instant as she realizes just how serious this is, and how I know full well that I'm risking a lot by telling her anything.

Finally I pick my cell phone up from the dashboard console and run my finger over the screen to open the live video feed from my basement. Izabel watches me intently while I wait for the video to appear. I watch it for a moment first to see if there's anything out of the ordinary. Cassia is alone in the room for now, pacing the floor and dragging the chain around her ankle behind her. She's wearing a thick blue robe over her nightgown that drops to her calves. She looks lost and anxious. I wonder briefly if Greta has been down there with her yet and then conclude that she must have because she had to have taken her breakfast.

I hesitate, collapsing my hand around the phone, and contemplate this whole thing quietly one last time, making sure I want to open the lid on this issue.

I hand Izabel the phone.

Reluctantly she takes it from my hand and peers down at the screen. After watching a moment, and looking back and forth between me and the feed, she asks, "Who is she?" and then she looks at the screen again.

"Her name is Cassia."

Another long pause.

Izabel looks up from the phone and at me for a longer time.

"OK," she says simply, waiting for me to explain.

"That's a live video feed," I say. "From my basement."

Her eyebrows crease with confusion.

"You have a girl in your basement? I don't understand."

I sigh heavily, having a difficult time trying to figure out how to tell her. What do I start with? What do I leave out? I have to be careful because Izabel is smart and will pick up on gaps in my story easily.

"I've been using her to help me find Seraphina."

"Using her how?" Already Izabel looks disapproving. "What does she have to do with Seraphina? How long have you had her down there? Wait—." She stops abruptly and looks at the screen one more time. When she raises her eyes to me again, full of suspicion and criticism, she says, "Is that a chain around her ankle?"

"Yes," I admit.

Izabel tries to shake off her initial feelings of disapproval to give me the benefit of the doubt. "OK, so you're interrogating her. She's involved with Seraphina's life of betrayal and murder and God knows what else. I get that." She sets the phone down in the console.

I can tell by the look of uncertainty on her face that she's not so sure any part of the excuse she just came up with is valid.

"No," I admit with hesitation. "Cassia is an innocent girl. I've been keeping her prisoner in my basement for about a year now. Since five months after the Hamburg and Stephens job went down in New Mexico."

Izabel freezes.

"A *year*?" she says aghast. "And she's *innocent*? Fredrik, what the hell is wrong with you?"

I shut my eyes softly. "Just calm down and let me explain."

She takes a deep, concentrated breath and just looks across the small confined space at me. "Victor was right," she says and it makes my head snap around the rest of the way. "When he sent you home from Seattle, Victor told me that he had suspicions about your involvement with Seraphina, that it's what's been distracting you. I didn't even know she was still alive until the other night, Fredrik." She shakes her head gently. "Hell, the only reason Victor told me anything at all was because I was so worried about you and the way you've been acting lately. But Fredrik, you can't do this to this girl, no matter what part she plays in Seraphina's life. Not if she's innocent. You need to let her go."

"Izabel," I say softly, hoping I can make her understand without telling her too much, "Cassia doesn't want to be let go. She's terrified of Seraphina. She *wants* to stay with me."

Lines deepen in Izabel's forehead as her brows draw inward.

It takes a moment to get her words together, but she says, "*Wants* to stay with you? Jesus, Fredrik, she has a *chain* around her ankle. She's locked in a *basement*." She motions her hands, emphasizing the words, trying to make me understand how ridiculous they sound. "If she wants to stay with you, why would you keep her locked up?"

"It's just a precaution. In case she tries to escape." Even to me my own words sound contradictory and stupid.

And judging by the forced smile in Izabel's eyes, she thinks so, too.

But then her expression shifts suddenly as if a reasonable explanation just crept into her mind. "You're in love with her," she accuses and it shocks me a little—I hadn't expected that, of all things. "You don't want to let her go because you're in *love* with her. It makes sense. And I can see something in you, Fredrik—I could sense something was different about you, and it didn't feel like anything...bad. Just different."

I want to say, *Izabel, you're way off the mark here,* because what she's saying is ridiculous, but at the same time it's a way out. If she thinks the only reason I'm keeping Cassia prisoner is because I'm in love with her it will seem less cruel and Izabel could possibly force herself to live with my decision and keep my secret, even if just for a little while longer, until I can get everything straightened out.

"And she must be in love with *you*," she goes on, her face lighting up with realization the more she puts the pieces together. "Stockholm syndrome. Makes perfect sense."

It actually amazes me how much everything she just said *does* make sense.

Only thing is, none of it is true.

Izabel leans over the console and pushes herself into view. "But Fredrik, this is crazy, even for you—"

"Oh, well thanks for that," I cut in with a faint smirk, trying to lighten the mood.

She smiles.

"You know what I mean."

Of course I do, but I couldn't help myself.

Then just as quickly as I had managed to inject a joke, I go back to the darkness and turn my eyes away from her, staring through the windshield at the cold, gray day.

"You know that Victor—hell, even *I*—will help you find Seraphina." She rests her body against the seat again, still facing me. I don't look back at her. "I know you think this is something you feel you have to do on your own—I completely get that—but it doesn't *have* to be that way. Not at the cost of that innocent girl. Fredrik, why do you need her to find Seraphina?"

My shoulders rise and fall with a heavy sigh and my gaze strays toward my lap where my fingers fidget restlessly. And then after a moment of quiet contemplation, I tell Izabel the same story that Cassia told me last night about how she and Seraphina met. Izabel listens the entire time with parted lips and an ever-growing look of horror and sadness slowly twisting her features. I try not to look at her eyes at all because I can sense how much the story is affecting her personally. And I begin to feel regret for telling her, Izabel of all people, who lived nine years of her life under the rule of a notorious Mexican drug lord who molested and raped and kept her prisoner long enough to turn her into the killer she is today.

By the time the story is over, Izabel can't speak for what feels like an hour but is just mere minutes. I see the raw emotions eating away at her brought on mostly by the things that Seraphina went through, the memories of her own life with Javier Ruiz and all the things from her past that she—just as I do with my similar past—tries every day to shut out of her mind. But also like me, no matter how hard she tries, the deepest scars *never* fade.

"Fredrik…" she says softly and then turns her head to face me, "…you have to let that girl go. You have to, now more than ever."

I shake my head no, though I didn't mean for her to actually see me do it—it was a reflex. I can't let Cassia go, and I won't, no matter how hard Izabel presses me.

*Why did I tell her any of this? What could I have possibly gotten out of it?*

I feel her hand on my forearm as I grip the steering wheel. Her fingers tighten around my bone. "You listen to me." Her voice becomes sharper, determined, and I finally look back into her eyes. "Look what she's been through. Think about what you just told me." She shakes my arm. "That cold bitch—regardless of the horrific things *she* went through—killed this girl's mother and father. She was traumatized as a child because of what your ex-wife did to her. She went through something that no one, goddammit *no one*, should *ever* have to go through, and now she's being kept a prisoner, chained inside a basement like an animal, and what makes it sicker is that she thinks she's in love with you!" Her rising voice fills the car, her fingers are digging into my arm over the top of my coat sleeve.

Izabel looks a lot like I do when I need to torture and kill someone to appease the painful memories.

I can't look at her anymore.

My fingers are white-knuckling the steering wheel.

Finally I feel her hand loosen and then fall away from my arm.

"I'll help you," she says gently. "I'll do whatever you need me to do, but you have to set that girl free. We'll put her in a safehouse to protect her until Seraphina is caught—"

"No."

Silence fills the car.

Consumed by regret and guilt and a plethora of other negative emotions slowly eating away at me, all I can say is, "I'm sorry for what you went through when you were with Javier Ruiz. And I'm sorry that I dragged you into this—I don't even know why I did—but I'm *not* letting Cassia go. I need her to find Seraphina. She's the only way I'm *ever* going to find Seraphina."

After a moment, Izabel says somberly, "Then you're not who I thought you were." I hear the door click open and a rush of cold air escapes into the car.

"Where are you going?" I ask carefully without moving a muscle.

She swings the door open all the way and gets out of the car. Leaning over and inside with one hand propped on the edge of the door she glares in at me, her eyes full of anger and disappointment and pain.

"If you won't let that girl go," she says through her teeth, "*I will.*"

She slams the door shut, cutting off the frigid air filtering through the car.

"Izabel, wait!" I'm out of the car in seconds and walking around the front and toward her on the other side. "You can't do that. You have to trust me on this!"

She stops at her door without opening it, crossing her arms tight against her chest as the wind pushes against her long white coat.

Disgusted with me, she shakes her head indignantly.

"I was wrong," she says. "You don't love that girl at all. You're still in love with that crazy bitch. And you're *so* in love with her that you're willing to ruin an innocent girl's life just to find her. As if what Seraphina did to her already isn't bad enough! I can't believe you'd *do* this, Fredrik!" Her voice cracks.

A small family approaches from the parking lot heading toward the conservatory. Hearing Izabel's shouts, the father takes his little girl's hand and pulls her closer between him and his wife. They watch us over their shoulders as they hurry up the walkway.

Izabel and I both wait until they slip inside the building before saying anything more, glaring into each other's eyes, hers filled with more anger and disappointment toward me than I ever wanted to see.

"I can't let her go," I say calmly, one more time.

She turns on her heels and jerks her car door open, intent on leaving me standing here.

"Izabel!" My voice rips through the air.

She stops, standing wedged between the door and the frame, her face consumed by rage, her body rigid and conflicted by its need to get away.

I sigh heavily, and look down at my shoes, letting regret and pain crush me from the inside out.

And then finally I realize why I brought Izabel here, why I need her so badly.

"I can't let her go…I can't because Cassia *is* Seraphina…"

She stares at me blankly, yet behind her eyes is a lake of shock and confusion and denial and she's drowning in it.

She steps away from the door, but leaves it open, and very slowly walks toward me. I study her quietly as she approaches, trying to decipher the seemingly impenetrable veil of perplexity that consumes her, and all I can make out from it is pain. Though I can't tell who she's hurting for: Cassia, Seraphina, me or herself.

The corners of her eyes begin to glisten with moisture. She steps onto the sidewalk and reaches out carefully to touch the side of my face, and the moment she does, that unnamed pain she harbors transfers from her and right into me. Her throat moves as she swallows her tears down. I realize in this moment that I do the same thing.

"Oh, Fredrik," she says softly, shaking her head.

But it's all she can say and she drops her cold hand from my face and rests her arm down at her side.

I choke back my own tears because they're fucking ridiculous and they don't belong in my eyes. I don't have that right. I don't *want* that right. Then I slide my hands into my coat pockets and straighten my face to look only like Fredrik Gustavsson, The Specialist, the Jackal—anything but the wounded man with the wounded heart who lost his right to weep or to care or to love, a very long time ago.

"I need your help, Izabel."

She nods several times.

"Tell me everything," she says.

# NINETEEN

*Fredrik*

———

Getting out of the cold and the small space inside the car—Izabel said she needed more room to breathe after what I just told her— we found a quiet place to sit together inside the Desert House of the conservatory. The bench is tucked away between rocks and yucca plants and cacti. It's very warm in here, a stark difference from the frigid temperature outside. Izabel and I removed our coats and draped them over our laps before we sat down. And I pulled my black beanie off and shoved it inside my coat pocket with my keys.

"Why do you keep looking at me like that?" I ask her about those sad green eyes filled with heartbreak and pity.

I won't accept pity. Surely she knows that.

"I just…well, I just know how much you loved Seraphina," she says with soft, pain-filled words. "I mean, I never knew the whole story, but I knew—I *know*—enough to know that this can't be easy for you. I-I just can't imagine—how is this even *possible*?"

I look down at my hands.

"Honestly, I don't know," I say with defeat. "I didn't know the extent of any of this until last night." I look over at Izabel. "She finally remembered her past, or what she believes is her past. Izabel, I had no idea—I don't even know what I'm saying. I'm as confused about all of this as much as you are." My gaze falls to my hands again, draped between my opened legs, my elbows propped on the tops of my thighs. I fondle my thick, dark textured ring under my fingertips uneasily, briefly remembering the engraving I had placed on the inside that reads: The Jackal. To always remind me what the darkness inside of me was born from. In case I ever want to forget.

"What do you mean that she remembered?"

Hesitating, I look out at the desert flora, searching for signs of visitors who might be on their way inside to tour the room.

"Cassia—*Seraphina*—has had amnesia since I took her from the shelter after the fire...

*One Year Ago –New York City*

*I had been tracking Seraphina for two weeks after seeing her on a news broadcast in Times Square, walking behind the reporter in a small crowd. I knocked a steaming hot cup of coffee onto my laptop when I saw her face flash across the screen. Six years I had been searching for her. Six years—since the night she killed the last of three innocent women because of me—I thought—, injected me with drugs, set my house on fire and dragged my body into the large field behind it so that I wouldn't burn to death. I never saw her again after that night until a year ago. I thought she was long gone by then. Dead, even. Because it wasn't like Seraphina to simply vanish. She liked the game. She lived for it. I expected her to leave me a trail of bodies—all women with blond hair—to hunt her down. So when I saw her that night after all that time, something dark and predatory triggered inside of me. Anticipation. Vengeance. Lust. Love...*

*I left Baltimore that day and went to New York City.*

*Two weeks later I found her where I should've thought to look all along, working as a singer in an upscale Jazz and Blues bar and restaurant. There were no traces of a 'Seraphina Bragado' anywhere that I could gather in New York, or anywhere else, for that matter. I had been using The Order's resources to run her name against everything for six years. She didn't even have a birth certificate or a credit card under that name. But that didn't really surprise me much because she was employed by another order, and like all of us, we never use real identification. But I had no idea that the reason I couldn't find anything on Seraphina was because she was living under 'Cassia Carrington'. She had an apartment in New York. She paid bills. She had a close friend who lived across the hall from her. And she was employed. Living a normal life out in the open and seemed to have been for a very long time.*

*Finally after years of searching, I thought I had her.*

*I went to the bar that night, dressed in my finest suit, the way she always loved to see me dressed, and I had a plan.*

*The bar smelled of sweet cigars and bourbon and women's perfume. I was intoxicated by the atmosphere. I had always loved places like this where the finest wines are served and the entertainment is classy and sophisticated. Seraphina, despite her profession as a killer, or her dark sexual needs that only matched my own, was quite a classy and sophisticated woman—when she wasn't killing people, or sharing blood with me during sex, of course.*

*I chose a table, small and round and darkly lit, just off to the left of the stage so that I'd be in sight, but not the first face she saw when she stepped up to the mic. A small handful of instruments occupied the stage behind where she would be standing, and two more tall microphones were positioned behind and to one side of hers where the backup singers would be.*

*Already it was bringing back so many memories of when we were madly in love for two short years.*

# THE SWAN AND THE JACKAL

*I had never been so anxious—my stomach had collapsed into a rock solid ball of hot muscle burning through my insides. My throat was painfully dry no matter how many times I sipped from my whiskey glass just to wet it. But I kept my composure flawlessly, not letting on to anyone sitting at the tables around me that deep inside I was ready to explode with anticipation and need that only Seraphina would understand.*

*The band came out on stage quietly and took their positions, and then the backup singers, dressed in matching lacy black dresses that hugged their bodies down to their knees.*

*Seraphina came out last.*

*She was beautiful. The most beautiful thing I had ever seen, just as she had always been since the day we met. Only this time, long, flowing blond hair draped her shoulders, fixed perfectly so that each side fell in a silky blond wave and ended in a half-curl just below each breast. Not a strand of hair was out of place. She wore a short cream-colored dress adorned with feathers and diamond-like flower sequins laid out in an intricate pattern about her hips and thighs. And tall high-heeled cream-colored shoes with sparkling silver glitter around the heels and the soles.*

*I was mesmerized by her. I had never seen her with blond hair and only a hint of makeup of natural rose-colored shades, or dressed in something so light and soft. Seraphina had always dressed in black. Wore her hair black. Colored her eyes and lips darkly. It was as if an angel had replaced the devil right before my eyes.*

*I had no idea just how true that thought was. Not then.*

*The music began to play and immediately the familiarity of it struck me numb. My hand tightened around my whiskey glass. My shoulders went rigid and I stopped breathing in the moment.*

*The lyrics to Wicked Game came through her lips, so sultry and soul-filled. Exactly the way I remembered her singing it to me years ago. Did she know I was there? Had she seen me enter the building, or walk through the room in search of the perfect table? Had she known I was in town all along and had found her? It was possible. Seraphina was a master assassin and spy. She was at the top of her game, difficult to hide from and impossible to escape once she'd found you. She had always been a step ahead of me.*

*But the more I watched her, the more I began to reject that idea.*

*A few times she made eye contact with the crowd, in between closing her eyes to emphasize particular lyrics. She moved her slim, curvy body in time with the slow beat, gestured her ring-covered hands out in front of her every now and then.*

*That anxious, hot ball that was my stomach had begun to set my chest on fire when the song went on and on and she never noticed me. I wanted to stand up and look her straight in the eye, but I didn't. I sat there appearing as calm as everyone else who was just there to enjoy the entertainment.*

*By the time the last chorus came, I thought surely I was going to have to move to another table so that she'd see me.*

*But then finally she did.*

*Her soft brown eyes locked on me from across the short distance. And then she looked away.*

*Seraphina didn't know me.*

*Even if she had been pretending, I would've detected it, the smallest hint of recognition. She had none. I was to her the same as any man who sat in the audience that night, making love to her with my thoughts, drinking from her soul as she poured it out across the audience in teasing amounts through her voice.*

*I was baffled.*

*And heartbroken.*

*I may have wanted to kill her—because I knew I had to—but I still loved her intensely, and when the only woman I have ever loved looked me in the eyes and didn't know who I was, I didn't know what to do anymore. With myself. With anything. It was hard* enough to live the past six years of my life without her, but I at least had hope that she was still out there and that we would be together again someday. But after this, my plan—there was no plan any longer.

After that night, I began following her and watching her even more closely. I went as far as breaking into her apartment on the third floor of her building and bugging her home.

Seraphina, living as Cassia, was as normal as anyone. The conversations she had with her friend from across the hall were about work and bills and rent and men, to which only the friend had much input on men. Seraphina was single, and according to the friend, had been 'manless for far too long' and needed to 'loosen up a little'. The two of them even had sexual relations which, I admit, excited me as I listened to them through the audio feed in Seraphina's bedroom. But they were just friends, letting off sexual steam because it was readily available and neither of them expected anything more from one another. Having sex with women wasn't out of the ordinary for Seraphina, anyway. She did it often when we were together, though only with me involved. Men—that's another story. I had been the only man she'd ever been with. Until Marcus from Safe House Sixteen. Again, that's another story...

But this Seraphina wasn't my Seraphina. She was nothing like her, and without the black hair and heavy, dark makeup, she hardly even looked like her. I began to think that maybe she had a twin that I never knew about. But I quickly rejected that idea, too, once I thought of her up on that stage, singing that song with the same notes and emotion that she had sang it to me.

She was Seraphina, after all, but she wasn't herself.

And I was determined to find out why.

Another two weeks passed and I was on my way to her apartment again one cold night in December when I heard police, ambulance and fire truck sirens blaring clamorously between the old buildings of the street she lived on. I smelled smoke. As I picked up my pace, my hands buried deep in my coat pockets, I hurried toward the building as a hot, orange glowing light burned against the surrounding structures. People were standing around on the sidewalks, watching and pointing, all huddled in night robes and big coats and scarves tossed messily around their necks. I stood among them, watching with a quiet horror as Seraphina's apartment blazed with licking flames into the cold, dark, night sky. The fire had started from her apartment and was quickly spreading to the rest of the building as the fire department worked swiftly to put it out.

I felt dead inside, like something had crawled inside my soul and died there. I thought she was dead. That apartment was engulfed in flames. But then from the corner of my eye, and past all of the shuffling emergency response workers clamoring to and from within the street, I saw her lying on her side on the frigid sidewalk surrounded by two EMT's and a pile of old furniture and boxes probably left outside after a recent vacancy in the complex.

I sucked in a quick breath, relieved to see that she was alive. And for a moment, I could've sworn, just before she was hoisted onto a stretcher, that she saw me from across the street, even through the darkness and the gathered crowd. And I could've sworn that she knew who I was for a fleeting moment. I could sense it, like a predator can sense fear.

My heart skipped two beats and rattled boisterously behind my ribs.

She saw me and she knew me.

The game was back on. Or so I thought.

Nearly thirty minutes later, when I had resolved in my mind that I was going to end up following her to the hospital, Seraphina was helped out of the ambulance by the EMT's. I faintly heard her rejecting their recommendation that she go with them to the hospital for further tests. Waving her hands about in front of her, she told them no, and then she left, walking in the opposite direction of the burning apartment complex and slipping into the dark shadows cast by the surrounding buildings.

Stepping off the sidewalk, I made my way through small pockets of gawkers and followed her.

The farther away she got, the quieter everything became. The sirens and the voices began to fade into the background. The emergency lights bouncing sporadically off the buildings were reduced to vague flashes in the distance. Where was she going? I began to wonder if she even knew herself.

With the blanket the EMT gave her draped over her shoulders, Seraphina continued with a severe limp, down the dark sidewalk heading deeper into the outskirts of the city. I kept my distance, staying in the shadows so she wouldn't see me. Did she know I was following her? And if so, where was she leading me?

Fifteen minutes turned into thirty. Forty-five. Nearly an hour of walking endlessly, up one block and down another, through traffic and past stores, I knew she had no idea where she was going, or even where she was. And if she was just fucking with my head—which was always possible—she was doing a damn good job of it.

I followed her all the way to a homeless shelter, where instead of even going inside, she sat down in front of the building on the cold, hard concrete of the walkway and wrapped the blanket tighter around her shivering and bruised body.

She raised her eyes when I stepped up in front of her.

"Hello," she said cautiously.

I tried searching her eyes for the same recognition I thought I saw in her earlier, but it wasn't there.

"What are you doing here?" I asked.

She looked up at me again, afraid to make eye contact. She pressed her bare knees together and clasped her hands around the knit fabric underneath the blanket. Puffs of breath moved through her lips. She wore no shoes.

"I'm just sitting down," she said with an absence of understanding in her own answer.

Leery of her, and halfway expecting her to slice my ankles open with a knife hidden beneath the blanket and then run away grinning back at me, I took a step back and crouched down in front of her, the ends of my long black coat touching the sidewalk.

Black streaks of soot were smeared across her reddened cheeks. The whole right side of her face was one large series of scratches, as if someone had grabbed her by the head and scraped her face against the asphalt until it bled. She shook from the cold and from her fear of me.

"P-Please just leave me alone," she said, looking up to keep me in her sights, but trying not to make eye contact.

"Sera—."

I stopped myself and said instead, "What's your name?"

She frowned.

"I don't know you. Please just leave me alone."

"Do you know your name?" I asked. "If you can tell me your name, I'll leave you alone."

She couldn't.

A large part of me still didn't believe her. I believed she was suffering from amnesia, yes, but I was still convinced that once she remembered who she was, the game of a lifetime would be back on and pick up where she and I left off six years ago.

And I wasn't about to lose it this time.

After coaxing—and manipulating her, taking advantage of her obvious vulnerability—I talked her into going home with me, and once I brought her to Baltimore, she became my prisoner. I would make her remember who she was and have her in my grasp the moment she did.

# TWENTY

*Fredrik*

———

"…Only, when she did finally get her memory back just days ago, I never expected it to be the memory of a girl who I never knew."

I stare out ahead of me, the words lost on my lips, my mind lost in the memories as if the events just happened all over again. I can hear Izabel's soft breaths expelling gently from her nostrils she's sitting so close. I can almost hear her thoughts, loud with confused ideas and broken sentences. She wants to say something, *needs* to, but can't quite figure out yet what to say.

"Didn't you tell her who she was?" she asks after a long pause, turning on the bench toward me. "If she couldn't remember, didn't you tell her her name?"

I shake my head once. "I almost did a few times, but I was so intrigued by the fact that she couldn't remember. Intrigued by her strange, delicate personality. The darkness inside of me wanted to understand her, to study her. I had never seen such frailty in a woman before, and to see it in someone like Seraphina—of all people—I was intrigued."

"What did you do then?" Izabel asks almost breathily beside me as she hangs onto every one of my words.

"I tortured her"—I pause, bearing the pain of the memory of what I'd done—"And the whole time I tortured her, my conscience was telling me that she was innocent. I ached for her as I drew blood. But I didn't stop. She was still Seraphina, after all."

*"Why don't you just tell me who you think I am?" Cassia cried from my interrogation chair as I stood behind her next to my tools. "Please! Please! I don't know what you want from me!" Sobs racked her body, covered by nothing but a pair of white panties and a matching bra.*

*"It's not going to work like that, love," I told her, stepping around the chair with a long razor in my hand. Her eyes grew wider than the sockets that contained them when she glimpsed the silver blade dangling from my fingers. "You're going to tell me on your own, who you really are. I want to hear you say it, love. I'm the one in control of the game now." I stepped right up to her side and peered down into her shrinking, tear-soaked face. "And I can do this for six more years," I taunted. "Until you remember. Until you tell me your name."*

*"My name is Cassia! Cassia Carrington!" she screamed so loud her voice momentarily went hoarse. She strained against the leather restraints that held her against the chair at her ankles, wrists, torso and forehead.*

*I positioned the blade in my fingers and started my cutting on her legs…*

"Cassia's admission of her name shocked us both, though I ignored that while I tortured her. She had remembered something about her life so soon. Just days before, when I took her from the street in front of the shelter, she couldn't remember *anything*. But she

had remembered her name—though not the name I wanted—
and it took absolute terror to make her see it again. I knew then
that it was how I was going to draw Seraphina out and bring her
back to me. With fear. And pain. And eventually..." I stop and
swallow down the guilt of my transgressions.

Izabel's hand touches my shoulder.

"Eventually what, Fredrik?" she asks in a soft voice.

*Eventually, with sex,* I want to say but can't bring myself to
admit aloud because I feel as though I've taken advantage of her
even though she wanted it every time. I feel guilty and ashamed
for defiling a girl so fragile and innocent. I feel unworthy of someone like Cassia because she is so kind and compassionate and pure.
And each time I was inside of her, I hated myself more and more.

Still facing forward, I say distantly, "That doesn't matter."

With quiet reluctance, Izabel accepts my refusal to tell her.

Her hand slides away from my shoulder at the same moment
the small family from outside earlier, enters the spacious room.
Izabel and I both make note of their presence, as they do ours,
choosing to walk in the opposite direction of us.

"What's wrong with her?" she asks, meeting my gaze. "She
seems very...I don't know, traumatized. Jesus, Fredrik, as much
as I hate her for what she did to you, I can't help but feel sorry for
her, too."

"I don't know what's wrong with her," I say with a pang of
helplessness." I lower my head, propping it in my uplifted hands.
After a moment, I raise my head again and slap the palms of my
hands down on my legs. "I could've dealt with anything. I was
prepared to kill her, Izabel, even as much as I loved her. I was prepared. Shit, I'd been preparing for it since she left me in that field.
I was ready to confront anything she threw at me. But not this." I
shake my head, my gaze fixated on a spot on the ground between
my shoes. "I never imagined anything like this."

"Why did you choose to tell me any of this?"

"Because I don't know what to do. I had a plan and it changed when I finally found her. So then I devised another plan, and just like the one before it, I've had to toss it entirely and start from scratch." I sigh deep and long and then straighten my back out of a slouch. "It's a mind-fuck of a problem and I don't think I'll be finding the answers I need to deal with something like this on Google."

The voices of the couple and their small child become more pronounced as they slowly draw nearer.

I stand from the bench, slipping my coat on. Izabel does the same.

"Fredrik," she says in a quiet voice, "Did you want my advice because you don't know what to do, or are you really just looking for validation of the choice you've already made?"

I frown faintly, but choose not answer. Because I'm not sure of the answer.

"I can't be with someone like Cassia," I say instead. "She and I are too different. Someone like her deserves someone better than me."

"What does that mean?" Izabel says carefully, though I get the feeling she understands something in what I just said more than even I do.

I think about it for a moment, but she helps by saying, "You said 'someone like her'. You didn't say Cassia. Why didn't you say Cassia?"

I understand now and it just makes my mood darker.

"Because when this is all over, there's a chance she won't *be* Cassia anymore."

Izabel looks at me with benevolent eyes.

"Then I guess in the meantime you should love the one who's there," she says just as the family approaches from behind.

Love? Was that an accusation, or simply an observation?

Izabel looks at me with a soft, understanding face, but then the moment is disrupted—thankfully—by the family who are now too close for us to talk anymore.

We walk down the pathway side by side, heading for the exit. Izabel glances over at me and adds, "Just out of curiosity, what did you plan to do to Seraphina when you found her?"

"*Everything*," I answer and leave it at that.

We make it back outside in the frigid air and head quickly to our cars parked side by side in the parking lot.

"I won't say anything to Victor," she says, standing at the door of her car, looking over the roof of my car at me. "Technically you're on leave, so this is all personal. He'll understand."

I nod, shivering beneath my coat.

"Thanks, doll."

"But when Victor calls you back to the field, if you're still considered out of commission because of this, I'll have to tell him why."

"I know," I say softly.

"For now, I'll look into Cassia Carrington," she says. "If you couldn't find anything on Seraphina Bragado, maybe I'll have better luck with her other name." I nod. "I'll let you know what I find out."

She pops open her door and starts to get inside, but stops and looks back at me once more. A sort of unnamed grief rests in her features.

"And if you need me for anything else...*anything*, Fredrik, you know I'll do it."

Neither of us blink for several moments as we stare at each other; the unspoken meaning of her offer playing between us like a tragic, inevitable event too painful to say out loud.

———

I stay away from my house for the rest of the day. I have a lot of thinking to do, though it'll take more than several hours to sort through my thoughts.

By six o'clock, I've come up with absolutely nothing. By eight, after driving around aimlessly for as long as I can, I've only grown more intolerant of this entire situation. I can't even think straight. I can't function enough on my own to form a reasonable sentence, much less a solution.

Because there *is* no goddamn solution.

I know that no matter what happens, all I can do is *let* it because it's going to, anyway.

"Would you like more coffee?" I hear a soft voice say.

Pulling my fingers from the top of my hair, I raise my head from staring down at my phone on the table. The pretty dark-haired waitress stands beside me with a smile, looking once toward my empty coffee mug.

How long have I been sitting here?

I shake my head. "No, but thank you."

She leaves me alone in my grief again and a part of me wishes she wouldn't. The old Fredrik would charm her for a little while, promise her things with my eyes that I know would excite her, and then wait for her after her shift was over. The old Fredrik would take her to the nearest hotel and tie her hands behind her back. He'd fuck her until there were tears in her eyes and she'd beg me not to stop.

But the old Fredrik is gone and the longer I subject myself to this 'problem', the more the even *older* Fredrik I feel I'm starting to become. The person I was before I met Seraphina, when I tortured and killed recklessly because I couldn't help myself. I've clung to my more disciplined self, the man that Seraphina helped me to be, all these years because I had hope I'd find her and she'd be in my life again someday. But now that I know it's not possible,

## THE SWAN AND THE JACKAL

I feel myself slipping back into the life of pure, unadulterated darkness that I led since I was a child and escaped my captors.

If I become him again, he will destroy me.

I won't be suitable as part of Victor Faust's new Order.

I will have to leave this place and the life I've built with those I've grown to care for, and continue on the lonely, self-destructive path of the Jackal.

# TWENTY-ONE

*Fredrik*

———

Greta has been spying on me from different windows in the house since I pulled into the driveway a half hour ago. I couldn't go inside. I still can't. Right now I prefer the quiet solitude of the car with the metal walls so close on all sides of me that it feels like my thoughts are better contained by them. They're all I can hear. Even though I don't like anything they're saying.

Aside from my conversation with Izabel and all the things I don't want to think about anymore, I also think about the women. Gwen from the bar. The waitress from the diner earlier this evening. I think about the last woman I had sex with. And the one before her. It never dawned on me until the woman from the diner that I'm less like myself even more than I thought. And I have been since shortly after I took 'Cassia' from the street that night in New York.

I can't enjoy other women anymore. Not without passionate guilt and regret that sits heavily in my chest for days after.

In the year that I've kept Cassia in the basement, Gwen was the first woman I ever brought home. I had intended to bring others before her, to do the things to them that I did to the women Seraphina and I shared, so that maybe it would draw out Seraphina's memories while she watched on the television screen. It's why I put a video feed in my bedroom to begin with. But until Gwen, I never could go through with it.

With Seraphina, it was normal.

With Cassia, I can't fucking do it.

A small sliver of light from the kitchen window blinks out as Greta drops the curtain back into place.

"I have to face this," I say quietly to myself.

After a long pause, I kill the engine and head into the house.

"She's asleep," Greta says when I walk into the kitchen.

I drop my keys on the counter.

"How is she?" I ask, removing my coat.

"She's good," Greta says with a warm smile around her eyes. "I think she's better since she's remembered who she is. More at peace maybe."

"She told you then."

Greta nods her graying head as her face falls.

"It's awful what she went through, Mr. Gustavsson. And while although I still don't like it that you keep her locked up like that— nor do I understand it—it may be for the best. Seraphina is dangerous. She needs help, yes, but she's dangerous."

I say nothing.

Greta walks around the counter and takes her long wool coat up from the back of a kitchen chair, slipping her arms into the thick sleeves.

"Why don't you take the day off tomorrow," I say. "I have no plans and I'll be with Cassia all day."

"Are you sure?" she asks warily.

I raise a brow. "That I have no plans?" I say with offense, "Or that I'm capable of taking care of her for twenty-four hours by myself?"

"I-I didn't mean that, sir." She folds her hands together down in front of her.

Sighing, I say, "I apologize," making note of my misplaced irritation toward her. "Just take the day off. I'll call you when I need you to come back."

I reach into my wallet and finger five one hundred dollar bills and place the money into her hand.

"This is just a little extra aside from what I pay you." She looks down at it faintly surprised, but mostly thankful. "I do appreciate your help with Cassia."

She says nothing, but words aren't needed to express the thanks in her eyes.

After Greta leaves, I lock the front door behind her and stand at the entrance of the hallway for a long time before willing my legs to carry me toward the basement door. I don't want to see her. I don't want to because of what she's doing to me.

I make my way down the concrete stairs lit only by a vague swath of light coming from her bathroom. I took my shoes off upstairs so they wouldn't wake her and the concrete is cold underneath my feet. But the air is warm; heat blasts from the vents in the ceiling making the basement feel somewhat toasty. But Cassia appears comfortable lying there with the blanket only covering her lower back and her bottom and the top half of her thighs. She lies on her stomach facing me with her small, delicate arms crushed beneath her. Her long flowing blond hair lies disheveled against the pillow. The chain locked to her ankle dangles off the side of the bed and extends far out across the floor.

I want to touch her, but I'm afraid. Afraid to wake her. To face her. To look into her consuming brown eyes and risk falling deeper into them than I already have.

But I can't help myself.

Sitting down carefully beside her on the bed, I reach out my hand and move her hair away from her face with my fingers. She stirs. And then her eyelids break apart and slowly she looks up at me.

"Fredrik"—my name on her lips always crushes me, makes me feel conflicted inside—"I missed you." She smiles and I feel her hand touching mine.

I look down at her fingers, intrigued by how easily her touch makes me emotionally submissive to her without her ever trying. After a moment, her slender hand blurs out of focus the heavier my thoughts become.

*What is happening to me?*

"What's wrong?" she asks so softly, so compassionately that I feel a weight in my chest.

Her fingers stroke the tops of mine.

I look at her eyes again.

"Nothing." I move my hand from underneath hers and place it on top of hers instead.

"Are you going to stay with me tonight?" she asks in a soft voice.

"Yes."

A small smile warms her face.

She moves her hand away and grasps the blanket, pulling it aside to make room for me.

I just look at her for a moment and then finally let go of the conflict that's been raging inside of me since I brought her here.

"No," I say evenly and I move the blanket away. Then I reach into my jeans pocket to retrieve the key. "Give me your leg, love." I take her leg into my hand and carefully unlock her ankle from the shackle.

Dropping the chain on the floor and the key carelessly beside it, I rise to my feet and then lean over, taking her into my arms.

"Where are we going?" she asks, draping her arms around my neck, her legs resting over my right arm.

"To my room."

Cassia lays her head on my chest as I carry her up the stairs and into the house, a place she's only ever seen on the television screen in her room since the night I first brought her here.

Carrying her through the dark hall and into my bedroom, I lay her down on my bed amid the dark sheets and thick comforter. The sensation of her fingers leaving mine when I step away from her does something to me that I don't fully understand. And against my strong need to let her hold onto me, I pull my sweater off and drop it on the floor. Afterward the t-shirt I wore underneath it. She watches me with soft innocence as I step out of the rest of my clothes and stand naked in front of her before crawling into the bed next to her. I always sleep naked. She knows this. I know she expects nothing by the gesture.

I just want her near me.

Cassia curls up next to me, resting her head on my bare chest. I pull her closer as if she wasn't already as close as she can be.

"Why did you bring me here?" She kisses my chest.

Tightening my arm around her I say, "Because I'm coming to my senses." I kiss the top of her hair.

"Fredrik?"

"Yeah?" I stare up at the ceiling.

"I'm sorry for what Seraphina did to you."

"Don't be. It wasn't your fault."

Her small breaths warm my skin as she exhales.

"It doesn't have to be my fault for me to be sorry for what she did." Heartbreak lies in her voice.

My head falls to the side so that I can see her and even in the dark bluish hue of the room I can see the tears glistening plainly in her eyes.

"Why are you crying?" I ask, wiping them away with my thumb.

Her gaze falls away from mine. She doesn't want to answer, but then she says, "Because I'm afraid that when you find her, you'll forget all about me."

I breathe in deeply through my nose, instinctively trying to force away the itching sensation building behind my eyes.

I roll over carefully on top of her, pinning her beneath me and gaze down into her softly pained face. My lips meet hers once. My hands cup the sides of her head, my fingers brush the soft, perfect contours of her cheeks. I'm intoxicated by her warm flesh against my own, the scent of her womanly skin, the heat of her sweet breath, the feeling of her rapid heartbeat thrumming down into my stomach and farther.

"Don't think about any of that," I whisper onto her mouth. "Because you have nothing to worry about." My lips cover hers.

I slip her panties off and put myself inside of her to a sweet gasp that expels uncontrollably from her lips. She tenses at first, but then surrenders and melts into me. I'm instantly delirious to the sensation of her small, warm body wrapped tightly around mine in every way. She moans against my mouth the deeper I go, whimpers into the side of my neck the more forcefully I thrust my hips against hers. The pit of my stomach aches with ecstasy—I've never felt this before. Never. Not like this.

My mouth devours her lips, kissing her hungrily, stealing her breath away. The wet warmth of her tongue tangled around mine alone threatens to send me into sexual bliss. And when my mouth falls away from hers it searches her neck and the little hollow at the bottom, and then her breasts, where I kiss them and lick them and bite them gently so that I don't hurt her.

"Please don't ever leave me again," she shudders against my ear, pressing her hips toward me to take me deeper.

The sensation of her mouth makes me thrust harder. But I stop and hold myself deep inside of her and say, "I won't leave you," and then push my hips forward again to the sounds of her soft, pleading moans.

Cassia's fingers wind within the top of my hair. Her thighs crush around my sides. Her head falls back against the pillow and I drag my tongue across the gentle slope of her throat exposed to me, until my mouth finds her lips again. I kiss her passionately, possessively. Because she is mine. She belongs to me just as she always has, and I don't give a fuck who she thinks she is. She is mine and she'll be mine until the day she dies.

# TWENTY-TWO

*Cassia*

———

I don't know what's happening to me.

But I don't like it.

Fredrik gets out of the bed so late in the morning that I expect to smell chicken pot pie baking in the oven for lunch. Greta always makes it for me on Thursdays. The sun beams brightly through the bedroom window, nearly blinding me, not because I just woke up but because I haven't seen the sun in a year. I'm quietly mesmerized by it as I lay on my side amid Fredrik's sheets letting the light bring a flurry of black and yellow spots before my eyes.

Just as Fredrik is about to leave the room with a clean pair of boxers and a t-shirt crushed in his large fist, he realizes I'm awake and stops suddenly in the doorway. He turns to look back at me as if he'd forgotten something and I melt into his blue-eyed gaze.

"Come shower with me," he says and then walks back over to the bed, reaching out his hand; a close-lipped smile plays softly on his handsome, stubbly face.

It makes me happy that he wants me to be with him for such a seemingly insignificant thing, but I can't help but wonder how much of it is because he doesn't trust me alone in the house unless I'm locked away downstairs. But I don't care about that and I try not to think about it. I'm with him now in ways I've only dreamed of since he brought me here.

But why this ominous feeling of sadness in my heart all of a sudden? How can I be so happy because Fredrik seems to have given in to my feelings for him, yet I feel such a strange and looming sadness growing inside?

I take his hand and he helps me out of the bed. I stumble at first, so used to the chain always dragging behind me, but I quickly get the hang of it being gone. I just wonder how long that will last, but I try not to think about that, either.

Walking me down the short hallway with my hand clasped in his, I'm in awe of such small things. The beautiful dark hardwood floor under my bare feet, the cream-white paint on the walls and ceiling that make the dark crown moulding bordering the ceiling stand out. The rich marble accent table sitting at the end of the hall with a small Greek statue displayed in its center. Even the light fixture in the ceiling above me, dome-shaped with beautiful crystal carvings, holds my attention longer than something as simple and boring as a light fixture normally would.

When I glimpse the door to the basement, remembering him walking with me through it last night, my breath hitches and my throat dries out instantly.

I stop in the hallway with my hand still clasped in his. I don't want to go any farther.

"It's OK," Fredrik says gently, tugging on my hand. "I'm not taking you down there."

Urging me to continue, we walk only as far as the bathroom door and I find myself breathing again once we step inside.

Fredrik opens the glass shower door and turns on the water. I feel strange standing here. Waiting. Wanting to look at the bathroom in awe the same way I did the hallway, but I want to look at Fredrik more. His hard, tanned body, the strength of his solid, bulging calf muscles, the perfect curvature of his oblique muscles and how they dip down into his pelvis in a strong, masculine pattern. His six-pack abs that I still can't get out of my head from last night as I grazed them under my fingertips when he was on top of me. When he was inside of me. Just thinking about last night makes me ache with need and tingle with warmth beneath my belly. Not just because of the sex, but because of how different Fredrik was from every other time before. He didn't just take me, he *cherished* me.

A blush warms my face when he turns from the glass door and looks at me with those magnetic deep blue eyes.

He guides me with him into the shower.

The steaming water streams down on me, and it's heavenly, but nothing is more heavenly than the feeling of his hands gently massaging the shampoo into my hair, or his lips on my wet shoulders, or the sides of my neck.

"Where would you like to go today?" he whispers against my ear.

A shiver runs up my spine.

Surprised by the question, I turn my head at an angle to get a glimpse of him behind me. His large hands steadily massage my hair.

"What do you mean?" I know what he means, but I can hardly believe he's even considering taking me out of the house.

His lips fall on the corner of my mouth.

"Wherever you want to go," he says. "You name it and I'll take you there."

Turning me around, he guides my head back under the steady stream of water. I close my eyes as he rinses the shampoo from my hair.

"I-I don't know," I say when he finally pulls me away from the stream and I can open my eyes again.

He smiles and looks a little surprised himself.

"You can't think of anywhere?" he asks. "Not *one* place?"

I look up, pressing my lips together in a hard line on one side of my mouth, pondering the possibilities.

"Manhattan. Greenwich Village," I say brokenly as I slowly recall the place. "I haven't had a good hot dog in a really long time."

Fredrik smiles and it makes me blush.

He does everything for me, washing me from head to toe, carefully cleaning around the healing, yet still very tender wounds around my ankle. And he kisses me under the constant stream of water. On the shoulders. The sides and center of my throat. The corners of my mouth. My forehead. My lips. And as much as I'd love to let him take me right here in the shower, I'm equally content that he doesn't touch me in that way, and is very self-controlled.

When we're done, Fredrik stands me in front of the steam-laden mirror, his chest and pelvic area touching me lightly from behind. He's hard, but still he doesn't lose self-control and it only makes me want him more.

I feel the tip of his finger tracing the scars on my back. Then he dips his head and his lips fall on them, one by one.

"Can you tell me where you got these scars?" he asks, kissing another one.

The question throws me off. Not because he asked, but because…I can't remember.

"I…I don't really know."

It frustrates me wholly. I thought I had remembered everything about my past. How could I not remember something as unforgettable as the scars on my back? Fredrik always touches them. Since the first night he brought me here, he's always had an interest in them. He would lie me on my stomach across my bed downstairs and gently pull my nightgown up to my shoulders. He would trace his fingers across the scars—just as he's doing now. And then the tip of his tongue as if he were tasting and savoring a memory. I never knew the scars were there until I asked him what it was about my back that he seemed to treasure so much.

"It's all right," he says raising his head. "You don't have to remember everything."

I feel like he's somewhat relieved that I don't know. But that's ridiculous. Why would he be relieved that I couldn't remember any part of my past when we've both fought so hard and for so long to unravel everything?

I brush it off and smile to myself, thinking of only him. Of us. Being here together.

But then scars flash across my mind that I *do* remember. Absently, I finger the ones on my thighs—six on each side—cut in a perfect horizontal line three inches across. Fredrik's hand touches mine, moving it away from them—the scars *he* made when he tortured me in that chair on the other side of the basement.

"I'm sorry I did that to you," he says, his voice laced heavily with sadness and regret and shame and guilt. "I don't want you to forgive me. Because I'll never forgive myself."

"But I do—"

He places his fingers over my lips. Instantly I'm compelled to shut my eyes and kiss them, but I don't.

"Things will be different from now on," he says with his lips against the side of my neck. Then I feel a soft towel rubbing gently against my back as he begins to dry me off.

"Fredrik," I say almost in a whisper, "what made you change your mind?"

He squeezes the ends of my hair with the towel, soaking the water into the thick cotton.

"None of that matters," he says. "I don't want you to think about any of that."

"But what about Seraphina?" I ask quietly, nervously.

His hands stop moving and I feel him sigh behind me.

"*Most* of all," he says regretfully, "I don't want you to worry about *her.*"

"But she's looking for me. And I know you can protect me, but I'm still terrified of her. I'm most afraid when you're gone. When it's just me and Greta here."

I feel the towel drop and then his hands cupping my upper arms. He kisses the top of my head, standing so much taller than me. And I know that it's just an affectionate gesture, but I can't help but feel it's also one of regret, or maybe even grief.

"Cassia, would you believe me if I told you she couldn't hurt you if you didn't think about her?"

I start to turn around to face him, but he carefully holds me still. Then he reaches out a hand and swipes it through the thick layer of moisture covering the large mirror.

My hands begin to shake, though I don't know why. My stomach ties into a nervous knot and I feel sick all of a sudden, my nerves frayed. I look down at the counter.

"I…I don't know," I stutter uneasily. "H-How would that keep her from finding me?"

*I don't know what's happening to me…but I don't like it.*

Fredrik continues to wipe the steam away from the mirror. I continue to look down.

He stops and drops his arm, fitting both hands on my sides, just above my naked hips.

"Well, I think you let her get to you too much, love." My heart leaps inside my chest every time he calls me that. "I want you to stop worrying about her. Just stop thinking about her and live your life. The way you are now. A prisoner to no one. Not to me, or to Seraphina. Can you do that?"

Reluctantly I nod.

Then I turn to face him, putting my back to the mirror.

Pushing up on my toes, I kiss his warm and delicious lips.

He smiles.

"I think I can do that," I say and smile back at him.

He makes me breakfast and we sit together at the kitchen table like a married couple, both of us with a mug of hot coffee, Fredrik peering down at the day's newspaper. But I can't help but make note of how much of that newspaper he *doesn't* seem to be reading because he keeps raising his eyes from it to smile—to grin—across the table at me.

I feel like a teenager with my first crush all over again, my face flush with emotion.

We talk for the longest time about everything and nothing. And sometimes I find myself lost in his deep and precious voice. I could listen to him talk all day and I'd never get bored or want any interruptions.

By the time breakfast is over, I've changed my mind about going to New York. Not only because it's ridiculous to go three hours away for a hot dog, but because despite Fredrik asking me to stop worrying about Seraphina, I can't. And New York was where she tried to kill me. She plagues my thoughts and haunts my memories.

"Why don't you want to go?" Fredrik asks.

I lower my gaze because I was never any good at lying and say, "I just want to stay in Maryland." I laugh lightly for good measure. "I've been here for a long time and I've never seen anything outside of this house."

Fredrik frowns.

I smile and say, "Oh no, love, I'm not blaming you," to assure him.

Something flickered in his eyes when I called him 'love'.

Why did I call him that? It doesn't matter. I like it. And it feels right. Natural.

He flattens the newspaper on the table and looks at me inquiringly. "So then if not New York, where would you like to go?" His gorgeous smile broadens. "I'm yours all day long."

My face flushes again.

"Why don't you pick a place?"

He purses his lips.

I want to kiss them…

*Fredrik*

---

It's all an illusion, the voice in the back of my mind constantly tells me as I sit across from Cassia in the finest restaurant in all of Baltimore. *It's all an illusion:* The two of us. Sitting here together like this. Like any normal couple would. It's an illusion, Fredrik. Over and over again. Because I have yet to let myself believe it. A part of me doesn't want to believe it. The old Fredrik. And the even older one. The parts of me that I've only ever known. What *is* this strange light I feel when in Cassia's presence?

It must be what a normal life feels like.

And while I feel a great sense of contentment, the light scares the hell out of me just the same.

*An illusion*, the darkness within me taunts. *This kind of life was never meant for you, so don't fall for it, or what's left of your life will come crashing down around you into pieces so small that they can never be put back together again.* Shut the fuck up!

Cassia's smile is so vibrant, yet so fragile that I feel the smallest touch of darkness can easily wash it away. She's wearing a pretty white sweater that fits loosely about her shoulders, revealing the softness of her collarbone and long, dainty neck. An elongated gray skirt clings to her hourglass form, down past her knees and drapes over a pair of tall black winter boots. I took her shopping when we left the house this morning. She was shy and at first didn't want me to buy her things. So I picked out outfits for her to wear and bought them anyway. And I dressed her. And while I dressed her, I kissed the scars on her back like I've always done. Scars left by cuts that I put there over time, one by one, as I made love to Seraphina.

We leave the restaurant and head back out into the cold, our shoes crunching in the mere two inches of snow that had fallen last night. I open the car door for her and help her into the passenger's seat. The car is already warm. I made sure to use the remote start before we left the restaurant.

"Fredrik," Cassia says softly from her seat, "I feel like I've known you forever." I look over at her and her face is flush with heat. I smile gently—though inside I'm not smiling so much—and she continues: "I know that if I told anyone else how I feel about you, despite the circumstances of how we know each other, they'd probably think I was crazy. Greta must think I'm crazy." Her eyes meet mine again. She's looking for confirmation or rejection of her theory. I don't have the heart to be honest with her.

I put the key in the ignition and unlock the wheel so that the car will remain running.

"Greta doesn't think that way," I say simply.

I don't look back at her this time.

"But it really doesn't matter what anyone else thinks," she says with uncertainty. "Does it?"

I glance over briefly.

"No," I say, though I don't know what I'm saying, or even if I should be saying it at all. "The way anyone chooses to feel about someone else is their choice and their business." I tried to be vague.

She smiles and folds her hands together on her lap.

"But I really do feel like I've known you forever," she repeats. "I...can't explain it. But it feels right." She smiles.

*Does she want me to agree?*

*What does she want from me?*

I put the car in reverse and pull out of the parking space.

I spend all day with Cassia, just as I promised. She eventually began to loosen up and suggest places she'd like to go, things she'd like to do. It didn't surprise me much that everything she chose was simple and not lavish or expensive. I would've gladly spent every dollar I own on her, bought her the most extravagant car. I would've done *anything* for her. But all she asked of me was to spend an hour and a half watching a movie in the local theatre. We ate popcorn and drank soda and sat close together with our shoes propped on the back of the empty seats in front of us. I hadn't done anything like that in—I've never done anything like that. It was odd. But it was liberating and immature and unsophisticated, and I'd do it again. If she were with me. And Cassia, for such a small-framed woman, has a massive appetite—so did Seraphina. In addition to the lunch and then the popcorn, she had her fair share of fast food before the day was over.

Shortly after nightfall, we find our way to a nice bar in the better part of town. Cassia's choice. She's been calling the shots since before the movie.

"I used to sing in a bar and restaurant," she says from the passenger's seat. "When I lived in New York."

"Really?" I ask, trying to sound surprised.

People come and go from the building in front of us all dressed in casual slacks and nice sweaters and long coats, couples arm in arm, some vaguely tipsy as they leave and make their way to their cars in the parking lot.

Cassia watches them in a soundless, thoughtful manner; her memory of her time singing in New York surely playing through her mind.

She looks over and smiles. "Yeah, I sang. It was my job, though."

I smile in return.

"I bet you have a beautiful voice." *The most beautiful voice I've ever heard.*

Cassia looks down at her hands in her lap, her face turning red underneath that soft skin.

Then she giggles and says with a grin, "OK, yeah, I *am* pretty good," but is immediately embarrassed by the confession.

Leaning over the console toward her, I cup her chin in my hand and close my lips around hers, stealing her breath away. I can't stop. *I've missed you.* I don't want to. *But you're not you anymore.* I should stop, because I know that nothing good can come from this. But I can't.

*There* has *to be a way.*

The kiss breaks. I stare into her soft brown eyes, savoring the taste of her mouth lingering on my lips.

*It's all an illusion*—No…it's not.

"Fredrik," I hear her voice say, but it's faint at first while I'm locked in my own fighting thoughts. "Is something wrong?"

I snap out of it.

She smiles at me curiously. "Why don't we go inside?" she asks about the bar just feet from us.

Suddenly I have a new plan. And this time I'm going to *make* it work. I look at her in silent contemplation, and within a matter of seconds I know what I have to do.

"How about we skip the bar," I suggest, kissing her lightly on the lips. "I think I'd rather spend the rest of the night alone with you. We can kick back and watch TV. We can soak in a warm bath together." Anything but the bar. Anything but what might help bring back more memories. The night Greta took off her shackle and they danced and sang to Connie Francis was the night that Cassia got her memories back. Memories I never expected, but nonetheless.

Cassia smiles. "OK," she says without reluctance or question. "Then let's go home."

Home. Seraphina has come home.

# TWENTY-THREE

*Fredrik*

—

I never imagined feeling this way about anyone. Seraphina will always be a part of me, but *this* part of *her* that I'll likely never understand, has been filling the holes in my soul that have been empty since I was a boy, ever since the day I brought her here. The holes that Seraphina's darker half could not fill. I've never known light. Only darkness. I've never experienced tenderness or frailty or compassion, until Cassia. How can one person be so many things? Wear so many faces? Accommodate so many desires?

I give Greta another full day off and I spend the next day with Cassia as well. And then the next. But by the end of the weekend, something much deeper than frustration begins to grow within me. Resentment of the truth? Knowing that what I want so badly, in reality I can't have? And to make matters worse, I begin to realize that just because something good is standing in front of me, I can't so easily forget who I really am inside. The need to pacify my vengeance and bloodlust is growing strong again—stronger now that my darkness feels threatened by something more powerful that is trying to hold me back, to keep me from being me. And the only thing that'll quiet the brutal voice in the back of my mind is to find an unwilling participant and do what I do best.

I'm trying so very hard to ignore it.

Cassia sits beside me on the arm of the leather chair in my living room. Her fingers wind gently in top of my dark hair.

"Can I ask you something?" she says suggestively as I'm glimpsing her naked thighs on the thick chair arm beside me.

"Of course," I tell her.

I keep my eyes on the iPad in front of me on the coffee table, trying not to let myself become distracted by her.

But like ignoring my dark side, that's not so easy to do.

"How did you make love to Seraphina?"

My eyes shut in a soft, brief moment of regret. Cassia's fingers continue to wind through my hair, sending shivers down the back of my neck.

"I think it's better we don't talk about her." I run my fingertip over the screen, pretending to be preoccupied. But all I can think about is the way her skin smells and how warm her hip is pressed against my arm.

"What was she like? In bed, I mean."

"Cassia—." I stop myself from sounding angry and let my breath out in a heavy sigh. "Please, you promised you wouldn't do this."

She slides off the chair arm and straddles my lap.

I swell uncomfortably beneath the fabric of my pants, but I can't will myself to readjust it because I don't want to move her even an inch from my lap. She's wearing a gray tank top with no bra and a small tight pair of pink cotton panties. I glimpse down between her legs spread with her thighs on either side of me, her knees pressed into the cushion, and my head begins to spin with need.

"Fredrik…please." She softens her gaze to the point of frowning and I fight not to be putty in her fucking hands. "The way you were with me all the times before—you were different. Sometimes rough, other times you looked at me before you took me as if you were fighting something inside. Something predatory, primal." She moves her little hips on my lap with purpose. I can't breathe. "You were always holding something back with me. And now…" she leans inward and slides her tongue between my lips once. I can't see through my tingling eyelids. "…now you treat me with such frailty."

"Would you prefer that I didn't?" I ask with a purpose of my own—I want to make her feel guilty so she'll drop this. "What, you don't like it?"

She pulls away from my lips and tilts her head dejectedly to one side. "No, no, I *do*." She rests her hands on my shirt-covered chest. "Sometimes I feel like I could come just when you touch me. I *never* want you to change. I need you to be the way you are. The way you make me feel…I've never felt it before."

"Then what does it matter how I was with Seraphina?" I tilt my head in the same manner, looking up at her. "Why do you care?"

"Curiosity, I guess." She shrugs and somehow even that is sexy to me. "Maybe I want you to—"

A streak of jealousy shoots through me all of a sudden and she notices the change right away.

"Cassia," I say trailing my fingertips down the softness of her bare arms, "You say you've never felt it before, the way you feel with me—have you been with other men?"

Her face falls and she looks downward at her hands now resting between her panties and my stomach. She doesn't look ashamed. She appears as blank as she did when I asked her a few nights ago where she got the scars on her back and she couldn't recall.

Her eyes meet mine with reluctance.

"Not that I can remember," she says. "*Never* when I lived in New York. But before that—I don't know."

"Can you remember *anything* before New York?"

She shakes her head and now looks ashamed.

"Come here," I say, cupping the back of her head and pulling her toward my shoulder where she rests the side of her face. "Don't worry about it."

"Fredrik?"

"Yeah?"

"If I had been with other men, would you still keep me here with you?"

My hand stiffens in her hair and I press her tightly against me, wrapping the other hand around her back.

*I don't know.*

"Yes," I tell her. "It wouldn't matter to me," I lie.

With any other woman other than Seraphina, it wouldn't matter to me who or how many men she has been with. But Seraphina was different. She wasn't a virgin when we met, but I knew by her refusal to talk about her first time, that it was someone she *needed* to forget. Seraphina called *me* her 'true first'. She despised men. I was the only man she could ever love. The only man she would ever let touch her. Seraphina *killed* men for touching her—if I didn't get to them first. But I was the only one. Until Marcus at Safe House Sixteen. And I killed him ten days after I found out.

Cassia raises her body from mine and looks into my eyes smiling soft and coyly. And again with purpose, she presses herself against my hardness below and I lose my breath. A low, guttural growl rumbles quietly through my chest.

"Cassia," I say, ready to hoist her off of me, tucking my hands underneath her thighs, "we shouldn't do this right now."

What has gotten into her? Not that it bothers me—quite the opposite—but I get the feeling she's jealous of Seraphina and is trying to take her place in all ways, not just in my heart.

She frowns.

"Don't do that," I say.

"I'm sorry, I just—"

Reaching around her with one arm firmly around her waist so she doesn't fall, I grab the iPad from the coffee table and toss it on the floor. Seconds after, I swipe away the files I had been reading about Kelly Bennings and Paul Fortright in Seattle. Photographs and sheets of white paper scatter about the accent rug. I lean over forward and Cassia instinctively grabs me around the neck to keep from falling backward, and I fit my hands about the upper legs of the coffee table, pulling it closer.

I lay her down on it on her back.

"What are you doing?" she asks with curiosity but no insecurity—she has an idea of what I'm doing.

"Whatever I want," I say, fitting my fingers behind the elastic of her panties and pulling them off.

Grabbing her ankles, I prop her feet on the edge of the table.

Her eyes grow wider.

My dick gets harder.

Her thighs fall apart before me, spreading like butterfly wings. I help her hold them still, grasping them with both hands, until she holds them still on her own.

"If you swear to me you'll never ask about Seraphina again"—I slide my middle finger between her nether lips, up and down twice before spreading her apart. She gasps.—"I'll do this for you. Anywhere you want me to do it. Whenever you want me to do it. And often when you least expect it."

Her fingers curl firmly around the sides of the table, white-knuckling the grain. Her chest rises and falls with little pants that make me hungrier for her.

I lean over and drag the tip of my tongue between her wet lips and she shudders and gasps.

"But you have to fucking swear it."

I lick her again and push my index and middle fingers deep inside of her. Her head pushes back, arching her neck against the coffee table, her long blond hair stark against the dark grain.

"I swear it." She shudders.

With my fingers still inside of her, I flick my tongue against her clit.

"Not very convincing, love."

I pull completely away from her, letting my back fall against the oversized leather chair, my long legs fallen open, leaving me the perfect view of her exposed naked body. My hands drape casually over the chair arms.

"I swear it, Fredrik! I swear it!"

"Don't raise your head," I tell her.

She lays it back down.

"I'll never ask about her again," she goes on pleading and it just makes me want to put more than my fingers or my tongue inside of her, but I won't.

"Hmmm," I say, glancing upward at the ceiling, biding my time. "I'm still not sure I can believe you. I mean, you did promise me once before—"

"I swear it, Fredrik—I'll never even speak her *name* again."

That gets my attention.

I raise my back from the chair and brush my hand against her thighs, only grazing the warmth between her legs to get to the other side.

"Say you promise," I say gently.

"I promise," she says in a shivering whisper.

I stick my middle fingers inside of her, sliding them in and out carefully. A series of soft moans escape her. I play with her for a little while. Because I like to touch it. I could touch and probe her for hours and never get bored.

More gasps, sweet and cock-throbbing, each and every time.

Finally my head falls between her trembling thighs and I lick her with furious intent, working my fingers inside and out at the same time. Cassia gasps, clutching the edges of the coffee table. Her stomach sinks in and she sucks in her breath to breathe in pants, revealing the outline of her ribs.

I hear keys jangling in the front door, but I don't stop.

All I care about is sending Cassia into a delirious fit, splayed out right here in my living room.

"Oh Fredrik! Please don't stop…"

*I don't plan to, love.*

I suck her clit repeatedly into my mouth, pressing my lips hard against her pelvic bone.

I hear another gasp, though it's not coming from Cassia. I only stop when her thighs clamp around my head and she looks toward the living room entrance with an expression of horror.

Greta is standing there with her mouth agape and eyes wider than Cassia's legs had been.

Without raising my body, I look across at her and say, "Do you mind waiting outside for about"—I figure it out in my head quickly—"a couple more minutes?"

Greta, making me feel like she hasn't been laid in a very long time, takes a few seconds to get her thoughts together.

"I'll be in the car," she says, moving quickly toward the door. "Just wave at me when…you're done."

The front door opens and closes so fast she probably ran the last few feet.

"Oh my God, I'm *so* embarrassed!"

"Don't be," I tell her while grasping her thighs firmly with both hands and spreading them away from my head. "Now be still."

"But I can't—"

"Oh, yes, you can. Trust me. Now lay your head back down."

Promptly, she does what I tell her and I go back to work.

———

While Cassia is in my bedroom getting dressed, Greta is re-entering the house with absolutely no eye contact. Not that that's unusual, but this time for very a very different reason.

"I am so sorry, Mr. Gustavsson." She sets her purse on the counter and then goes to drape her coat over the back of a barstool, but she misses and it falls to the floor instead. She bends over and tries again, fumbling it all the while. "You told me to let myself in. I just didn't—"

"Don't worry about it." I step toward her. She steps to the side, dropping her gaze. I walk around her and toward the refrigerator. "It was my fault. I knew you'd be here, but…well, things happened that I didn't anticipate."

"*I'll* say," Greta mumbles under her breath.

I let it slide.

Cassia enters the room, dressed in her gray tank top and a pair of my running pants covering her little pink panties. She can barely look Greta in the face, unable to contain the redness in her own. It's so fucking cute I want to put her on the counter next.

"Hi Greta." Cassia waves her hand daintily.

I open the refrigerator and take a water bottle off the top shelf.

"Hi Cassia, dear. I uh, take it you've been doing well the past few days."

I shake my head at their awkwardness, but say nothing.

If Cassia were standing on a beach, she'd look like she was shyly shuffling her toes in the sand.

How can she and Seraphina be the same person?

"Yes, Greta," Cassia says with an unrelenting smile, "things have been wonderful."

Greta's eyes finally find their way to mine, but she doesn't look at me for long, just long enough to expose the uncertainty hidden within them. I let that slide, too. She's just very motherly when it comes to Cassia, and quite frankly, I'm beginning to appreciate that about her even more now.

Suddenly realization sinks in and Cassia's smile drops as she turns to me. If Greta is here it can only mean one thing.

"Are you leaving?" Her sad eyes draw inward. It crushes me a little inside.

"Yes." I twist the cap off the water. "I have to meet someone in about an hour. It's very important."

It's important, but it also has me on edge. I almost don't want to meet Izabel at the coffee shop because I'm afraid of what she's going to tell me.

Cassia steps up to me.

"I don't want you to go."

I set the water down and place my hands on her shoulders and lean in to kiss her forehead. "It won't be for long. You'll be all right."

Greta begins unloading the dishwasher, pretending not to be listening, but she's hanging on every word.

Cassia's expression appears tortured. I know she doesn't want me to leave her, but this isn't only about that. She doesn't want to go back into the basement and although I haven't verified that's going to happen, she knows that it will.

I take her hand and she lets me.

We leave Greta in the kitchen and I walk with Cassia down the concrete stairs, turning on the lights as I pass. I admit that even to me it feels like walking into a prison though I haven't been the one confined in this place. I wish I could let her live freely in my house, able to look out the windows or even to go outside whenever she wanted. But right now that's not possible. And it may never be.

"You promise you won't be gone long?"

She lays her head on my chest, her arms bent and pressed between us, her fingers clutching my dress shirt.

I cradle the back of her head in my hand, tightening my grip around her. "I promise."

Raising her face, she looks up at me with apprehension.

"Fredrik?"

I kiss her forehead.

"What is it?"

"I'm afraid."

Cupping her face in both of my hands, I kiss her trembling lips.

"Don't be afraid."

"But I am. I'll always be afraid." Her fingers tighten around the fabric of my shirt.

"Fredrik?" she repeats, though this time with reluctance.

I soften my gaze, letting her know that it's OK to talk about Seraphina—this is different.

"Can you promise me that you'll never let her hurt me again?" The corners of her eyes well up with moisture. "I know that you love her"—she tugs my shirt harder, seizing my wandering gaze—"I know you will *always* love her. But please, don't *ever* let her hurt me again."

Looking her in the eyes and seeing only Cassia for the first time I say, "I'll never let her hurt you again." I kiss her forehead. "And I don't think I want to find her anymore."

Cassia says nothing else as I lock the shackle around her ankle and make my way back up the concrete steps.

*Cassia*

—

I felt a smile try pushing its way the surface of my face, but it died too soon. My hands drop to my sides and I just stand here in the center of the room, the chain stretched out beside me on the floor. I should be happy about the last thing he said—I *want* to be, but I feel strange.

I don't know what's happening to me.

But I don't like it.

*Fredrik*

———

With my coat already on and my keys in my hand, I head to the front door but stop at the kitchen entrance.

"Greta, you need to understand something."

She sets the dish towel on the counter and walks around it toward me, her eyes never leaving mine as she senses the importance of what I'm about to say.

"Cassia is dangerous"—Greta's eyebrows harden instantly—"and you need to be careful around her."

"Forgive me, Mr. Gustavsson," she says stepping right up to me, "but I thought you were past this. You told me the first week I began caring for her to be careful around her. You said it was because she couldn't be trusted, but you—"

"I know what I said," I cut her off. "I know I eventually told you that it was OK, but the truth is I never should've allowed you to let your guard down around her. That was a mistake on my part."

"Cassia is harmless," she says, crossing her arms covered by a knit blue sweater. "How can you say she's dangerous after all this time? After what…" she narrows her eyes, "…after what you've been through with her?" She's referring somewhat to what she saw when she walked through the door tonight.

"Listen to me," I say with authority. "I'll tell you more when I find out tonight in my meeting with Izabel. Hopefully I'll have a better understanding. But until then, I want you to be on your guard around Cassia at all times."

"I will," Greta says, dropping her hands to her sides and walking back around the counter. "But let me just say for the record—and you can kill me for saying it if you want—I trust her more than I trust you. Sir." Her words were bitter, but heartfelt. She resents me for keeping Cassia a prisoner, for treating her like an animal—in her eyes—for even entertaining the thought that someone as sweet and caring as Cassia is, could be dangerous.

"Your opinion is noted," I say and open the front door. "I'll be watching the cameras, so don't do anything stupid."

"I won't, sir."

# TWENTY-FOUR

*Fredrik*

———

I pull into the parking lot of the coffee shop and find that Izabel is already here waiting for me fifteen minutes early. She's not smiling when I approach her table in the far corner of the store. The only smile on her face is the lamentable kind when you're about to give someone you love some devastating news.

I want to turn on my heels and walk right back out the door. Maybe if I don't listen to what she has to say none of it will be true.

I sit down on the empty chair across from Izabel.

I say nothing.

Izabel takes a thick white envelope from her purse on the table and sets it in front of her covering it with her manicured fingers.

I despise that envelope. It's about to ruin my life and I want to set it on fire.

Tearing my eyes away from it, I look only at Izabel.

"How has she been?" she asks.

"Actually, Cassia has been perfect," I answer, as if that fact is going to negate everything she's going to tell me. "No signs of her remembering that she's Seraphina. I even let her out of the basement for the first time in a year. Took her out to eat and to the movies, you can believe that—Me. At the movies." I didn't realize how big my smile had gotten over the short time, but I couldn't help myself as I recalled the past few days alone with Cassia.

Izabel looks sympathetic and the smile dissolves from my face.

"Fredrik, can I ask you a personal question?"

"Sure."

I lean back against my chair and interlock my fingers across my stomach.

Izabel keeps her hands on top of the envelope and I get the feeling she doesn't want me to see what's inside as much as I don't.

"Was your childhood anything like mine?"

That takes me by surprise.

I've never told Izabel about my past. The only two people—that I know of—other than Seraphina who know anything about it at all are Victor Faust and our ex-employer, Vonnegut. They knew because it was their business to know before I was recruited by The Order. But even still they don't know everything.

No one knew everything but Seraphina.

"Somewhat like yours, yes." I look at the wall behind her head.

"Victor won't tell me much about you," she says gently, "because it isn't my business unless you tell me yourself. I know this and I accept it. But I wanted to ask in case you felt close enough to me to tell me."

"What does my past have to do with what's in that envelope, Izabel?" I still won't look at the envelope. I see it in my peripheral vision, but I can't force myself to look at it directly.

"It's just a question, Fredrik."

"No, it's more than that," I say and then lower my voice so the barista behind the counter won't hear. "But yes, I was a sex slave, just like you were. Only I was one for a much longer time. And I wasn't anyone's favorite."

I didn't mean for that last part to sound resentful or harsh, but by the offended look in Izabel's eyes, I'm assuming it came out that way.

Sighing with regret, I shut my eyes briefly and place my folded hands on the table. "I didn't mean that how it sounded."

Izabel softens her expression and nods gently. "I know."

"But I don't know why any of this matters," I cut in. "What does my past have to do with Seraphina?"

"It has nothing to do with Seraphina," she says. "I just want you to know that I'm here for you no matter what. You and me, we're alike in many ways and I know that I was alone for a very long time because of the life I was forced to live. I had no one. Except for the girls who lived in the compound with me, but my relationships with them were always short-lived. They were either sold, committed suicide, or were murdered. I had no one, Fredrik. And I know how it feels to be alone and in a horrific life not of my choosing."

She leans forward, sliding the envelope to the center of the small table, but not yet ready to give it to me. Her eyes are sad and filled with understanding.

"Not just recently," she goes on, "but since the night I met you in Los Angeles, I saw in you the same loneliness and torment that was in me before I found Victor. People like you and me, we think we're hiding our pain and darkness from the rest of the world, but we forget that we can see it plainly in *each other*."

I reach for the envelope, but she's reluctant to move her hand away. Finally she relents. I slide it over to me and keep my hand on top of it. But I'm not ready to read the contents.

"I appreciate the heart-to-heart, Izabel, but—"

"Fredrik, I'm afraid for you."

"Why? Because of this?" I tap the envelope with the tip of my finger without looking down at it. "I can handle it. Whatever it is I'm about to find out, I can deal with it."

"But I just want to say that Seraphina is *not* the only person in this world who has ever cared about you."

My fingers crush around the edges of the envelope.

"Maybe not," I say, "but she's the only person who truly understood me."

Izabel nods pensively. "Yeah, but she doesn't have to be."

"What's that supposed to mean?" I laugh suddenly. "Are we going to have a love affair?" I joke, grinning at her.

Izabel smiles and rolls her eyes a little, but trades humor for determination quickly.

"I'm just saying that I'm here for you. I would do just about anything for you. I hope you believe that."

Finally I look down at the envelope, then carefully pull the flap out of the inside, opening it.

"James Woodard tracked the information down on Cassia Carrington," Izabel says as I'm unfolding the thick sheets of paper and my heart is pounding violently inside my chest. "It wasn't hard to find."

Looking down into the text printed on the paper, I read with an open mind and a crushing heart:

# THE SWAN AND THE JACKAL

**June 25$^{th}$**

**Patient: Cassia Ana Carrington**

**Age: 13**

**Primary Diagnosis: Dissociative Identity Disorder**

—

The patient shows no signs of conscious deception. It is my professional opinion that Carrington genuinely believes that a young girl her age named Seraphina Bragado, is who murdered her parents and set their house on fire. Carrington has told me in great length and with complex detail the story of how she 'met' her second personality, Seraphina Bragado, and each time she tells the story, it is exactly the same as before. I've tried to confuse her with details, but she always corrects me. She believes one hundred percent that everything she is telling me is real.

Carrington as 'Seraphina' confessed to me that she killed Carrington's parents because she was trying to save Carrington, to spare her from going through with her father the same that Seraphina went through with hers: brutal physical abuse, sexual molestation and rape. This is not uncommon for patients with DID, to create a personality that is emotionally and mentally stronger than themselves, who can do the things that the primary personality is too afraid or weak to do on their own. In Carrington's case, Seraphina became the part of her who was brave enough to face the abuse of her father and deal with her mother looking the other way and not stepping in to help her.

**August 1$^{st}$**

**Patient: Cassia Ana Carrington**

**Age: 13**

**Primary Diagnosis: Dissociative Identity Disorder**

—

Evidence has concluded that the fourteen-year-old boy, Phillip Johnson, who went missing from Carrington's neighborhood six months before Carrington murdered her parents, that Carrington was responsible for his murder as well. Johnson's body was found in the woods behind Carrington's house, covered by tree branches and brush. 'Seraphina' is who told us where to find the boy. 'Seraphina' claimed that Johnson tried to kiss Carrington, and so to protect Carrington, Seraphina led him into the woods and stabbed him to death.

**September 21st**
**Patient: Cassia Ana Carrington**
**Age: 14**
**Primary Diagnosis: Dissociative Identity Disorder**

—

The patient has not reverted back to her true self for quite some time. She insists that she is Seraphina Bragado and I'm beginning to feel that this alter personality is slowly taking over. It concerns me how long this might last. The treatment to help Carrington cannot be successful if Carrington is not the personality that I'm treating.

**October 29th**
**Patient: Cassia Ana Carrington**
**Age: 15**
**Primary Diagnosis: Dissociative Identity Disorder**

—

Carrington came back this week, but it was a very brief encounter before 'Seraphina' took over again. But in that brief moment, I've finally found the patient's trigger, or one of them, at least. Carrington does not like mirrors. Seraphina has no issue with looking into a mirror, but Carrington will go out of her way to avoid them. I believe that when Carrington looks into a mirror it isn't her own reflection she sees staring back at her, but rather that of Seraphina's. But I do not believe that looking into a mirror every time will change her personality and she will become Seraphina. After further testing, it is apparent that there is no real pattern to when Carrington becomes Seraphina, but only that sometimes seeing her reflection in a mirror can trigger the change.

**April 20<sup>th</sup>**
**Patient: Cassia Ana Carrington**
**Age: 17**
**Primary Diagnosis: Dissociative Identity Disorder**

—

Cassia Carrington hasn't been herself in over a year. I've come to the conclusion that Carrington's case is one of the worst I've ever seen when it comes to how long an alter personality remains the dominant. It's as if Cassia no longer exists and Seraphina has taken over fully.

A side note: A small group of people—two men and one woman—came to the institution today to see Carrington. They claimed they were from a government organization, provided the proper identification—their names were even in the system listed as permitted visitors—and they spent three hours alone with her in an unobserved room. Cameras and voice recorders were prohibited. I asked 'Seraphina' after they had left what they discussed with her. She would not answer.

**May 1<sup>st</sup>**
**Patient: Cassia Ana Carrington**
**Age: 17**
**Primary Diagnosis: Dissociative Identity Disorder**

—

Carrington is no longer at the institution. She was transferred—under mysterious circumstances, in my opinion—to another institution in New York, but I was not given any more information on the transfer other than that. I have been ordered by my superior to drop Carrington's case and remove her files from my possession.

I stare at the paper in my hand, letting the text blur out of focus. Then I let it drop from my fingers onto the table. I have no interest in reading the other ten or so pages.

"I'm sorry, Fredrik."

"Don't be sorry. I told you I can deal with this."

I fall against the back of my chair and throw my head back, laughing gently. "Unbelievable." I cross my arms over my chest. "I fell in love with probably the most mentally fucked up woman on the planet."

Izabel isn't laughing, nor is she even smiling at my poor attempt at humor. I guess she was right when she said we can't hide pain from each other.

"OK," I say, motioning my hands, "so she's sick. I knew that already. As a matter of fact, this whole multiple personality thing, in the back of my mind, I knew that's what it was. But I didn't want to believe it. I mean it *is* rare, after all. Why did it have to be her? This is ridiculous. I can't even—" I don't even know what I'm saying anymore.

I drop my hands in my lap and stare at the creased paper in front of me. Izabel remains silent, listening, watching, wanting to say something to make this all better but she knows as much as I do that there's nothing that *can*.

"So then I can get her help," I say, looking across at her. "She's been fine as Cassia—holy fucking shit, Izabel; Seraphina never actually existed. When I married her in private, when I made love to her, all of the things we did together; she was and always has been Cassia Carrington. Seraphina never existed." The revelation nearly sends me over the edge, and what's left of my own mind into oblivion.

"I can get her help," I repeat, resolved to do just that.

"Fredrik," Izabel speaks up carefully, "I don't think there's anyone or anything that can help her."

"Why would you say that?" I feel my eyebrows hardening in my forehead.

She glances at the paper in front of me.

"You should read the rest of it."

I shake my head.

"I'm not going to read anymore. Seraphina is sick. She needs help. And I'm going to get her help." My voice begins to rise. "What, you think shrinks and doctors just put people like her away because they're sick? No. They put them through therapy and give them medication—"

"Yes, they do," Izabel adds with caution and sympathy, "but not the ones who murder innocent people. I've read the entire file Fredrik. Her parents may not have been innocent. She killed them and they deserved it. But that boy, Phillip Johnson, he wasn't the first innocent person who Seraphina killed. There were several others after him. All male."

*And then the innocent blond women six years ago—there's no telling how many people Seraphina killed that I never knew about.*

"Which side of her did, or *do* you, love more?"

I look up. "I never said I still loved her."

"You didn't *have* to say it."

I look back down.

"I loved Seraphina because she was like me," I begin, seeing only Seraphina's face and short black hair and dark makeup in my mind. "I was a different kind of monster when we first met. She was the answer to everything. She helped me control my urges and showed me a way to still be myself without risking getting caught. We were *perfect* together, Izabel. I never prayed and I never dreamed of anything, but she was both the answer to my prayers and a dream come true. She was *everything* to me."

"And what about Cassia?"

I picture only Cassia now with her long, beautiful blond hair and natural beauty because she never wore makeup—only now I know why: she couldn't look into a mirror in order to apply it.

"Cassia gave me something that I never got from Seraphina. She gave me peace. She made me see a light in the darkness that is my life and she made me feel as normal as anyone else." I lock eyes with Izabel. "She is my light."

Izabel looks at me for a moment—pain and regret lay in her features.

"You need a whole person, Fredrik," she says thoughtful and determined. "I have to believe that one day you'll find her, a love who is both light and darkness, who understands you and fulfills you the way that Seraphina did, but who can also give you peace." She interlocks her fingers on the table and leans forward. "But you can't do this with *her*, and you know it. She's not a whole person. And she's gone too far—in every way—to ever become one. She could snap and turn at any moment, and you know that, too."

I look away. I don't want to hear any of this. Because I know it's true.

"You'll find her—"

"No," I cut in; my eyes boring into hers. "If it can't be Seraphina—Cassia—then it'll be no one." I grind my jaw. "I'm not desperate for the love of a woman, Izabel—you're entirely mistaken if that's what you think. I never wanted Seraphina when I first met her. I wanted to be alone and the last thing I needed was her, or any other woman, shadowing my every move.

But because she understood me and because I had been emotionally alone all my life, I fell in love with her. That couldn't be helped. Love betrayed me, just like life did the day I was born in a convenience store restroom to a mother who didn't want me." I lean over, pushing myself farther into view so Izabel can see the resolution buried on the surface of my face. "There will be no one after her. There will be *nothing* after her except the shell of a man I was before we met."

"What does that mean?" She appears worried—for me, no doubt.

I begin stuffing the paper back into the envelope and then shove it down inside my coat pocket.

I stand from the table.

"It means that I might not fit into yours or Victor's world anymore."

Izabel stares up at me from the chair; her long auburn hair blanketing the shoulders of her white coat, gathering atop the fuzzy white faux fur around the border of the hood lying against her back.

She rises to her feet, tall in height wearing a pair of tall-heeled bronze-colored boots. Her cheeks are still faintly reddened from the cold outside.

"She helped you kill, didn't she?"

My heart stops. I glance across the empty room at the barista behind the counter, and then down at the floor.

"No," I answer. "She helped me find the right people." I look at her again and continue to speak lowly. "People who were tied to her hits. Those whose death could be covered and accounted for under her Order. They were all people who deserved it and who I knew one hundred percent deserved it." My eyes fall away from her so maybe she won't see the shame and guilt hidden within them.

"Who did you"—she looks at the barista once and whispers even lower—"how did you do it before Seraphina?"

My shoulders rise and fall. I sit back down.

"People off the streets," I say. "Drug dealers. Pimps. Gang members. People few would notice missing. But—." I stop myself.

"But what?"

Glancing down at my shoes I go on: "A few times—and I mean a few—I'd take an innocent person by mistake. I tortured a man last year. It was around the time you fled Mexico and were on the run with Victor. I...well, like I said, I tortured him. Found out before I killed him that he wasn't the man I was looking for." I look straight into her eyes, regret at rest in mine. "I tortured an *innocent* man, Izabel. A father of two daughters. Didn't even have a parking ticket."

"But you didn't kill him. Right?" She looks hopeful.

I shake my head. "No. I didn't kill him. If it hadn't been for those instincts of mine—though they kicked in a little late that night because my head was so clouded by need—I never would've stopped. I never would've listened to him tell me he wasn't who I thought he was. I let him go and"—I laugh suddenly—"and as if it would make it all better, like slapping a goddamn Band-Aid on a gunshot wound, I gave him half a million dollars—would've given him more if I'd had it, but I hadn't been paid by The Order in three months."

"But you didn't *kill* him," Izabel says with a small smile of urgency.

I'm *not* smiling.

"No, you're right," I say. "I didn't kill *him*."

Her face falls just as quickly.

"There was one," I say with reluctance, picturing the victim's face. "A woman. Not long ago in San Francisco. She was the sister of one of Dorian's hits." Her eyes get bigger now that she knows

I was the one who killed the woman because no one knew what had happened to her until now. "Long story short—she claimed she was in on the murder that her brother had been involved in. She confessed while I held her captive in the opposite room while Dorian took care of the brother—she wasn't supposed to be there. I'm sure you remember the report." She nods. "But I was in desperate need of bloodshed. It had been a month since my last interrogation. She confessed and I obliged."

"But she was lying, wasn't she?"

I nod slowly.

"That explains the look on your face when in the meeting with Victor. When Victor showed you and Dorian the information found on the sister."

"Yes," I say with a heavy heart. "She *wanted* to die and used me to do it for her. I still wonder how François Moreau all the way in France, seemingly with no ties to these people, knew about me killing her."

"François Moreau," Izabel says, "was the client who ordered the hit on the brother."

Baffled by this information, at first I can't summon words.

But that isn't important right now, so I leave it alone.

She reaches into her black purse on the table and retrieves another envelope, placing it in front of me. Leery of it after having just read the news from the first envelope, I only glance at it.

"Anyway, speaking of Paul Fortright and Kelly Bennings," she says, sliding the envelope closer, urging me to take it but still I don't, "you were right."

"About what?"

She nods toward the envelope. "Open it and see for yourself."

Hesitating at first, I finally do as she suggested. Reading over the paper about Kelly Bennings, it's really no surprise.

I drop the paper on the table and look at Izabel.

With a shrug I say, "So why are you showing me this?" finding no connection between it and Seraphina, the reason she brought me here, and quite frankly, the only thing I care about right now.

She glances down at the table, her long fingers tapping against the wood grain seemingly out of slight nervousness. Then she says, "It's why I asked you if Seraphina helped you to kill. I didn't know for sure, but from what little I did know, I had a feeling it was Seraphina who helped you with your urges. In some way."

Still not understanding what's she's getting at, I cross my arms over my chest and glance between her and the paper, waiting for her to go on.

"I, umm, well, I thought you might need someone to take your pain out on." She pauses, unsure either of her words or my coming reaction to them, though probably both. "After what you found out about Seraphina tonight. I *know* this is hard for you." She's becoming more confident, more determined to make me understand. "You can pretend that you can handle it, but—"

"You're offering me a *victim*?" I accuse, having a hard time deciphering her intentions. I know that's what she's doing, but what is still unclear is—"Wait...does Victor know about this?"

She doesn't answer.

And she can't look at me.

"Izabel, *Jesus Christ*, you're offering me a victim who's involved in one of our contracts and Victor doesn't know about it?" I shake my head and slide the paper back across the table to her, refusing the gesture.

She smacks the palm of her hand down on top of it.

"Look, I've never really had a family before," she argues, "other than Mrs. Gregory, before I met Victor and you—and twist my tits off for saying it, even Niklas." She pushes the paper back toward me. "You're family to me and I want to help you. I meant what I said about telling Victor everything. And I *will*. But I'll tell him when I'm ready. Right now, I want to help you."

"I don't need this, Izabel." I remove my hand from the table completely and stand up. "I can find my own victims. I sure as hell don't need you putting your ass on the line for me. Victor will *kill* you."

She blinks, stunned, and rears her head back. "Thought you said he'd never kill me?"

"You know what I mean." I sigh. "Look, Izabel, I appreciate it. I really do. But I can find my own."

"I *want* you to kill her," she hisses through her teeth, as if she had been holding it back the whole time.

I stop in my tracks just as I'm about to leave her sitting there. "What?"

She stands up beside me.

"I was going to do it myself when I found out what she did," she whispers harshly. "I was ready to get on a plane last night. I even told Victor I was going to visit Dina—which I would've done afterward so it wouldn't have technically been a lie, so don't look at me like that." She grabs the lapel of my coat and wrenches me closer. "But then James Woodard gave me the information on Cass—Seraphina, and I knew then that killing Kelly Bennings would be a job better off in your hands. You need it more than I do." She lets go of my coat. "I don't actually *need* it. I just *want* it."

"Why do you want it so badly?"

Her nostrils flare briefly.

"Because of what she put her daughter and the client's daughter through, all for a fucking *man*!" She looks behind me at the barista. A customer enters the store. "That bitch *deserves* to die, or to at least be tortured—who better to do it than you? Any so-called mother who would risk ruining her daughter's life because of a man, deserves whatever's coming to her." She takes her purse from the table and tosses the short strap over her shoulder.

I search her face for what I already know is there: pain for what her own mother did to her, for taking her away at a young age to live with a Mexican drug lord who held her captive for much of her life. Any other day I might mess with her head and accuse her of just using me to do her dirty work, but I know that's not it. Izabel doesn't need anyone to do her dirty work. She's more than capable. And she likes it.

"You need this, Fredrik." She starts to walk past, but stops in front of me and looks at me with her soft green eyes. "You're my family," she says, "and I think you should let me help you the way Seraphina used to. And now after what you said before, about becoming the shell of the man you used to be, I'll make it my job to help you. Because I refuse to lose any members of my family. Do you understand?" It was more a demand than a question.

I say nothing, but I know I don't have to. I look down at the paper and then take it into my hand.

"Thank you, Izabel," I say and she nods and walks out of the coffee shop.

# TWENTY-FIVE

*Fredrik*

———

I couldn't bear to see Cassia again tonight. I need time to figure out what I'm going to do, because in the end I'm going to have to do *something*, and I'd rather it be of my choosing than to be blind-sided by whatever fate has in store. Though as history proves, I expect to be blindsided, anyway.

But more importantly, more than my need to take a step away from Cassia, my need for bloodshed must be nurtured.

I called Greta minutes before I left for the airport and told her to stay away from Cassia until I came back:

*"But what if she needs me for something? How long will you be gone?"*

*"No more than forty-eight hours,"* I said. *"Cassia will be fine on her own for that long."*

As usual, I could detect the frustration in Greta's voice though she tried very hard to hide it.

What Izabel did for me—well, it concerns me, and I'll address it more when this is all over because I can't deal with all of these things at once. But I won't be letting her risk herself for me like this. Besides, the last thing I need is for Victor to think something is going on between us. He wouldn't think twice about putting a bullet in my head when it comes to that girl. Unfortunately, I'm all too familiar with the feeling. I felt that way about Seraphina. And now, Cassia…

Dorian stretches his legs out, one into the aisle of the plane, and slouches far down into his seat. I stare out the window beside me into the blackness of the night sky forty thousand feet in the air over Washington State.

"I don't know what's gotten into you lately," he says, resting his head against the seat and crossing his hands over his stomach, "but you're really beginning to disappoint me."

I want to laugh at the seriousness in his voice.

"I was warned," he goes on, "that working with you wouldn't be easy. Like you were some kind of Sweeny Todd two-point-o."— I laugh softly to myself, anyway—"But truthfully, I'm finding you to be more wishy-washy than anything."

"Well, I could always offer *you* a seat in my chair, if you'd like," I say with a grin.

"Yeah, thanks, but no thanks, asshole." He readjusts his position, pulling his foot from the aisle. "But I *am* going to request a reassignment after I help you with this."

"You won't need to," I say, staring at the back of the seat in front of me. "Victor assured me that the Seattle job would be our last one working together."

His head falls to the side to face me.

"Really?"

I nod.

"Hm," he says sharply. "Wonder why he hasn't said anything to me about it yet."

"I don't know." I glance over at him briefly. "Perhaps the Seattle job wasn't over when you thought it was."

He shrugs and looks at the seat in front of him.

"I guess that would explain why we're going back," he says.

Yes, that might make sense if Victor was the one who sent us back to Seattle, but this time it's personal. Izabel was right—I need a job of my own to take off the edge. Like a drug addict needing a fix, I suppose. I never claimed to be any better than one.

I have a very special date with Kelly Bennings. For me *and* for Izabel.

Dorian glances over again

"No offense, of course," he says. "I'm just used to working with people more like myself. You know what I mean?"

I nod, still not looking at him.

"I know perfectly well what you mean," I say. "And I need to be free of you as much as you need to be free of me."

Dorian laughs under his breath.

"But I don't see there being many more like *you* waiting to take my place when I'm gone," he says with an air of comical disbelief.

"No, there won't be. Because men like me prefer to work alone."

"It's a lonely fucking world out there, Gustavsson." He closes his eyes. "I think if I were anything like you, I'd probably go crazy by myself, doing that demented shit that you do."

In a big way, Dorian is right. My life *is* a lonely one. And if I had my way with things, Seraphina never would've betrayed me years ago. She never would've killed those three innocent women. She never would've ran and left me to live in solitude without her. But more than anything, if I had my way, she wouldn't be sick and none of it would've ever happened to begin with and we'd still be together. I wouldn't *have* to be alone.

But it all goes to show that we're all probably better off on our own, anyway. Attachments make us weak and vulnerable. They fuck with our emotions. And I don't like my emotions fucked with.

Dorian and I are in Seattle before six the next morning. We get a rental car and find a hotel where we spend some of the day going over location information on Kelly Bennings and the client who hired us to take out Paul Fortright. According to the files there *is* a connection between Bennings and the client, Ross Emerson, who claimed that Fortright molested his daughter. All the information I need is right here in my jacket pocket. The rest is—and was—gut instinct and I've yet to be wrong about a person's guilt—except, of course, when a victim *pretends* to be guilty, which was a first for me and completely threw me off. But instinct can be a deadly weapon when one knows how to utilize it. I mastered mine when I was a boy. Because if I didn't, I never would've escaped my masters and I would've died a slave.

By nightfall, Dorian and I are waiting in the car parked in the front of Kelly Benning's current place of employment—a liquor store. Two hours later, after following her to a gas station, a fast food restaurant and finally to and from none other than the client, Ross Emerson's apartment, we have her stuffed in the trunk after she finally makes her way home and parks in the driveway.

Now, we're back in the same warehouse we used to interrogate her the first time, and she's just as defiant as she was then.

With my handkerchief, I wipe her spit from my face and then shove the handkerchief in her mouth.

"Mnnmmmnn!" Her stifled screams are most certainly filled with curses and threats. "Dmmnmmm-Mnnnmmooo!" The whites of her bugged-out eyes are in plain view. She thrashes against the wooden chair, causing it to jerk back and forth scraping against the concrete.

I really wish I had *my* chair to strap her to—makes things so much easier.

Dorian remains off to one side of the room, gun hidden away in the back of his pants, a look of impatience and discomfort on his pretty-boy face as he stands with his back against the steel wall.

Collapsing my hand around the back of an empty chair in a corner, I lift the legs from the floor and walk with it back over to Bennings, setting it down in front of her. Just like the last time. She glares at me through pale blue eyes framed by unkempt dishwater-brown hair. Her shouts and threats continue to come out as muffled nonsense, indecipherable yet completely obvious at the same time.

I cross one leg over the other and cock my head to one side. Then I glance down at the dirty gauze around her hand tied to the arm of the chair and I smile faintly, recalling what I felt when I drove Izabel's knife through it—complete and utter satisfaction.

I pull my own knife from the inside of my coat. Bennings' eyes lock on the blade and she stops screaming.

Leaning forward, I place the edge of the knife against the bare skin of her shoulder and drag it down the length of her arm without cutting her. I had stripped her before I tied her to the chair, and she sits in nothing but her miss-matched panties and bra, her bony legs shaking against the wood, her ribs clearly visible—she's about ninety pounds of wicked bitch. Pale skin that isn't beautiful, but sickly. Dark circles blemish the area underneath her eyes. I wonder what her drug of choice is, but don't care enough to ask and resolve to believe it must be heroin.

*But does Kelly Bennings really deserve to die?*

Still practically in her face, I say calmly, "If you spit on me again, I'll cut out your tongue."

She nods furiously with tears in her eyes.

Hesitating only a moment, I reach up with my latex glove-covered hand and remove the spit-soaked handkerchief from her throat—shoved back far enough that she couldn't have spit it out on her own—and drop it on the floor beside my feet.

"What the fuck do you want from me?!"

I tilt my head to one side.

"And lower your voice," I tell her, "because you're beginning to give me a headache."

Her eyebrows draw inward and she looks at me as if to say *What the fuck do I care?* but won't dare say it aloud. At least not yet. This one is bold and almost entirely fearless—it's just a matter of time before that mouth of hers gets her into more trouble.

"You set up that hit against your boyfriend, Paul Fortright, with Ross Emerson," I say, leaning back in my chair again.

"*What?* What the fuck are you *talking* about?"

She's not a very good liar when she knows she's done for.

"You know exactly what I'm talking about." I set my knife down on the top of my leg, covering it gently with my hand. "But what's even worse than setting up the hit on him, is that you were in on it with Ross Emerson to try and have Fortright put away in prison for child molestation—death would've been a better sentence."

Bennings' eyes grow darker and her mouth falls open.

"You're—You're *insane!* Why in the *fuck* would I do something like that?"

"Because you're a worthless bitch," I say simply, cutting in. "A waste of air"—I twirl my white gloved hand in the air above my shoulder—"It bothers me immensely that you're breathing mine right now." I drop my hand back on top of the knife. "You and Emerson set up the hit when the molestation accusations failed to put him away. To get Fortright out of yours and Ross Emerson's life. You—"

"You're crazy! Fuck you, you psycho motherfucker!" She thrashes in the chair again. "Let me out of here! Let me go!" She starts to scream at the top of her lungs.

"Shit, man, shut her up!" I hear Dorian say from the wall.

But I'm already leaning forward with the knife pressed against her arm again before Dorian finishes his sentence. I cut long and deep and blood pours from the slit. Bennings cries out in pain and agony as the left side of her body glistens with dark, red, *wonderful* blood.

"AHHHHH! FUCK!" Tears shoot from her eyes.

Finally she stops screaming and all that's left for her to do is tremble and stutter and bleed.

"A-All right! I helped Ross! I did! But what does that matter to you?! You people were supposed to kill him! That's what you were *hired* to do!"

I flash the blade in her view and she shuts up in an instant.

"You were willing to ruin an innocent man's life for another man. You could've just left him." My voice never raises.

She struggles against her restraints regardless of knowing she'll never free herself from them.

"I couldn't just leave!" she hisses. "Paul is a bastard! He threatened to take our daughter if I ever left him!"

"You don't care about your daughter," I say.

She looks shocked. And hurt.

I'm not buying it, and as much as I know she wants to believe it herself, I know she's not fully buying it, either.

"I love my baby girl! How can you say something like that to me?"

I inhale a deep, aggravated breath and adjust my back against the seat.

"Oh sure," I mock. "You love her enough to have her *innocent* father put in prison for child molestation." I cut a long deep slit down the length of her other arm just because I feel like it. She screams out again, but I continue calmly through her screams: "Not to mention, what you and Emerson put Emerson's daughter through with the police, brainwashing her to make her believe that she was molested." I've no physical proof of this, but I know it's a fact, nonetheless. "You and your love affair are the lowest of the low, Miz' Bennings, I have to say."

I'm just now noticing that at some point Dorian left the area. I knew it wouldn't be long once I started the cutting. But then again, he has another job to do, which is why I brought him along to begin with.

"Look, I-I don't know why you brought me here," Bennings stammers with thin quivering lips. "But Ross will pay you to let me go. H-He will pay you double what he was going to pay your organization to kill Paul. Just call him. Please. His number is in my cell phone. In my coat." She looks across the room at her clothes sitting in a pile on the floor.

"That won't be necessary." I cross my other leg and pull away from her, sitting as casually as if I were in a boring meeting. "But I'm interested in knowing why you believe that Ross Emerson would do something like that for you." One side of my nose curls into a faint snarl as I look her up and down. "Look at you—you're disgusting."

Shocked and thoroughly insulted, Bennings lashes out, "Go fuck yourself!" and it still amazes me how defiant and stupid this woman is to be in the situation she's in and can't keep her mouth shut.

I smile.

"So are you going to tell me?" I ask, tapping the bloody knife against my pant leg. "Or am I going to have to resort to more drastic measures of interrogation?"

As with anyone, I *really* hope she doesn't talk.

Bennings stares coldly at me, harsh lines forming around the edges of her pale blue eyes. Strands of her hair are scattered about her face and neck and collarbone, stuck to her skin by sweat even though it's cold in this warehouse.

I raise both brows asking her in gesture, *So what's it going to be?*

"Ross would do anything for me," she begins. "And I'd do anything for him. Anything!"

"Why?"

"Because we were meant to be together. Because I love him. Because he loves me. What more does there *need* to be?"

I smile again and look upon her thoughtfully.

"A valid reason to intentionally ruin or take away entirely, the life of an innocent person," I say, but find myself thinking only of Seraphina in this moment of personal divergence. "If you can give me one good reason, one valid and justifiable reason for what you and Ross Emerson did to Paul Fortright and the two defenseless children the both of you used to get what you wanted, then I will let you and Emerson go."

Bennings' trembling mouth snaps shut, her thin, cracked lips stretching into a hard line.

Then it dawns on her and her widening eyes dart to and from me and all around the cold, dimly lit, spacious area.

"What do you mean, let *us* go?" she asks carefully at first, but then her voice begins to rise. "Where is he? Tell me! Where is Ross?" She struggles against her restraints.

"He's in the other room," I tell her, glancing over my shoulder at the metal door that once led into an employee break room.

"You're lying," she accuses, but the worried look on her face says the opposite. "You're just saying that to—"

"To *what*?" I taunt her. "You have no more information that I need, Miz' Bennings, other than the last fairly simple question that I asked you." I smile faintly and shake my head. "But you and I both know that it's not a question you'll ever have an acceptable answer to. Because there's not one."

"The answer I gave you is enough!" she roars, her disheveled hair falling more about her face and sticking to her lips. "Yes! We love each other, you fucking bastard! And yes! We'd do *anything* for each other, even if it means ruining another person's life! Because that's what love is! It's the meaning of unconditional! *You* would never know!" She spits on the floor and looks at me with such hate and violent retribution in her wet and narrowed eyes.

I grit my teeth privately at her last comment.

Without taking my eyes off her, I call out to Dorian, "Bring Emerson in here!"

The sound of the metal door to the break room opening echoes through the large, empty space and Emerson steps through first with Dorian behind him with a gun pointed at Emerson's back.

"Ross! Ross!" Bennings cries out, nearly knocking herself over within the chair.

Leaning forward and tapping the blade of my knife against the top of her bare leg I say, "Volume, Miz' Bennings. Remember what I said about the volume of your voice and the attachment of your tongue."

She swallows hard and lowers her voice.

"Ross, I-I'm so sorry"—more tears stream from the corners of her eyes—"I'm so sorry!"

Dorian forces Emerson to walk the rest of the way with only the gun as incentive, while Dorian makes sure to stop next to me and not put himself in view of the hidden camera I have on them.

Ross is a short man with curly dark hair and broad shoulders and a look of terror and cowardice. Early thirties. Work boot construction-type who smells of cigarettes and cheap aftershave that he finds easier to pull off than showering. He wants to look at her, but he's scared. He keeps his dark eyes on the floor, his hands tied behind his back.

"Ross—"

"Please, Kelly, just be quiet," Emerson says in a low, defeated voice. "Don't make this any worse."

"Are you...pissed at me?" Bennings asks with intense worry.

Emerson shakes his head. "No, baby, no. I love you, you know that."

I roll my eyes and glance at Dorian. "Help Mr. Emerson have a seat, why don't you?"

Dorian grins. "I'd be delighted," he says properly and with a broad smile.

Two shots ring out. Emerson's cries fill the space as his knee-caps are taken out by the bullets. He falls to the cold floor onto his side, the side of his face hitting the concrete.

"What the fuck is *wrong* with you?!" Bennings screams. "He didn't *do* anything!"

I shoot up from my chair and wrench Benning's lower jaw in my hand, forcing her mouth open—always keeping my back to the camera. She tries to cry out but begins to choke on the saliva and tears draining into the back of her throat as I force her neck back. I grab her fleshy tongue amid her screams and her struggles and her gnashing teeth, forcing two fingers into the warm, flabby muscle underneath it, and my thumb on the top to maintain my grip; her eyes pried open by terror, all the bones and muscles in her body solidifying at once.

I put the blade to center of her tongue.

"Please! Don't hurt her! I'm begging you!" Emerson cries out from the floor, unable to lift himself into a sitting position, much less to his feet.

I pause indifferently with the blade still on her tongue.

"I know what we did was wrong," Emerson speaks out through troubled breaths and painfully twisted features. "Paul threatened her," he goes on. "Said if she ever left him and their daughter, that he'd make her life a living hell. That he'd take cus-tody of Abigail and force her to pay child support." He stops only long enough to catch his breath and let more pain shoot through his legs. "The plan was my idea. To accuse him of molesting my daughter. We just wanted him in jail. Out of the way. It was better than *killing* him."

I shake my head with disbelief.

"Better to live a life banished by society and by his own daughter because he wears the label of a child molester?" I laugh lightly and press the blade a little harder against Bennings' tongue, drawing blood. She cries some more, her eyes opening and closing from exhaustion and fear, but she doesn't dare struggle knowing that one wrong move could take her tongue off.

Emerson has no rebuttal.

"Do you see me, Mr. Emerson?" He looks up at me from the floor, pushing through his pain. "Tell me, what do you see when you look at me? Be completely honest. I won't hurt you for telling the truth."

Bennings' eyes move back and forth, at me and in the direction of Emerson, but he's too low against the floor for her to see.

Emerson appears baffled by the question, and leery of it just the same. It takes him a moment, but finally he begins to stammer. "Y-You're a man of justice."

I look upward in an annoyed and disappointing manner.

Dorian laughs from behind.

"That's fucking hilarious," he says. "He's being kind—*I'll* give you an honest answer."

"I didn't ask you," I say without looking at him.

"Well, I'm just sayin', you want the truth, I'm your guy." He laughs again and says below his breath, "A man of justice. Fucking hilarious."

I look only at Emerson.

"I said I wanted the truth."

"But...that *is* the truth."

With deep aggravation, I release Bennings' tongue and she gasps sharply, sucking back the saliva that had accumulated in her mouth that she could not swallow.

"You tell me the truth, Miz' Bennings." I know she's the only one of them that will. "What do you see when you look at me? This is your chance to get it off your chest without any repercussions."

Bennings sneers hatefully. "You're a sick *fuck—that's* what you are. Deranged. Demented." She spits on the floor again. "I bet you cut people into little fucking pieces for enjoyment, don't you? When I look at you I see a man who's not right in the head. A *sick fuck.*"

I smile gently and take a step away from her.

"What you're really seeing," I say, "is a man created by people like you. Evil incarnate who dance their way through society dropping poison on the tongues of the innocent. You deface, despoil and destroy the light in those who are still too young to control their own paths, by stripping them of their light and leaving only darkness." *Me. Izabel. Cassia.* "You're an infection. A malignancy. And you're right, Miz' Bennings, I *am* a sick fuck. I revel in what I do. I covet it. And I'll never stop because being a sick fuck who takes pleasure in torturing people like you who made me this way, is the only thing I can ever imagine being." I stab my knife into Bennings' uninjured hand, straight through the bone and the tendons and into the wood of the chair arm beneath it.

"FUUUUUCKKK!" she cries out.

Emerson cries out too, reaching a hand out to her, but still unable to move.

Casually, I step backward and out of view of the hidden camera and turn to Dorian.

"You might want to go wait in the car," I tell him.

"Don't have to tell me twice," he says, shoves his gun into the back of his pants and heads toward the exit.

"Jesus!" I hear him say to himself as he gets farther away. "I've *got* to get a reassignment."

The tall metal door closes behind him and I look back at Bennings and Emerson who know that this night has just taken an unfortunate turn.

I waste no time and get right to work.

# TWENTY-SIX

*Fredrik*

———

"How is she?" I ask Greta over the phone, sitting in my car at the airport after just arriving back in Baltimore.

"Well, from the video feed," Greta says, "she's doing just fine. But I don't feel right about this, Mr. Gustavsson. Cassia knows I'm here and it must be confusing to her why I haven't been down to see her yet."

"She'll understand."

Greta hesitates, likely rearranging the words she had been about to say, and says instead, "Will you be returning soon?"

"Yes. I'm already back in town. I have a few things I need to take care of and then I'll head that way. Expect me no later than midnight."

"Yes, sir."

This is it.

This is the moment in which I have to make a decision. I can't go back to that house until I figure it out. I can't because one look at her and my mind and emotions and decisions will be dictated by her and all my reason will leave me.

My hands tighten around the steering wheel as I stare out the windshield at the cold evening where exhaust swirls chaotically from the tailpipes of running cars. I watch people come and go from the airport parking lot, dragging their wheeled suitcases behind them through a lightly dusted snow-covered sidewalk. Businessmen. Couples returning from vacation or arriving here to spend the holidays with family. All normal rituals catered to by normal people. I've never dreamed of being like they are. You have to know a normal life before you can miss it and dream about having it again.

The only life I miss is the one I lived with Seraphina.

I leave the airport and find myself in the same diner I was in a few nights ago, and for the same reason—I can't go home. And the very same waitress who served me that night is also here on this night. She steps up to my table with a bright white smile and average-sized breasts and long dark hair pulled into a ponytail at the back of her head.

"Back again so soon?" she says, holding an order pad in the palm of her hand. "Can I start you off with some coffee?"

"Yes, thank you." I smile slimly and lay my arms across the table.

Watching her walk away, I study the perfect shape of her body—the curve of her hourglass hips, the roundness of her ass, the naked skin on the back of her neck where little strands of chocolate-colored hair have broken free from the ponytail holder.

But all I can see is Cassia.

Before the waitress comes back with the coffee, I've already left the diner and am heading straight for my house.

It's just after ten o'clock at night. There are two lights burning on the upstairs floor—the kitchen and likely the television in the den. I stare at the house for a long time, thinking about Cassia. About Seraphina. About how any of this could've ever happened.

I've made a decision.

I'm going to help Cassia. No matter what it takes, I'm going to help her get better. I remembered on the drive home what I had read in the files Izabel gave me:

The treatment to help Carrington cannot be successful if Carrington is not the personality that I'm treating.

But Cassia is here now and she has been for a year—*more* than a year because she's been living as her true self for a while, made a life for herself in New York. That has to mean something. That has to be good news. I will get her the best care in the world.

I'm going to help her.

I step out of the car and into the cold air, walking briskly up the sidewalk toward the front porch. But before I put my key in the doorknob, my instincts start going haywire. Greta never once peeked through any of the curtains while I sat in the driveway in the running car. I've not seen her shadow moving through the lights in the house. She's not eager to open the door for me.

The pit of my stomach grows into a heavy knot.

My mouth has run dry of saliva.

My heart is heavy.

I open the door carefully and peer inside the dimly lit house finding it eerie how quiet it is; only the low volume of the television in the den making any kind of noise.

"Greta?" I call out carefully.

No answer.

Then I hear the pipes squeaking and I recognize it right away as the shower being turned off. Letting out a heavy sigh of relief, I finally close the front door behind me and make my way into the kitchen, dropping my car keys on the counter. Slipping off my long black coat, I drape it across the seat of a barstool. Then I prop my hands on the counter and drop my head in between my rigid shoulders, looking down at the black marble counter.

"I thought you'd never come back," I hear Cassia's voice behind me.

Raising my head slowly, I turn it to see her standing there where the hallway wall and kitchen meet, dressed only in one of my button-up dress shirts. Her long blond hair is wet, lying against her back.

But something's very wrong with this picture. *Everything* is wrong with this picture and that voice in the back of my head is roaring in my brain.

Leery of her—confused, shocked, concerned—a gamut of emotions keep me stone-still, with my hands still braced against the bar, my shoulders as stiff as rock.

She walks toward me and I still can't will myself to move, and then she passes me up and moves around the bar.

"Where's Greta?" I ask carefully.

Cassia opens the fridge and peers inside, but I get the feeling it has nothing to do with any real interest in anything that's in it.

"Was *that* her name?" she says so casually that it sets my nerves on edge.

Then she closes the fridge with a beer in her hand and looks right at me. Popping the cap off on the edge of the counter, she places the bottle to her lips and takes a small drink, never taking her eyes away from mine.

"Where is Greta, Seraphina?" I ask once more and inhale a deep breath, trying to contain my calm façade.

Seraphina smiles, but it's a casual, innocent smile and not one of malice.

She sets the beer on the counter.

I finally straighten my back and let my hands fall away from the bar and down at my sides.

"I've missed you so much, love," she says and it wrenches my heart. "I'm not sure how you found me, or what I was doing downstairs with a chain around my ankle, but you found me fair and square and I always knew you would."

She walks back around the counter and steps right up to me—the scent of her skin intoxicating and familiar, her closeness even though still a few feet away, enough to make me relent, to want to push her violently against the wall and bury myself inside of her.

My heart is breaking.

I swallow hard and say, "Yes, I found you," but it's all I can get out.

Seraphina steps closer, placing the palms of her hands against my chest and her warmth sinks through my shirt and right into my skin.

"I was going to run," she says softly as her head slowly descends toward my heart. "I was going to leave, but I'm tired of running, Fredrik. I just want to be with you again. Where I belong."

My arms have collapsed around her body and I didn't even know it until looking down and seeing them there.

I shut my eyes softly and take her in, all of her, because it's been so long since I've felt her this close to me, was able to inhale her scent and feel the heat of her body against mine.

But I force myself quickly back into reality.

I pull away from her gently.

"What's wrong?" she asks, looking up at me with a slightly tilted head.

"Where is Greta?" I repeat.

"She's in the basement," she says as if it really doesn't matter. Then she smiles and grabs me by the hand. "Come with me, love." She pulls me along and reluctantly I follow her past the den where the television is glowing against the dark walls and then toward my bedroom.

That voice inside is screaming, but I continue to shut it out, my mind too perplexed and excited and regretful and relieved to do anything else.

Seraphina practically dances into my room.

She stops at the bed where she looks back at me while fitting her fingers around the buttons of my shirt she's wearing, breaking them apart. Then she stands before me naked, the dress shirt pooling around her bare feet.

I shake my head. "No," I say, taking a step back. I want her. I want her more than anything right now, but my conscience is beating the shit out of me. "I'm not doing this with you, Seraphina."

"Why not?" She approaches me, her slim, shapely hips swishing seductively as she moves, snake-like, the way only Seraphina could ever move.

Dragging her fingertips down my chest, she searches for my buttons next, but I carefully place my hands on top of hers and push them away.

"You can cut me, love," she whispers, turning her back to me so that I can see the scars I put there, and just imagining it makes me hard. "I know it's been a long time. How have you managed?"

I step away from her when really what I want to do is give in, to feel her underneath me again, to taste her love for me again.

But I can't. All I see in front of me is Cassia. Maybe it's the long blond hair, or that she's wearing no makeup, I don't know, but all I see is Cassia. And I could never hurt *her* like that.

"What's wrong with you?" Seraphina asks, starting to get impatient.

She looks up into my tortured eyes with her perplexed soft brown ones and then she steps closer, her mouth turned downward, her expression full of remorse.

*I can't do this.*

"Fredrik?"

"I…Seraphina, I can't do this." My hands come up and I spear my fingers through the top of my dark hair and then hold them there. "You betrayed me." I feel my voice rising, the anger inside of me rising. "I loved you. You were *everything* to me. My dark angel. My salvation. My sanity." I'm the one with tortured eyes now, I know. I look right at her. "I've looked for you for six years. SIX YEARS!"

My hands fall away from my head and become half-fists in front of me.

She steps even closer, her hands out in front of her too, reaching for me in her slow and careful steps.

"I know, Fredrik…I know and I can never forgive myself."

"You betrayed me!" I feel my face twisting in anger.

"I know!" Seraphina's eyes begin to glisten with moisture. "But I betrayed you because I loved you! Not because I loved someone else!"

"YOU DESTROYED ME, SERAPHINA!" My voice rips through the house.

She flings herself into my arms.

"But I love you! I've always loved you! Why can't you *forgive* me?" With her arms bent between us, her fingers grasp desperately at my shirt. "If you loved me so much, why couldn't you *forgive* me?!"

"I DID!" I thought I pushed her away, but I guess it was just my mind that did it—I'm holding her now instead. "I forgave you a long time ago, Seraphina. For years, I kept telling myself that when I found you I'd kill you." A tear falls from both of her eyes and trails down her cheeks. "But I knew, the deepest part of me knew, that I wouldn't be able to go through with it. I would've tortured you. Yes, I would've done that much. But I couldn't kill you."

Her hands move up to the sides of my neck and her touch sends a warm shiver through my body as if I'd just downed a shot of whiskey.

"But I'm here now," she says, looking into my eyes with all of her dark passion and love and sincerity—all of the things about her that I've hungered for for so long. "I'm here now and we can be together again. We can be like we used to be." She grasps my shirt tighter with emphasis. "We are a one of a kind pair, Fredrik. There is no one else out there like us. Apart, we'd die alone. Together, the way we were meant to be, we can be happy again."

Like the angel on my shoulder telling me to do the right thing no matter how sweet the wrong thing tastes, I see Cassia again. Cassia's face in front of me speaking with Seraphina's delicious, poisonous lips.

And I know that nothing can ever be the way it was.

Finally I manage to pull away from her, shaking my head not only at the words coming out of her mouth that I want nothing more than to believe, but at myself for giving them too much thought.

Her bright brown eyes narrow suspiciously.

"Who is it?" she asks with acid in her voice.

Stunned by her sudden change of attitude, I just look at her.

"Who is what?" I finally say.

"Was it—"she rears her head back, her eyebrows thickening in her forehead—"was it the old woman? Did you forget about me and replace me with an *old woman*?"

"No," I say with my hands out at her, trying to calm her down.

But I'm stunned again when instead of shouts and anger and accusations, she cries.

Seraphina falls to her knees, her face buried in her hands.

"I'm so sorry, love," she says in a shuddering, tortured voice. "I shouldn't have left you. I shouldn't have given myself to that man—I can't even remember his name."

"Marcus," I say it for her and I'm no less bitter about it today than I was six years ago.

"It's my own fault," she says. "I was afraid of love. I was afraid of *you*."

I kneel on the floor beside her and pull her against me wrapping my arms around her. This isn't the Seraphina that I remember. This isn't the woman I fell in love with. Seraphina was strong and proud and the only time I ever saw her cry was that night she killed that woman in my interrogation chair because she thought she was someone else.

Because she thought the woman was Cassia.

"Seraphina?" I say softly into her wet hair. I squeeze her tighter and stroke her back. "It wasn't Greta. I didn't fall in love with Greta."

Seraphina lifts her head from the crook of my arm and peers into my eyes.

I take her face into my hands and lean in kissing her softly on the forehead.

She appears confused. Worried.

"I fell in love with Cassia," I say.

Her whole body becomes rigid underneath my hands. Her eyes widen and lock in place as if she'd just seen the most traumatizing thing ever.

Then she shoves me away and jumps to her feet so fast that all I can do is jump back to mine.

"CASSIA?!" she roars. "You love *Cassia*?!"

I reach out grabbing her by her upper arms.

"YES!" I scream into her enraged face plagued by the worst betrayal. "You *are* Cassia! Don't you see?! Please tell me that you understand!" Tears are burning the back of my throat and the backs of my eyes, but I won't let them fall.

I shake her again, roughly, as if I could shake Cassia back to the surface again, but I know deep down that I've lost her.

I've lost her.

I've lost both of them, every part of the only woman I've ever loved or ever *will* love.

I've *lost* her…

"She betrayed me, Fredrik!" Seraphina shoves her body against mine, but I hold her still. "I spent years of my life in a goddamn mental institution because of her!"

"You *are* her!" My hands tighten around her arms so harshly that I know I must be hurting her. "You. Are. Cassia!" I want to make her understand. I just want her to be normal, to be…she can never be normal.

"Don't do this to me again," I say through an anguished voice, though I don't know what I'm saying—it's my heart talking, not my rational mind.

She breaks away from me and runs toward the bedroom door, but I grab her around the waist before she gets too far away and I wrench her back into my arms.

"Let go of me!" she screams.

"No. Not until you tell me who you are." I hold her close with her back pressed into my chest, my arms tight around her warm, naked form, my lips near her ear.

I want to cry.

"You know who I am! Now let me go!"

"Tell me your name." I can't open my eyes. I just want to savor this moment with her.

I just want to savor it.

My hands are shaking. My heart is alive again, but I know not for long. It's afraid. Afraid of what's going to happen to it when it knows she's gone forever, when every part of her is gone forever.

I squeeze her tighter, clutching her naked body against mine as if it's the last time I'm ever going to see her again. The tears are burning. Fucking burning!

"I'm Seraphina! You know me, Fredrik! I'm your wife! The only woman who has ever loved you!" Tears roll through her body and her struggling begins to subside. "*Please…*"

Suddenly she melts into me, surrendering not only to me but to the pain my words have caused. The weight of her body begins to drop as she slides down.

"Why would you love her," she says through uncontrollable tears, "of all the people in this world, why Cassia?"

I hold her tight and we're both sitting against the floor, her still wrapped in my arms, but now *wanting* to be here. I stroke her hair and kiss her temple and still the fucking tears are burning.

"Because she is you," I say softly into the side of her face. "And because you are her. I can help you if you'll let me, but you *have* to let her go. You have to let Cassia go."

*Please let her go…*

"I killed that woman in the basement," she says about Greta and even though I had a feeling she did, it's still difficult to hear her admit it. "I killed her because she wouldn't set me free." She sniffles back her tears. "I strangled her with the chain around my ankle. And then I took the key from her pocket to unlock myself."

"You didn't have to kill her," I say calmly, but I am anything but calm inside.

I continue to stroke her hair.

"Yes I did."

"Why? Why did you have to kill her?"

She turns around, her fingers clutching the sleeves of my shirt.

"Because she kept calling me Cassia." Her voice is calm and distant as though she's remembering it. "And because she wouldn't set me free."

She looks up into my eyes and it takes everything in me not to break down in front of her.

"I love you, Fredrik. I always have. You're the only person in this world that I've ever loved."

I choke back my tears and crush her against me. She cries into the side of my neck. I picture the two years that we were together, two short years that felt like forever. How she helped me and molded me and made me a better man and loved me. I picture how she loved me.

"Tell me your name," I say once more, hoping that this will be it, that she'll understand. "Just tell me your name and everything will be OK."

The silence between us seems like an eternity as I wait for her answer. My heart has stopped beating. My breath is caught in my lungs.

*Please let her go...*

"My name is Seraphina," she says and my heart fades to black and my breath releases in a long, drawn-out breath of anguish and sorrow.

Reaching for the knife just inches away underneath my bed, and with a heavy black heart, I move it between us and bury the blade in her chest. The burning tears finally burst through to the surface, and I let out a cry I never knew I could make. The warmth of her blood flowing onto my hand and onto my chest, I can feel it but I'm afraid to look at it. For the first time in my adult life as an interrogator and torturer, I don't want to see the blood because it hurts too much.

Her head falls back, bobbing unsteadily on her neck as she looks at me. A tiny trickle of blood seeps from one corner of her mouth. I lean in and kiss it away as sobs roll through my chest.

I haven't cried like this since I was a boy.

"I'm so sorry...I'm *so* sorry it had to be this way," I say through troubled breaths and a burning throat. "You're the only death I'll truly regret until the day I join you."

She reaches up her hand weakly and touches the side of my face. I do the same, letting my hand leave the knife and touching her cheek instead. Blood smears across her face from my fingertips.

She chokes and coughs up more blood.

"Don't regret," she says, but I don't know which one she is. "You saved me."

"Cassia?" I can't see through the tears in my eyes.

She smiles faintly and strokes my bottom lip with her fingers and I know that it's her. Cassia.

I kiss her bloody lips and embrace her tighter, feeling the handle of the knife pressing against me. Her eyes are getting heavier, her body weaker, her arms limper. I push her wet hair over her forehead where more blood stains her face, but I can't stop touching her, caressing her, being here with her in her last moment. *Our* last moment.

"I always loved you," I whisper onto her lips. "Everything about you, Cassia. And I always will."

Her hand falls away from my face and her head falls back limply on her neck. And when I see her dead eyes staring up at the ceiling I choke on my burning tears and crush her body against me, wailing until my chest hurts.

# TWENTY-SEVEN

*Izabel*

———

Fredrik's front door is unlocked when I arrive with the cleaners. I got a call from Fredrik two hours ago.

He wasn't himself:

*"Fredrik, what's going on?" I asked, surprised to hear from him again so soon.*

*Silence ensued.*

*"Fredrik?"*

*"I need you to come here," he said in such a quiet, distant voice that I wondered if he was calling me in his sleep.*

*"Is everything OK?" I said into the phone.*

*"What's going on?" Victor asked, rolling over in our bed and draping his arm over my waist.*

*I pulled my lips away from the phone and turned to Victor. "I don't know—something's wrong," I said quietly and I couldn't hide the worry and grief in my voice even if I'd tried. "I need to go see him."*

*I turned back to the call while Victor was switching on the bed-side light.*

*"Fredrik," I said with urgency, "I need you to tell me what's going on. I'll come there right away, but I just need to know what to prepare for. If anything."*

*I felt the bed move as Victor stood up and walked butt naked across the room to our bathroom.*

*Still not hearing Fredrik's voice on the other end, I sat all the way up in bed and draped my bare legs over the side of the mattress.*

*"I killed her," Fredrik said and my heart stopped—out of shock, but mostly it stopped for Fredrik.*

*I gasped and shot up from the bed.*

*Victor was looking right at me as he came back out of the bathroom.*

*"Tell him you'll be there soon," he said with a nod.*

*I thanked Victor with my eyes and said into the phone, "Fredrik, I'll be there soon. Just stay where you are. Don't leave, OK? Promise me you won't leave."*

*Nothing.*

*"Fredrik?"*

*My eyes never left Victor's then and I knew they must've been full of worry and fear. Fear only for Fredrik.*

*The phone went dead.*

*For a long time I just held it against my ear, thinking maybe he was just being really quiet. Finally Victor took it from my hand and it pulled me out of my worried and paranoid thoughts—would Fredrik hurt himself? Was he capable of doing something stupid? The thoughts put my nerves on edge.*

*"Get dressed and go see him," Victor said softly. "I'll make a call and have a car meet you there."*

*I nodded short and rapidly and then scrambled to get my clothes on. And before I left, Victor came up to me, kissed me on the lips and said, "And when you get back, I think it's time you tell me about Seraphina Bragado being in his basement."*

*He knew all along.*

*I stood there frozen before him, worried about what he was thinking of me, of Fredrik—of me and Fredrik. I was scared. I don't know why, but I was scared. Maybe because I knew that I could never, no matter how hard I tried, ever hide anything from him.*

*Victor kissed me on the mouth and brushed my hair away from my face with the side of his hand.*

*"I understand," he said. "Now go help him and keep me updated."*

*I nodded.*

*And then I left.*

Entering Fredrik's front door quietly, I peer in around the frame before I step all the way inside. The house is nearly pitch dark, only the faint blue hue of the moonlight beaming through few windows. It's quiet. So quiet. Not even the dripping of a faucet or the humming of the refrigerator or the central heat can be heard. But I hear my heartbeat, pumping blood anxiously through my heart.

Two of Victor's men start to enter the house behind me.

"Wait," I say, putting up my hand. "Stay on the porch until I tell you to come in."

Stopped in the doorway, they nod and step back outside, leaving the door open partway.

Walking carefully through the house, I stop in my tracks at the entrance to the den. Fredrik sits on the center cushion of the sofa with his long legs bent and his arms resting against his thighs, his hands dangling between them. His back is hunched over, his shoulders stiff.

He's staring at the floor in front of him. I glance over to see that the coffee table has been shoved off to the side, sitting crookedly against a leather chair.

"Fredrik, I'm here," I call out to him softly.

I approach him with caution—my heart tells me that he needs me, but also that's he's not in his right mind and he could be dangerous.

He won't speak.

I step a little closer. My heart is breaking for him.

"I'm here—"

"I need her out of the house," Fredrik says without looking up at me or moving a muscle in his body other than his mouth. "And the body in the basement."

I want to ask who 'the body in the basement' belongs to, but it's not the right time for that.

I nod even though he doesn't see me and call out to the cleaners—men designated to clean up our crime scenes—on the porch, "Come inside! And be quick about it!" Once they're standing at the den entrance I add, "There are two bodies. One in the basement, the other I don't know, but just find them and get them out of here."

They nod and walk away quickly to follow my orders.

I turn back to Fredrik, stepping up closer, the light sound of my boots tapping against the hardwood floor.

Finally I step all the way up to the sofa, remove my long white coat and set it on the cushion next to me as I sit down. Fredrik still won't look at me. He won't speak. He won't move. And I don't know what to say because there really is nothing that I can say to make him better.

We sit quietly for several long minutes while the cleaners move through other parts of the house. Thankfully, they know better than to carry the bodies back through the den and I hear them going outside from a back door, instead.

I look over Fredrik, as still as a statue, and I feel like I've lost my best friend, that his mind is gone because his heart is gone, and it's devastating to me.

Will he ever be the same?

Something tells me the answer is no.

A sort of darkness has consumed him entirely, inside and out, something so awful and merciless and unforgiving that it impregnates me with sorrow, and I feel hopeless all over again like I felt when I was imprisoned by Javier back in Mexico. I want to reach out and lay my hand upon his arm, but I'm too afraid.

Why the fuck am I afraid?

I do it anyway, relieved that Fredrik doesn't move his arm or refuse me. But he's not necessarily accepting of it, either, I know.

I wonder if he even notices.

"I would've done it for you," I say carefully. "It didn't have to be you, Fredrik."

He says nothing.

"You did what had to be done," I say even more carefully this time because I feel I'm walking a dangerous line with these kinds of words. "You gave that girl peace. I believe that." I pause and then add, "If it had been me, it's what I would've wanted."

"I know I gave her peace," he finally says, but still doesn't move.

Trying to comfort him, I brush my hand across his arm once before resting it in the bend, my fingers tucked into the inner part opposite side of his elbow.

"I'll stay here with you," I say gently, "if you need me to stay. I can sleep here on the sofa."

"No." He shakes his head and finally moves his arm so that my hand will fall away from it. "I'll be fine. I just needed someone else to remove the bodies."

"I understand," I relent, though I know that Fredrik is anything but fine.

"Maybe you should go—"

His head jerks around to the side and finally he looks right at me; the tortured look in his eyes puts me on edge. "I said no."

I nod.

But after a few seconds, I push away the part of me that wants to give in to what he says and I say what I really feel:

"I know you loved her. Both sides of her—I know. And I know that you feel like you'll never be able to live with yourself for how it all ended, or that you'll always be alone because you think there is no one else out there like her. I know."

I stop, expecting him to have already cut in and told me to shut up and leave, but still he offers no words of his own and I don't know how to feel about that. Relieved that he's listening to me? Concerned that he isn't? Worried about what's going on inside his head that's so all-consuming that I have to be surprised he hasn't spoken against me either way?

When still he shows no signs of rebuttal, I go on:

"This may sound insane—actually, I know it's going to sound insane—but I felt that way when I killed Javier."

Nothing but silence.

"After being with Javier for so long, it didn't matter that he raped me or kept me prisoner, because he was all I knew. I brainwashed myself into believing that only he would ever love me, that only Javier would ever want anything to do with me. And when I killed him, I felt like I killed the other half of me. If it wasn't for Victor—"

"One day, Victor Faust will be the death of you, Izabel," he cuts in and I'm stunned by his words. He looks over, locking his eyes on mine. "If you want to help me, you can by keeping that in the back of your mind. One way or another, you're going to die because of him, *because* you love him."

I want to argue, to fight back and tell him that he's wrong, but I know he's hurting and I can't make this about me. I won't.

He looks away.

"Tell Victor that I'll accept any sentence he feels fits my offensives."

"Fredrik—"

"Please just go," he says looking down at the floor. "I give you my word—I'll be fine. I don't want you worrying about me, least of all."

"But—"

"Please, Izabel!" he snaps.

I stand up and look at him for a moment before taking my coat up from the cushion.

I don't even bother putting it on as I begin to walk away.

Stopping at the den entrance with my back to him, I say evenly, "I'm going to help you. Just like I did with Kelly Bennings. For as long as it takes."

Once again, he says nothing, and with a heavy heart I leave the house and step out onto the porch just as the cleaners are making yet another trip outside from the backyard. But all three of us stop mid-stride down the sidewalk when a vociferous *crash*, like glass breaking, fills the night air coming from inside Fredrik's house. And then more glass. And the sound of furniture crashing against the walls.

I feel the cleaners' eyes on me, but I can't tear mine away from the house where Fredrik is feeling the worst pain he's ever felt, just on the other side of those walls.

# TWENTY-EIGHT

*Fredrik*

———

Every last bit of furniture, I destroy, flinging chairs and shattering tables against the walls as if rejecting its right to exist if Cassia can't exist. If Seraphina can't exist. Anything that gets in my way, I move it with violent, resentful force.

I scream at the top of my lungs before grabbing the last standing chair and hurling it through the den and into the television screen. The glass shatters and what's left of the frame falls over onto the floor sending pieces of glass scattered across the hardwood.

I follow suit, unable to maintain my footing, and fall against the floor on my bottom in the center of the room, surrounded by destruction—destruction of objects, but also the destruction of what was left of a man. Sitting helplessly with my legs bent at the knees, I do the only thing fate will allow me to do in this moment—I cry into the palms of my hands, letting the pain do with me whatever it wants. The same way I did when I was just a boy, after I had been beaten and raped and broken. Only this time, the pain I feel inside is a hundred times more unbearable.

Blackness. All I see is blackness though my eyes are wide open as I look downward at the floor. And in that fucking blackness I can still see her face. Her light brown eyes and plump lips. Her soft, creamy skin and near perfect complexion. Long blond hair. Short black hair. And I know that she will haunt my soul for the rest of my days, however many of them there are left to suffer.

And I know I deserve it.

Without another thought, I jump up from the floor and rush into the kitchen, flinging open the cabinet underneath the sink. On my hands and knees, I shove the top half of my body through the opening, furiously swiping away bottles of cleaner and other various supplies. When I don't find what I'm looking for, I jump to my feet again and do the same to all the cabinets, tossing out boxes of food onto the kitchen floor. Finally, in the cabinet above the microwave, I find a bottle of lighter fluid and I storm toward the hallway with it clutched in my hand, but tripping over debris on my way and falling. My back hits the wall as my hands hit the floor to brace for the impact, but as soon as I'm in control of my body again, I pick the bottle of lighter fluid up from beside me and hurl myself down the hallway. Swinging open the basement door, I fly down the steps taking them three at a time and almost falling again, but I make it to the bottom of the stairs unscathed.

I spray the lighter fluid everywhere, starting with Cassia's bed and when the bottle is empty I toss it on the floor and just stare at it without moving until my legs become numb beneath me. I look at the chain stretched across the floor and then at the corner of the room where I often found Cassia sitting when I came home.

Sobs roll through my body and I'm unable to stop them.

Tearing my eyes away from all that is left of her, I look around the room for anything I can use to set the fluid aflame, and when I find nothing I'm up the stairs and back down here again so fast it feels like I never moved from this spot.

Cassia's thin white nightgown lies in a small silky pile next to my feet. I reach down and take it into my fingers, wanting to put it to my face and breathe in her scent one last time. But I don't. I set it aflame with the lighter in the other hand and then toss the quickly burning fabric on the fluid-soaked bed. The room is engulfed in seconds.

And I realize as I stand here watching the flames lick the walls, that I've come full-circle and there is no going back.

# TWENTY-NINE

*Fredrik*

———

*Two months later...*

Victor Faust owns a fancy new building just outside of Boston and he's quite proud of it, though one wouldn't know by his expressionless face—oh wait, he just smiled. I walk alongside him toward his private office, impressed with the building so far with all of its Old World charm, original stone walls and newly furnished marble floors and stunning artwork in large intricate frames. It's certainly fitting of a man like Faust, and I have to say, as much as I love the rich, modern style, I could get used to this. But it's a special building for all of us in Victor's new Order, because it's the first place we've been able to meet and conduct business that feels more like a business than a hideout in a back alley somewhere.

We're out in the open—somewhat—hiding in plain sight.

The word is that Vonnegut is threatened by Victor—by *all* of us. And while although we still have to watch our backs every minute of every day, we're gaining the upper hand.

Sometimes I think the only reason Victor ever chose to hide in the first place had everything to do with Izabel. He would do anything to keep her safe—of course, he can't tell *her* that.

We step into the private office with scaling walls lined by bookshelves packed with leather bound books from floor to nearly the ceiling. A large elongated table sits as the centerpiece of the vast room, occupied by eight high-back dark leather chairs on each side and one at each end. Attending this meeting today other than Victor and myself are the usual: Izabel, Niklas, Dorian and even James Woodard who Victor has decided to keep with us as his official information go-to guy. Woodard has grown on me, I admit. Dorian, not quite so much.

"Well, look who it is," Dorian says from his seat with a grin, "the guy bringin' crazy back."

Dorian was finally reassigned to a new member of our Order that I think might despise him more than even I did—a highly skilled spy named Evelyn Stiles who used to work for the CIA. But she hasn't been fully tested here yet and has no business at this meeting. James Woodard got in faster than the usual, but I trust Victor's judgment.

I take a seat next to Izabel. She smiles over at me, but doesn't say anything. The two of us haven't spoken much since the night I killed my wife two months ago in Baltimore. But the distance I put between us has been all my doing. I can't have her involved in my life the way she wants to be—or the way she used to be. I'm not the man I was when Izabel—as Sarai—and I first met. And as long as I'm in control of my life, that's the way it will stay. I don't want to love anyone—in any manner or situation—because to love is to *be* controlled. I will always care for Izabel and look after her and I will kill for her, but I can't let myself love her, not even as my sister, or my friend. I don't want Izabel, of all people, to end up like everyone else I've ever loved.

Despite the distance I keep, she still has it in her head that she's going to help me with 'personal' interrogations and tortures the way that Seraphina did.

But she is very wrong.

I have other plans for that.

Woodard smiles above that double chin of his and pushes a newspaper across the table toward me with his pudgy hand.

"You might like this news, sir," he says—always respectful, always terrified of me.

I glance at Victor once just as he's taking his seat at the head of the table, and then look down into the newspaper which has been folded over to the second page. It takes me a moment to realize it's a paper from Seattle.

Scanning over the text and images, my eyes fall on two small photos in one corner set side by side of Kelly Bennings and Ross Emerson in convict-style mug shots. As I read, the paper reveals how after a 'traumatizing and brutal kidnapping and interrogation by two unknown men' that the couple are 'facing years in prison after incriminating video evidence had been dropped off at the Seattle police department, which included their confessions and their crimes in full detail'.

I lean back against my chair, cross one leg over the other and say indifferently, "They're getting what they deserve."

I don't look at the newspaper again. And I don't think about it again.

"The reason I brought you all here today," Victor speaks up with one hand atop the other on the table, "is that I have significant news."

He has the room's full attention.

"Seems that Vonnegut has united with Sébastien Fournier's order in France and they're working together for one reason." He raises only his index finger from the top of his other hand. "I trust you all know very well what that reason is."

"Because they're fucking scared," Niklas chimes in, sitting to Victor's left; an unlit cigarette dangles from his lips.

Dorian shakes his blond head, smiling. "I say we just get it over with and take them *all* out."

"Can't kill someone you can't find," Izabel reminds him.

Vonnegut and Fournier have both proven elusive since Victor Faust went rogue from The Order.

"That's not entirely true," I speak up. "We've been taking them out slowly but surely by killing those loyal to them and taking control of those who aren't."

"Yes, Mr. Gustavsson has a point," James Woodard says and smiles across the table at me with a little too much admiration for my tastes.

I ignore him.

"Yes, but that's not even the most significant news I have for you," Victor says and all heads turn simultaneously back in his direction.

Victor pauses and steeples his hands in front of him.

"I have reason to believe—and for now I will not reveal my sources—that the U.S. Intelligence somehow knows about our operations. Not only are we being hunted by The Order, but we might also be hunted by the FBI and the CIA."

"What do you mean 'might'?" Izabel asks from Victor's right, her eyes filled with concern. "And what exactly do they know?"

Everyone, including me, want the same answers, so no one interrupts.

"What they know is also something I'm going to keep to myself for now," Victor says evenly, looking at no one in particular. "It doesn't surprise me that they know some things—operations like ours which continue to grow cannot be entirely inconspicuous—quite impossible, actually. But I *will* say that they know enough to lead me to believe that there might a mole our midst."

I look at Woodard. Woodard looks at me until he realizes *why* I'm looking at him and he shrinks his back against his chair and opts for looking at the table instead. Izabel looks at Niklas. Niklas looks at Dorian and then looks right back at Izabel with the same accusing eyes she's casting his way. Dorian looks at me. There sure is a lot of suspicion at this table.

We all look at Victor, though only with question on our faces.

"Someone at this table is a traitor?" Izabel asks.

"Well, it sure as fuck isn't me," Dorian says.

Woodard puts up his inflated hands. "I-It ain't me neither."

Niklas pulls the cigarette from his lips and slouches in his chair, draping one arm over the back casually and coolly. "Yeah, well other than my brother," he says with pride and confidence, "I'm the last person at this table who'd involve this shit government in *anything.*" I picture Niklas spitting on the floor to show how deeply his aversion for the U.S. government and intelligence goes, but he doesn't.

"*You're* my first pick," Izabel accuses, her pretty features twisting into a smirk.

Niklas flips her off.

"Oh, how mature can you get?" Izabel scoffs.

Victor inhales a noticeable breath and all eyes fall on him again.

"I never said the mole—if in fact there is one—was at this table. And truly, it could very well be that Vonnegut, as a last ditch attempt to get rid of us, is the one who provided the CIA and the FBI with the information. I have my suspicions, but the dilemma is that if they *do* know how and where to find us, why haven't they made a move?"

"That's a good question," I say and then add, "If they know, how *long* do you think they've known?"

"I'm not sure," Victor admits. "But I want all of you to be on the lookout for anything suspicious—of course, not that you don't already do that."

THE SWAN AND THE JACKAL

Dorian and Niklas both laugh.

"That's daily life for me," Dorian says.

Niklas nods, agreeing.

Victor changes the subject—a little too soon, in my opinion—and says, "Next order of business is a fifty thousand dollar hit in Miami. I'm assigning this one to Evan Betts"—he looks to his left—"and Niklas."

Niklas doesn't look pleased.

"You're putting me with a newbie?" In fact, he looks outright offended.

Izabel, on the other hand, is all smiles.

"Betts may be new," Victor says, "but he's good. I want to see more of his work and I'll only pair up newcomers with someone from this table that I feel I can trust."

Niklas appears more accepting now, but Isabel's smile turns into a sneer.

The meeting goes on for another twenty minutes and as it's coming to a close, everyone leaves but myself and Victor, who requested that I stay.

I've been out of commission—by Victor's orders—since what happened two months ago. I had expected more of a sentence than the 'time off for personal issues' that I feel I was given, but Victor didn't see my keeping Cassia a secret from him, a betrayal. It only further proves that Faust is not a tyrant leader, but a man with a conscience—though he sure goes out of his way to hide that fact.

But my time off alone to deal with what's left of my life didn't have the sort of effect that anyone at the 'round table' might've expected. I didn't grieve or come to terms or have any epiphanies. I didn't remove any heavy burdens from my shoulders, or bathe in the sun, or reflect on my life and force myself to be positive and move forward.

No, I didn't do any of that.

Instead, I stood in front of a mirror.

Naked. Still bloody after torturing and killing a man who led a notorious gang in Detroit. I stood in front of that mirror as the shower water got hot and I saw the shell of my former self looking back at me with new insides. New darkness. New demons. New memories. New everything. And yes, I did move forward, but not in the direction of the light.

That finite glimpse of light I experienced with Cassia was an illusion.

"I have to be honest with you," Victor says standing behind me. "I'm not convinced you're...yourself."

I nod, standing with my hands clasped together behind me.

"And you would be right," I admit.

Victor walks slowly around the table away from his chair, also with his hands clasped behind his back just as mine are.

"If you were anyone else," he goes on, "I wouldn't risk it, but all I'm asking of you is to back away from our operations at the first sign you feel that something you might do could compromise us. Can I trust you to do that?"

I nod again. "You have my word."

Victor glances at the wall and then looks back at me as if he had used that brief moment to decide what to say next.

"I have every bit of trust in you, Fredrik, but I would be fooling myself to believe that you're not walking the thin line between sanity and self-destruction. I've seen that look before—in fact, I saw it in the mirror once."

How ironic—the things we see in those malicious, mocking pieces of glass.

"I would ask how you, of all people, ever walked that line," I say, "but I know you won't tell me."

Victor smiles faintly.

"And you would be right," he says in the same even tone as I had said it to him moments ago.

"Despite my acceptance of all this," Victor says dropping his smile, "I do have to make something very clear."

I say nothing and just listen. This is the part where Victor hangs up his suit of understanding and steps into his threatening one.

"Izabel"—I knew he would begin his sentence with—"has it in her head that she's going to—"he motions a hand, twirling three of his fingers as if allowing the right term to materialize on his tongue—"*aide* you in finding people to torture, but you and I both know that's unacceptable. Correct?"

"Yes, you are correct," I say with a nod. "I don't need her help, nor do I want it. I did it on my own before, and I can do it again. If she tries to help me, I'll tell her that you'll be the first to know about it."

"I appreciate that."

I pause, wanting to ask a personal question, but not sure if I should probe.

I decide to, anyway.

"Does it bother you," I say, "that she and I were so close?"

"No," Victor answers truthfully. "Not in the way that you might be thinking. I trust Izabel alone with you—with any man— if that's what you're referring to."

"In a way it was, yes," I say. "But really I meant it in every way. She kept things from you in order to help me."

"You are her family," he states. "She's never really had one. I'm glad that you're there for her. You can give her things that I may never be able to give."

I shake my head once, rejecting his words with all due respect.

"Not anymore."

He doesn't look surprised.

"You do know that it'll crush her if you push her away."

I nod.

"Better to push her away now than to be the reason she ends up dead later." Part of that was also meant for Victor to heed, but I may never know if he understood the hidden message.

Victor leaves it at that and gestures his hand toward the tall, heavy wooden door behind me.

"It's good to have you back," he says.

"Thank you."

Izabel stops me in the hallway lined by off-white walls and shiny floors. Victor walks in the opposite direction, leaving us to be alone.

She waits until he rounds the corner at the end of the hall before she turns to me and says, "I know he probably threatened you because of me, but look, Fredrik—"

"He didn't have to threaten," I stop her. "I told him that if you ever try to help me that I'll tell him about it right away. And I mean that." I hold my unwavering gaze on her.

"But you're...Fredrik, I'm afraid for you. I just want to help."

"And you *can* by staying out of my way and out of my business."

A flash of hurt and conflict passes over her face.

"Why are you doing this?"

I start to walk down the hall, stepping around her.

"Fredrik. Stop. Please."

Finally I do, but only to let her get it all out, to say whatever's on her mind now because it'll be the only chance I ever give her.

I stand still with my back to her.

"I'm not going to let you destroy yourself," she says with buried anger and not-so-buried determination. "I don't give a shit what kind of face you want to wear—tell me to fuck off, I don't care—but I won't let you fall away. From us. From me. From yourself."

I turn around to face her with my hands folded together down in front of me, my wrists touching the fabric of my fine black suit.

"You're a little late for that, I'm afraid," I say, turn around and walk away; the sound of my dress shoes tapping against the floor left in my wake.

# THIRTY

*Fredrik*

——

*Baltimore, Maryland*

Yanking back on the woman's long dark ponytail, I ram my cock inside of her, my hips thrusting powerfully against her ass cheeks, her hands grasping the hotel bed sheet in a fit of pleasure and desperation.

"Holy fucking shit!" she says with one side of her face pressed against the mattress. She wrenches her bottom lip between her teeth as I slam into her harder, my cock swelling inside of her.

She gasps, parting her lips, unable to close them. "Oh my god, please…don't stop! Don't fucking stop!" She's nearly crying. I can feel the tension and anticipation tightening around my cock as if to keep me from pulling out of her before her explosive moment. I slam into her cunt harder and lean over and across her body, sticking my fingers into her opened mouth, hooking her cheek. Pulling back her ponytail with the other hand, her neck arches stiffly and awkwardly—if I pull any harder her neck might break.

I thrust in and out of her violently, satisfying all of my demons, but not myself. Not yet. She begins to whimper, forcing her ass toward me so that she can take me deeper.

A tear rolls down her cheek and discolors the sheet beneath her face.

I stop and pull out of her when I sense she's going to come and I stand up from the bed, my cock throbbing painfully against my lower stomach. I take it into my hand and work on it myself slowly to maintain, but decelerate my own climax.

The woman, still with her ass raised in the air, lifts her face from the mattress and looks across the room at me as if I'd just punched her mother.

I snap the condom off and toss it in the trash next to the nightstand.

"Why'd you—"

"Come here," I tell her, jerking my head back once and taking a seat on the chair at the small table by the window.

With slight protest on her face, she still gets up from the bed and does as I tell her. Standing naked in front of me with that perfect body and nicely rounded ass and curved hips, I really do want to fuck her some more, but that'll have to wait.

"Get on your knees," I tell her.

She does, and already assuming she knows what I want her to do, she takes my cock into her hand without my direction—gawking for a moment at the size, I suppose—before she begins to lower her mouth down on it.

"Did I tell you to do that yet?" I ask her, looking down at her under hooded eyes and an even expression.

She shakes her head, looking up at me with green doe-like eyes and with my cock still in her hand.

I make her wait a few long seconds as I study her knelt between my legs, the way her ponytail rests against the center of her bare back, the heart shape of her bare ass. She looks the same way I imagined she'd look naked when I visited her at the diner and thought about fucking her.

She never once lets go of my cock. She wants it and she doesn't care where. She likes having it in her hand. And I don't mind one bit.

"Now put me in your mouth," I say. "Slowly," I add just before her lips begin to slip over the head.

My cock fills her mouth, stretching her lips around it—also like I imagined. I tilt my head back and groan a little as she takes me into the back of her throat.

I raise both of my hands to the back of my head and interlock my fingers as I watch her between my splayed legs. I'm turned off when she stops to apologize for scraping me with her teeth—not because she scraped but because she apologized. I say nothing and let her get back to work.

But she does it again.

I stop her mid-sentence, collapsing my large hands about the sides of her head and forcing my cock into the back of her throat. "I don't care if you scrape me, sweetheart—I *like* the pain."

She gags a little as she takes me all the way in, but doesn't stop, or protest the force I continue to put on her head. I hate those gagging noises, but they excite me just the same—her discomfort, her pain, the burning tears in her eyes.

I'm a sick bastard.

Finally I explode in her mouth, throwing my head back, my fingers wound tightly in her hair and holding her down so she'll swallow.

And she does. Like a good girl.

We rest for a little while. I never get up from the chair. I just stare toward the wall, thinking of no one but her, though I can't remember her name. Kate. Kira. Kali. I hope she doesn't ask.

She comes out of the bathroom, parading herself toward me. Shy, not-so-shy, whorish, innocent, dominant, submissive, a bitch, a sweet girl—she'll be anything I tell her to be.

And that's precisely why I don't like her much.

I had moderate hopes for this one before I brought her here.

Trial and error, Fredrik. Trial and fucking error.

"Why don't you let me ride your cock," the girl whose name surely begins with a K says with a grin in her eyes.

*Why don't you just ride my cock and not ask my permission?*

"Yeah," I say aloud, "I want you to ride my cock," and then I tear open another condom package from the nearby table and put the condom in her hand.

"Put it on me first," I tell her.

Again, she does exactly what I tell her, and—I admit—she does it well, sliding it down on me with careful precision, making sure to cop a feel of my balls when she's done, before letting go and standing up between my opened legs.

Placing her hands on my shoulders to steady herself, she steps over my lap and straddles me on the chair. I'm hard again in under a second. I close my eyes softly when I first feel her warm, wet and swollen nether lips rubbing against my shaft.

She fucks me for a while. And when I'm tired of sitting on the chair, I bend her over the end of the bed and fuck her there for a little while more. And when I'm tired of that, I fuck her against the wall. And when I'm tired of standing, I lay with my back against the bed and let her ride me some more before finally giving in and telling her to sit on my face.

A couple of hours later I'm coming out of the shower when she says to me from the bed, "Ready for another round?" with a suggestive smile plastered all over her very beautiful face.

I barely look at her as I step into my boxers after picking them up from the floor.

I glance at my Rolex.

"Sorry, but I have somewhere I need to be soon."

She pouts. "Ah, come on. I'll make it worth it. I promise." She pats the mattress with the palm of her hand.

Stepping into my dress pants I button them and then buckle my belt.

"You've already made it worth it," I say evenly. "But I've really got to go."

While buttoning my gray dress shirt and tucking the ends into my pants, she gets up from the bed and walks naked the short way across the room. She steps right up to me and places her hands on my chest, but I turn sideways away from her and finish up the last buttons.

I notice her shoulders rise and fall with one heavy, disappointed breath.

"Well, you mind giving me your number?" she asks. "I'd like to see you again."

I slip my arms down into my suit jacket and then put on my long black winter coat.

"Sorry, but that's not going to happen," I say.

"What do you mean? Why not?"

I don't look at her as I make my way to the door.

"The sex was great," I say, turning to look back at her and hoping to leave her with her dignity, at least. It was never my intention to make her feel used. "But we won't be seeing each other again."

She just stares at me with a slack mouth and her eyebrows bunched in her forehead.

And I walk out the door.

—

I only came back to Baltimore for one thing and it certainly wasn't the sex.

I drive to the opposite end of town and park beside a dumpster on the side of a convenience store building, locking my doors with the press of the button on my key ring when I get out. The smell of gasoline from the car filling up at the pump fills the air. I walk slowly toward the front double glass doors and push one open to the sound of an electronic bell alerting the clerk of a new customer entering the store—the clerk doesn't look up from whatever he's doing behind the counter. I step into the heat to the stench of fried food, dirty mop water and bleach. A young boy with scruffy blond hair comes out of the restroom from a door on the other side of the drink coolers and zips past me, pushing the tall glass door open with all the weight of both of his skinny, boyish arms. A burst of cold air rushes inside. I watch the boy from the door for a moment as he runs toward the car at the pump, swings the back door open and jumps inside. Seconds later the car pulls onto the street and drives away.

I turn my focus back to Dante Furlong working behind the counter.

Making my way toward him, I take my time, nonchalantly scanning the various overpriced gas station junk foods and individually wrapped snack cakes and tiny cans of bean dip displayed on outside shelves. Everything is lined in an orderly fashion. The floor has been mopped recently. Dante has been hard at work—on something other than selling heroin and letting addicts suck him off for a fix.

Finally Dante looks up.

He does a double-take.

The smile that only got as far as his eyes flees at the sight of me. He sucks in a sharp gasp and falls backward against the shelves displaying various medicines—two-pack Tylenol's and

Advil's and cold and flu capsules—and merchandise falls from the brackets into a scattered mess against the floor.

"It's you!" He points a shaky finger at me. "Look, man, I haven't...I-I haven't done anything since that night! I swear it!"

He got himself a pair of upper dentures, I see.

Still stumbling backward into the shelf as if he could walk right through the wall behind him, more merchandise ends up on the floor until finally he realizes he has nowhere to go.

His entire body—dressed quite decently in a nice white shirt and a pair of clean blue jeans—shakes feverishly. His beady blue eyes seem as big around as my fists can be; the wrinkles and lines around them and in the corners deepen and stretch and pulsate. His curly black hair has been washed and doesn't look oily underneath the burning fluorescent lights above us in the ceiling. He has certainly changed since I tortured him two months ago.

I step the rest of the way up to the counter and stand with both hands buried in my coat pockets. Dante's eyes move back and forth from my face to my hands, likely worried about what I might be hiding in them behind the fabric of my coat. Needles to shoot him up with? Pliers to pull out the rest of his teeth? A knife to cut out his tongue, perhaps? A gun to put him out of his misery?

None of the above.

"Look, I didn't say nothin' to no one," he stutters with one hand facing me, palm forward. "I haven't said shit. I haven't *did* shit." He looks around the store. "I've got myself a real job here. It doesn't pay jack, but it's an honest job." Then his voice rises and cracks when I still don't respond: "I haven't done *anything!*"

"I know," I finally say. "I've been keeping tabs on you since I let you go that night."

Looking down at a box of gimmicky gum on the counter, each wrapped individually in clear plastic wrappers, I point and say, "Do you mind?"

"Sure, sure, yeah," he says quickly, gesturing both hands at the gum. "It's on the house, man. In fact, you can have anything in this fuckin' store you want." He smiles squeamishly.

I take a single piece of gum from the box and remove the plastic wrapper, popping it in my mouth.

"I see you got new teeth," I say and then start chewing.

He nods rapidly. "Y-Yeah, I uhh, well there's a nice dentist on the other side of town who helps addicts tryin' to get clean. I didn't actually lose my teeth because of Meth or anything"—I smile and continue to chew—"but he helped me. Got me a denture for real cheap and put me on a payment plan. I'll have it paid off in a few more months."

I slip my hands back inside my pockets.

"How would you like a set of permanent implants?" I ask.

Dante's eyebrows draw inward confusedly.

"I don't know what you mean?" He's extremely nervous.

I think I smell urine.

I make a face. "This gum tastes like shit," I say.

He nods rapidly again, uncertain and still fearful of my every movement and word. "Yeah, kids like that stuff…"

"Well, Dante," I go back to the important matter, "I have a job proposal for you. That is, if you're interested in hearing it."

Silence.

He doesn't know what answer he wants to give, but is sure he knows what answer I want to hear.

He opts for the in between.

"Umm, I'm not sure I understand."

Bringing the little plastic wrapper up to my lips, I spit the gum back into it and then toss it in the trash can pressed against the counter on the floor.

"I've been giving it some thought," I begin still in the same casual manner I walked in with, "and I believe you're the right kind of man for the job. You can pay off those dentures with just a fraction of your first paycheck and afford dental implants within a month. Of course, you'll be put through some tests—medical, among other things—and like with any honest job, you'll be subject to piss tests every now and then, but I think you're the right man. What do you say?"

"Umm, well"—he scratches his head—"what exactly is the job? I mean, uh, I guess I'd want to know what was expected of me…well, I mean, if it's OK I know before I agree?"

Yes, that's definitely urine I smell.

I pull out a cashier's check with his name on it and put it on the counter, sliding it into his view.

He glances down nervously, having a difficult time looking only at it with me standing close enough to grab him when his guard is down.

"Holy fuck…" his voice trails off and finally keeping his attention on me is put on the backburner as the five figures next to his name dance in his line of sight.

He takes the check into his hand as if to make sure that it's real, then finally he looks back up at me through those blue eyes wide on display underneath his curly black hair.

"You can make that much every month," I say. "As long as you perform at the job to my complete satisfaction and approval and as long as you stay clean and don't fuck up."

His eyes are finally smiling again, just like they had begun to do when I first walked into the store and he hadn't noticed who I was yet. Now his whole face is smiling. Greedily. Like a pirate standing over a chest of gold. The job could be sucking *me* off once a week and he'd likely agree to it for that much money.

"I'm your guy," he says.

I smile faintly and pull out my wallet from the other pocket, opening it and fingering a twenty into my hand. I toss it on the counter.

"I'm going to pull my car around to the pump," I say. "Give me twenty bucks."

He nods and takes the money.

"Wait, uhh," he calls out as I start to walk away—I stop and turn to face him. "How do I—?"

"I'll be in touch," I say and push open the glass door.

Dante Furlong became my private assistant. He knows a lot of drug dealers and addicts who can never be reformed, and whores, or 'lot lizards' who have killed men—truck drivers and husbands looking for some 'strange'. Dante knows just about everyone in the crime ring not only in Maryland, but most of the surrounding states. He knows the lingo. He knows the ins and outs, and where to find all of the people who will one day end up in my chair.

Sometimes when thinking of Seraphina—because I do think of her as well as Cassia—I wonder why I didn't just find someone like Dante a long time ago. With him there are no attachments, no risk falling in love, no risk losing love. I can look Dante in the eye and kill him if I have to without thinking twice about it, or regretting it, or hurting over it. And when I want to fuck, I can find the Kate's and the Kira's and the Kali's and the Gwen's. No attachments. No looking back. Just moving forward. Onto the next willing woman who I can break beneath me.

And every single day of my life, I fight against the pain that tortures my black heart, the pain that I know will never go away. The pain of being alone and without her. Without anyone. My interrogations for Victor's new Order become more brutal with every job. My tolerance for my victims, lessened. My ability to offer mercy, practically non-existent. And during my personal tortures of those who Dante brings my way, I become more sadistic and let fewer and fewer live.

A part of me—but just a small part—worries that I will someday come to the point when I kill each and every one of them. Because the more I kill, the more I immerse myself in the pain of others, the easier it is to shut out the screams in my head and the images of the two faces of the woman that I loved.

My beautiful swan. My savior and my undoing.

# -BONUS SCENE-

*January 1, 1979 – Stockholm, Sweden*

Holding her rounded belly with both shaking hands, the tall dark-haired woman pressed her back against the glass door of the convenience store and shoved it open. Her dirty running shoes squeaked against the tile floor as she forced her way inside, nearly knocking over the bread stand. Pain seared through the lower half of her body, stopping her in her desperate tracks toward the back of the store in search of the restrooms. She doubled over and bit back the pain, one hand now gripping the wall beside her to help her keep her balance. Only when the agony subsided could she will her legs to move again.

Pushing herself forward she came to another stop when the wall ended.

There were no restrooms.

Deep, heavy, desperate breaths calmed her for a moment, momentarily suffocating the panic inside. She closed her dark eyes and leaned the back of her head against the wall behind her. Her long navy coat hid her filthy clothes beneath it, and her pants drenched with amniotic fluid, but it did nothing to hide her protruding stomach that she thought would hold on for one more month before bringing her to this moment.

Her darkest moment.

Another contraction burned through her body like a scorching-hot fire raging through her insides. Her hips and lower back squeezed in on themselves, heaving her over forward and almost knocking her legs out from beneath her. She cried out in agony, her teeth clenched, her sweating, dirt and tear-stained face contorting in a horrific expression.

"Miss," the store clerk called out in the Swedish language from behind the counter. "Are you all right? Should I call an ambulance?"

With difficulty, the woman carried herself on her trembling legs back toward the front of the store, both hands latched on to her pregnant stomach as if she was afraid the baby was going to burst through it at any moment and leave her to bleed to death on the floor.

"Var är toaletten?!" she cried through bared teeth and heaved herself against the counter. "Var är toaletten?!"

The clerk pointed reluctantly to the back of the store, his eyes wide and filled with concern. "Utanför," he said.

The woman stormed back outside and went around the side of the building, the fingers of one hand clinging to the bricks to provide her balance. She could feel the baby's head already forcing itself through the birth canal, causing her legs to bow and her pain-filled walk awkward and precarious.

"Ahh!" she cried out and curses followed.

Flinging open the restroom door, she struggled to make her way inside the dimly lit space occupied by only two stalls and one sink with a flickering fluorescent light burning above it. Choosing the larger of the stalls, she fell against the two-way swinging door, shoving it open with a vociferous *bang!* as it slammed against the metal stall wall. She flung herself inside and then sat on the grimy floor beside, furiously tearing at her pants to get them pulled down to her knees.

She pushed. And she screamed. And she pushed again. And she screamed again. She felt faint, but the pain was merciless and wouldn't allow her to pass out. She reared her head back, banging the back of her skull on the stall door behind her. *Bam! Bam! Bam!* She wanted to knock herself out so she couldn't feel the pain anymore. But in one's darkest moment Fate never grants such wishes.

She pushed again and she cried and whimpered and cursed God and the man she thought cursed her with this pregnancy when he emptied his seed inside of her nine months ago. But the baby was coming early. Perhaps she was cursing the wrong man. She didn't know and she didn't care anymore. Her hands were wrapped around her thighs from the outside, the tips of her fingers digging into her trembling, sweating flesh. The pressure between her legs was so intense, so all-consuming, she thought she would die from it alone. She hoped that she would.

One more push and the pressure released in a moment of encompassing relief that actually managed to make her laugh with elation.

Everything was quiet as the woman lay with her back pressed awkwardly against the stall door, her knees drawn up, her legs wide open before her. She tried to catch her breath. She didn't want to look at the child she knew lay in a pool of fluids between her legs. The child that wasn't crying.

*Don't look at it, Elin. Don't look at it!*

Reluctantly she looked anyway, raising her back just slightly from the metal. The baby was turning blue, the umbilical cord stretching from his little belly to the placenta still inside the woman named Elin.

With a filthy hand, she wiped the tears from her cheeks.

*Leave it to die, Elin. You can't live with a child. Leave it.*

She shook her head, fighting with the voice in her mind that always got its way.

Always. In one way or another.

Instinctively she reached out for the baby, taking the slippery little boy into her shaking arms and began to rub his chest and clear his throat with her finger. She didn't know why, or what good it would do, but she did it anyway. She didn't want him. She knew she couldn't keep him. But she didn't want to be a murderer. Of all the things she was—whore, drug addict, waste of air—she *refused* to be a murderer.

Breathing into the baby's tiny mouth, finally a small cry emitted from his lungs, a small bloodcurdling scream that filled her ears both with relief and distress. Holding the screaming child against her swollen breasts, but not letting him eat, she reached for the toilet paper and rolled every last bit of it out onto the dirty floor. She laid him atop it and then fumbled inside her coat for the knife she always carried with her for protection. She cut the umbilical cord and soon after delivered the placenta.

He wouldn't stop crying. His little fisted hands moved in a mechanical-like motion above his chest. His rounded face and dark head of hair covered in a thin, white cottony film of sorts turned beet red and purple as he wailed perpetually.

*Don't feed it. Leave it, Elin.*

Finally the voice in the back of her mind won the war with her conscience. Like it always did. Like it always would.

She left the baby boy on the floor of the restroom beside a stinking toilet and she never looked back.

Many minutes later the store clerk entered the restroom with the authorities and found the baby lying atop a pile of toilet paper, and beside the only part of his mother that had been there for him since conception.

After the child was cared for in the hospital and the news of 'the baby who was birthed and abandoned inside a public restroom' had died down in the media, he was sent to live in an orphanage where he was named after the store clerk who found him: Fredrik Mikael, later given the surname 'Gustavsson' by the treacherous woman who ran the orphanage the children called 'Mother'.

A child wasn't born on that day. A child *died* on that day. His innocence. What he *could* have been. *Who* he could have been. His birth was the beginning of a very long and cruel life.

No, a child wasn't born that day, but a killer *was*.

# OTHER BOOKS BY J.A. REDMERSKI

**Speculative Fiction/Contemporary Fantasy**
DIRTY EDEN

**Crime & Suspense**
KILLING SARAI *(#1 – In the Company of Killers)*
REVIVING IZABEL *(#2 – In the Company of Killers)*
THE SWAN & THE JACKAL *(#3 – In the Company of Killers)*
SEEDS OF INIQUITY *(#4 – In the Company of Killers)*
THE BLACK WOLF *(#5 – In the Company of Killers)*
*More to come…*

**New Adult Contemporary Romance**
THE EDGE OF NEVER *(#1 – The Edge Duology)*
THE EDGE OF ALWAYS *(#2 – The Edge Duology)*
SONG OF THE FIREFLIES
THE MOMENT OF LETTING GO

**Young Adult Paranormal Romance**
THE MAYFAIR MOON *(#1 – The Darkwoods Trilogy)*
KINDRED *(#2 – The Darkwoods Trilogy)*
THE BALLAD OF ARAMEI *(#3 – The Darkwoods Trilogy)*

# ABOUT THE AUTHOR

J.A. (Jessica Ann) Redmerski is a *New York Times, USA Today* and *Wall Street Journal* bestselling author and award winner. She is a lover of film, television and books that push boundaries and a sucker for long, sweeping, epic love stories. Things on Jessica's wish-list are to conquer her long list of ridiculous fears, find a shirt that she actually likes, and travel the world with a backpack and a partner-in-crime.

To learn more about Jessica, visit her here:

www.jessicaredmerski.com
www.inthecompanyofkillers.com
www.facebook.com/J.A.Redmerski
www.pinterest.com/jredmerski
Twitter - @JRedmerski

CPSIA information can be obtained at www.ICGtesting.com
Printed in the USA
LVOW11s1445270716

497997LV00008BA/268/P